Carter-Krall Publishing

Literature that lasts forever

Carter-Krall Publishers
42155 Rue Saint Dominique, Suite 207
Stone Mountain, GA 30083

Printed in the United States of America
Published by Carter-Krall Publishers First Edition

Cover photograph by Angus Wilson
Cover art by Carter-Krall Design Team
Typesetting by Carter-Krall Staff

Copy edited by Pentouch Literary, LLC

Granddaddy's Dirt/ Brian Egeston
ISBN 0-9675505-8-0
Paperback

Library Of Congress Catalog Number
2001118672
First Edition October 2001

Granddaddy's Dirt

Brian Egeston
www.brianwrites.com

Carter-Krall Publishers

Other Novels by Brian Egeston

 Cଓଞ

Crossing Bridges

Whippins, Switches & Peach Cobbler

Dedication

For my amazing wife, Latise.

This book is written with warmth to heal the pain of your loss. Please find peace in knowing that the existence of your ancestors inspired these words. You needn't miss your grandmother, for she resides in you, taking cover in your spirit. Your grandfather's love knows no boundaries, except your precious heart, because for you, he will always melt. Your family is beautiful, for it is merely a reflection of you.

Acknowledgments

I must first begin by saying, Thaaaank ya God!
Now:
Background Music
<Begin humming the melody for J.B.'s 'Doin' it to Death'
aka James Brown's Gonna Have A Funky Time>
Hit It.
Electric Guitar *Dun-Dun-Dun-Dun, Duuuun, Dun-Dun-Dun-Dun*
Base Line- *Bomp-Bomp-Bomp, Bommp*
Bomp-Bomp-Bomp, Bommp

My church has moved up to the first spot on the acknowledgements list. Ray Of Hope Christian Church, the church that God stops by to visit when he's in town, and he's done so several times this year. Pastor Hale and Pastor Felder, I'm growing because of your seeds. HAAA-LLELUJAH! Glory to yo' name fatha! Don't y'all get me shoutin' before the book even starts.

Dun-Dun-Dun-Dun, Duuuuun, Dun-Dun-Dun-Dun
(Keep it going)

The Mutotas at the African Spectrum Bookstore.
Minister Rice and family for claiming my victory before I left for each book event. My good friend, Jesus Christ, thanks for going with me each mile. I wanna be like you when I grow up.

The Black Writers Alliance held together with the super adhesive glue of Tia Shabazz and her wonderful family. Prolific Writers thanks for support and good dialogue. We wouldn't be family if we didn't fight. Thanks John, Dom, and Theresa. Marlive and The GRITS on-line book club and Tee from RAWSistaz, if your injury flares up, sue me using my "pen name". Brothas Well Read Book Club, great job! Thanks as always to my test readers, Dejuan and Jounrey. Great job.

My beloved brothers of the soul-Omega Psi Phi. Man, y'all continue to support and surprise me everywhere I turn. It means more to me than you'll ever know. Thanks to all the Ques that ensure I am NEVER alone at a book signing.

Independent bookstores that gave me a chance- Medu, Nubian, Alke-Bulan Images, X-Pressions, Mahogany, Legacy Books & Café, Books-n-Bites, Pyramid, Shrine of the Black Madonna, Black Images, Hidden Talent, It's a Mystery to Me, Peek-A-Boo, and all the others who welcomed my words. You know what? I wanna thank the bookstores that refused to give me chance as well, thanks.

All those authors who knew their books were good enough when the P.I.M.P.S. told you it wasn't. Everyone has a story to tell and no one has the right to silence you. Stay on the undergoing reading railroad, freedom is just around the corner.

<KEY CHANGE>

The WONDERFUL schools I've visited during the book tour. Thank you for allowing me to speak into your lives.

Rainbow Elementary- Decatur, Georgia
Carver High School- Birmingham, Alabama
East Middle High School- Nashville, Tennessee
McGarrah Elementary-Morrow Georgia
South Hampton Elementary- Birmingham. Alabama

Art Silverman Sr. producer at *All Things Considered*, thanks for letting me in the door and reminding me to keep it simple.

88.3 and the "Say It Loud" Youth Program. KATV Channel 7 in Little Rock, thanks for the welcome home spot! Thanks to the men who changed my life at the Carol Vance Unit of the IFI in Richardson, TX. My home is still filled with the residue of your blessings.

Thomas Lux, thanks for your strong, opposing views on polysyllabic words. It helped me, stupendously...oops, sorry.

Zelda Oliver-Miles and the ENTIRE city of Birmingham, thanks for making me feel famous; you so awesome it don't make no sense. Angela and Michael at Barnes & Noble, you've pushed me further than you could ever know. Vanessa, Tina and the whole Journey's End crew, love is a many splendid things as is your infinite joy in my heart.

Brandon Massey, my partner in crime and tour buddy— e-books forever! Through sweet cigarettes and adolescent gas passing, we made it.

Dun-Dun-Dun-Dun, Duuuuun, Dun-Dun-Dun-Dun
'Gonna Have a funky good time'

My faithful and trusty Black Male Writing Mentors and associates, Mr. Robert Flemming (the mentor a student dreams of having), Franklin White, Mat Johnson, Brian Keith Jackson, Timm Mcann(Blonde Beloved aka Akhi-halik!), Marcus Majors, Vincent Alexander, Travis Hunter and so many other brothers doing their thing.

The P&P LA connection Parry and Portia; Lawd Almighty!

Tennessee State University alumni chapters across the country, thanks for extending big blue love all over the country. My State Farm buddies Teresa, Denise and their wonderful husbands. Thanks so much for hospitality and love.

A special thanks to the gracious book clubs, hosting intimate and funny discussions. Books make people talk and talking brings people together.

Andrew Harper, and all my other Parkview High School classmates from 1988. If you only knew how I think of you and miss you all the time, you'd move in with me.

Special thanks to K.K. Snyder and Mary Braswell at the Albany Herald. I appreciate your help and support during my tour and research in Albany.

This project could never have been accomplished without the thorough journalism from the staff at the Atlanta Journal Constitution. Your 1994 flood articles are so vivid I felt the splashes. Timothy C. Stamey, your report on Tropical Storm Alberto was absolutely stellar. Many thanks to your talents and support from the U.S. Department of the Interior and U.S. Geological Survey. Edward N. Rappaport, your account of Alberto's trek across the Atlantic Ocean was an amazing tutorial of geography, oceanography, and meteorology. I hope I have done justice to your work and the entire National Hurricane Center.

My Motorola family and friends, especially the Galvin family, thanks for showing me the way.

The residents of South Georgia, know that you have already worked together and survived and now you can work together and grow.

For the souls made homeward bound in 1994, rest easy and enjoy the heavenly ride. You will never be forgotten.

Wynfield Quail Plantation in Albany, Georgia, thanks for fast answers. It was extremely valuable and your place is beautiful, cyberly speaking.

Shon Griggs from Ray of Hope security, thanks for covering me on the roadtrips, Boi, I got you! I got you, bruh!

Oh yeah, recognition to Mr. Geoffrey Royal who beat me up and down the Hillendale golf course in North Carolina by at least 10 strokes. You are the most gracious winner I have ever seen. It would be my honor and privilege to tee it up with a gentleman like yourself, anytime.

To those who have dipped their spoon of trust into my wholesome and warm peach cobbler, may the sweetness solidify our friendship

The fellow writers in my diverse circle of writers of which I am proud to know. I love you for your literature and I love you for your lives. Thanks to my mom, Delores Egeston for making me a writer in the womb and coming to grips with the fact that—I write books for living. Love ya!

If I've omitted anyone, I've got 29 more books to write. I'm sure I'll get you in one of 'em.

Last but of course not least, Thaaaannnk ya God!

"...Despite my personal failures there must be possible a fiction which, leaving sociology and case histories to the scientists, can arrive at the truth about the human condition, here and now, with all the bright magic of the fairy tale."

Ralph Ellison 1953 after receiving the National Book Award

Contents

PART I
Andrew's Allegory
1977-1980

⚜

One
While on the Way Home...

———————— ᘓᘔᘓ ————————

IN THE DEEPEST BOWELS OF HELL'S CAULDRON, THE temperature often reached—*flame broil*. On the longest stretch of Highway 257 leading to Albany, Georgia, the temperature was known to reach—*combustible obliteration*. On this night, the sins of each locale would form a dichotomous fusion, which would only be quenched by generational gestures of humanity.

Albany was a city of diverse icons searching for identity amongst Georgia's red clay, the Bayou's Spanish Moss and Florida's swaying palms. The stretch of road offered no solace from the skin-scorching sun. Mirages meandered, making mockery of the distant images. Drivers often found themselves wondering what had compelled them to make the drive initially, but more importantly, how to avoid future trips. Air conditioners were run at maximum settings. As a result, maximum prices were paid at gas stations. Those without air conditioning paid by purging their pores as sweat fled their bodies like water plummeting down a fall.

Andrew Scales and his wife, Virginia, knew all too well the sweat-saturated car seats and drenched clothes which accompanied a summer drive on the highway. They'd learned from many trips to Atlanta and back home to Albany that the best route was one in the cool night air. Although the night air was considerably cooler than the day drive, it was merely a dark layer of humidity. It felt as though skin could be peeled from one's body like a snake shedding its seasonal inconvenience. They'd made the Atlanta-Albany trip so frequently, Andrew could practically drive through each bump and crack in the road without headlights.

Virginia was usually a chatterbox from Atlanta to Macon and then became comatose with sleep from Macon to Cordele. Upon arrival at the water tower of Cordele, she resumed her chattering ways. Her welcome-to-Cordele verbiage lasted long enough for the pasty taste of summer sleep to make her speech flavorless, uncomfortable, and borderline toxic. Andrew was grateful for his wife's road slumber. He had low tolerance for her late night conversations as well as the added staleness in the air. However, he remained cordial.

"You sleep good?" Andrew asked of his wife.

"Not really. Why you let me sleep so long?"

"Let you? What was I gon' do, as dead to the world as you be? Pull over and give you mouth to mouth? Not wit' dem logs you cut when you be snorin'. Sound like a lumberjack," Andrew offered, teasing his wife with a smile.

After thirty-five years of marriage, her beauty still melted his rock-candy heart. Even inside the car, illuminated only by the green instrument panel, Virginia's glowing wide eyes shone brightly. She'd been a looker ever since they'd met at Albany State in the forties.

"Andrew Scales, I don't know why you even tell that lie. I don't bit mo' snore than the man on the moon," Virginia responded jovially to her husband. As she turned to look out of the window at the nothingness that could be seen in the dark night, Andrew prepared another comment about his wife's hearty snoring, but was suddenly interrupted by colorful flashes appearing in the black air.

Peering into the small rearview mirror, he noticed the patriotic display of lights behind him. Red and blue strobes flickered like an Independence Day celebration. Absent was the white contrast seen in the stars sprinkling the earth's nightly backdrop. Those stars would the only witnesses of events yet to occur.

Andrew began to decelerate his automobile while accelerating his obscenity for being pulled over so close to his destination.

"What does this fool want with me? I wasn't even speedin'. Somebody got to do somethin' about these cops with a license to harass anybody they want to," Andrew said to no one in particular. The car finally came to a halt, but Andrew's swearing continued as a lanky officer exited the cruiser. The policeman burned their retinas by leaving the lights glowing in the reflection of the rear and sideview mirrors. Reflections of the lights on Andrew's side were blocked, then cleared, blocked and cleared by the sway of the policeman as he sauntered up to the driver's side of the car.

It was here on this same stretch that Andrew had watched his own father disrespected and beaten by local authorities and hypocrite clergymen. While leaving a field playing catch all afternoon, the father and son were confronted by a group with nothing better to do than hate. As one of them constrained Andrew, the others took turns planting hands and feet over the father's body. That was the day it began and ended. No more ball playing in the field. No more recreation. Now there was only work, a father with an evil disposition and a complete disregard for authority. It was the genesis of Andrew's wicked ways.

Once the officer reached Andrew's door, he knocked on the window and gestured for Andrew to roll it down. Andrew obliged and felt the purging of his cool conditioned air out into the humidity. The officer, already sweating, looked at the driver for a moment, then glanced over at Virginia for a moment longer. The extra moment was laced with impure thoughts preceding his perverted grin.

Andrew inhaled the officer's breath, a mixture of oxygen and Jack Daniel's, or Wild Turkey and carbon dioxide or perhaps Jim Beam and malice. Regardless of the brand and its chaser, it most assuredly wasn't a breath mint. The officer had obviously been consuming late night liquor instead of the traditional coffee and donuts. After the looks, impure thoughts, and last-call leftovers, Andrew became fearfully angry. He didn't see an authoritative figure standing outside of his car. He saw a pale-faced disruption from his homeward journey.

Stubble garnished the officer's face as if a symbol of the long hours the man had been working. What's more, the officer was allowing the adhesive night air to invade every square inch of the car, and Andrew loathed being uncomfortable, in any manner.

"Evenin' all," the officer said, exposing a southern drawl thicker than the humidity invading the car. He stole more glances at Virginia.

"What can I do for you, officer?" Andrew asked directly, trying to convey the message that he was an inconvenience.

"Where 'bouts y'all headed?"

"Albany. Where else can we be goin' on this highway at this time of night?"

"Now hold on thar. You act like yer doin' me a favor by lettin' me pull you over. Did you know yer right brake light is out?"

"Are you kiddin' me!" Andrew lashed. "You pulled me over for somethin' you couldn't see unless you wouldn't 'a stopped me?"

"Calm down now, boy. I will put yer coon tail in jail for the night. I hope we ain't gon' have no problem out here wit' chu actin' outta yer place."

"Oh, no. It's too late for that!" Andrew exclaimed, opening his door to inject a verbal slashing. "See, you done stopped me for some nonsense, and on top of all that you gon' insult me in front of my woman. You might as well get ready, 'cause I'm 'bout to get in yo' butt 'til them red and blue lights stop flashin'."

"Andrew Scales!" Virginia yelled and reached for her husband. Before she had even formed the words in her mouth, she realized it was too late to intercede. Virginia knew that when her husband got an impulsive mission in his mind, there weren't many obstacles that could stand between him and accomplishing that task. This time the obstacle was a policeman and Virginia knew that the uniform would not deter Andrew from reaching his premeditated goal— the officer's beating.

"Boy, get *back* in that car!" The officer demanded as Andrew unbuttoned his shirt, exposing a once-chiseled physique that was now a resting place for hair and flab. Andrew ignored the officer. "Hold on one minute now!" the officer yelled as Andrew took a position of fighting trim.

Andrew was no stranger to conflict. He was an avid protester for civil rights and very active with the local NAACP chapter in Albany. He often boasted of marching with Martin Luther King, Jr. and serving as an aid for the SCLC. So Andrew had seen his share of run-ins with figures of authority. But now, at this moment, there were no water hoses and no barking dogs. As far as Andrew knew, the slightly inebriated officer had not even radioed the dispatch to inform someone of his traffic stop.

The officer was faced with two enemies of darkness. The angered black man standing before him and the dark night which would, unfortunately for him, be his only witness.

Andrew clinched hammer-like fists. His fingers were wrapped so tightly that fingernails were beginning to penetrate the skin in the palm of his hands. He opened his hands and took steps toward his opponent. Now the officer was fighting to sober up. He would need every sense and ability he could muster to contend with Andrew.

While the officer decided on which weapon he would use to arm himself during the battle, Andrew loaded his only available fighting tools—bare hands and anger. The officer unlatched his nightstick, attempting to gain the advantage in the fight, but his effort failed. Andrew lunged toward the officer, capturing his neck in his muscular grasp. Surprised and terrified, the officer was frozen in the vice-like grip noosing his neck.

Eyes bulging and skin transforming into a blood-filled shade of red, the officer retaliated, serving a stunning blow to Andrew's groin. Andrew quickly released the death-lock and grabbed his crotch, trying to relieve himself of the excruciating pain.

Reaching again for his nightstick, the officer managed to regain his composure and delivered a quick and sharp blow to Andrew's back, knocking him to the ground.

"Boy, I don't know what's don' got into you, but yer gonna die out here tonight. You should have got back in that car!"

The officer kicked Andrew in his ribs, forcing him to turn over on his back. He drew his revolver on the defenseless man lying underneath him. The officer cocked the gun and offered a little giggle at the weak fight Andrew posted. His giggle gave Andrew enough time to grab a rock larger than his own hand and hurl it at the officer's head. It landed in the center of his face, surely crushing his nose and possibly breaking bones in his ocular cavity. He grabbed his nose, dropped the gun, and lost sight of the nightstick lying at his feet.

Picking up the nightstick, Andrew, who now had the upper hand, planned to take full advantage of it. He smashed the stick into the officer's rib cage. Virginia began screaming at her irate husband as the officer was dropped to the ground by reciprocated blows.

"Andrew, please let that man be! Y'all gon' hurt each other," she yelled, as though she were viewing a family feud between two dueling cousins. The two men had no kinship, only a kill-ship. Virginia turned away from the commotion and shielded her eyes, fearing that the brutal vision might permanently place itself into her mind. It was too late, she'd caught a glimpse of Andrew kicking the badly wounded officer in the head, transforming him into a limp mass.

With life barely in his grasp, the officer reached down for his ankle and quickly drew his backup gun. Andrew was taken by surprise because he knew he'd gotten lucky with the first gun, but didn't see an escape from the new weapon. Noticing that the officer was a few pulses away from passing out, Andrew threw the nightstick in the direction of his enemy's hand. Suddenly, the quick sound of wood against metal was followed almost instantly by a loud pop. The officer had managed to get a shot off. Andrew heard a shrill sound come from the area of the car a second after the shot. It was Virginia. Panicked and confused she'd screamed while trying to bolt from the car without pulling the door handle and slammed her head into the passenger side window and was knocked unconscious. Andrew saw his wife slumped over in the car, seemingly lifeless. Making his way toward the still woman, Andrew was halted by flashes of past, present and future—the shot, his wife's body, and life without her. Fear froze his steps. Then his anger turned his attention, and body, in the direction from where the shot had been fired.

The officer was shocked himself that he'd actually fired

the gun. He could almost smell the anger on Andrew's breath and the dangerous sense penetrated the officer's oscillating heart. He was instantly panic-stricken with horror. The officer prayed that there were more bullets in the gun, then he begged God to give him strength to fire it one more time. The bullets were there, but the strength of sobriety failed him. Andrew, still staring at the shooter, rushed towards the officer, screaming at him for his wife's assumed revenge.

"Look what you did to my wife! You dead!" Releasing obscenities, Andrew reached the armed officer and began to wrestle him. The enraged husband was fighting for his wife's honor, which he thought was only a memory now. Andrew tussled with the officer and they rolled into the asphalt of the highway and back to the side of the road. Andrew began dispensing blows to the officer's now dismantled face.

With one last chance to escape his inevitable, but predicted beating, the officer clutched the gun tightly and brought it up between his and Andrew's chest and starting squeezing the trigger. Motionless time propelled the pulling of the gun, the squeezing of the trigger, and the preservation of Andrew's life. Another loud pop synchronized the time, motion, and reality.

Neither of the men moved after the shot was fired. They were both deathly still and silent.

It was after midnight, and three bodies were lying motionless in the Albany night. No one was around to check for pulses, call an ambulance, or call the coroner.

Two
Day of Discovery

⸙

ON THE FOLLOWING MORNING BISCUITS BAKING—ACcompanied by the symphony of bacon frying in a deep black cast iron skillet—served as an alarm clock for those who could not wake with the sunrise. No one heard the front door open at one o'clock that morning, so the attendance of the house was unknown, only assumed. Ingrid, Andrew's oldest daughter, was the conductor of the melodic morning meal. She was preparing food for her son as well as her mother and father. After retrieving eggs from the refrigerator, she noticed Virginia dragging sluggishly through the kitchen.

"Mama, how did you get that knot on your head!" Ingrid exclaimed.

Virginia's skin was a silky glow even in her golden years. So the bump was as peculiar as a purple stop sign. Ingrid stopped what she was doing and tended to her mother.

"Chile. Don't make no fuss over me. You bess be makin' sure you don't burn that bacon. Lord knows Andrew gon' be complainin' all day about crispy bacon. Did y'all water the garden yesterday?" Virginia rambled on, trying to imply that nothing out of the ordinary had occurred.

"Mama, what is that bump on your head and how did you get it?" Ingrid demanded. The bacon was reaching a decrescendo as it met its demise in the scorching grease.

Virginia paused for a moment, reflecting over the frightful incident. She was surprised that the police weren't waiting at the door for Andrew.

"Ingrid, I hit my head on the car window last night."

"When, mama?"

"Last night on the way back from Atlanta."

"But how did you get that big knot?"

"Chile, I told you. I hit my head on the window."

"Doin' what? I know you and Daddy wasn't foolin' around in the back seat at the rest stop again?"

"Girl, hush up talkin' like that. If you closed yo' mouth long enough for the draft to stop, I'd tell you." Virginia gathered her thoughts and mentally began reconstructing the scene on the highway. "Ingrid, somethin' happened last night on the way home. I'm not sure if I saw all of it but—"

"It wasn't nothin' *to* see." Andrew barged in and finished his wife's sentence. The words Andrew spoke were not at all those formulating in Virginia's thoughts. "We got pulled over by the police and that's what happened. Now, why y'all sittin' up here lettin' this food go to waste? You know I don't eat no burnt bacon, and this here bacon 'bout as black as the skillet. Bet y'all didn't water my garden either, did ya?"

"Andrew, watch yo' mouth while you talkin' to yo' daughter. They done came all this way to visit. She fixin' breakfast for you, and she don't need to be talked to that way," Virginia said, trying to draw attention away from Andrew's explanation of the night before.

"Mama, you know I ain't thinkin' about Daddy," Ingrid replied, waltzing over to her father and planting daddy's girl affection on his cheek. She wanted to soften him up before inquiring further.

"Now what happened last night, Daddy?"

"I done told y'all. Ain't nothin' happened! Why you keep talkin' like somethin' goin' on? If I say ain't nothin' happened, then ain't nothin' happened! Stop askin' me these crazy questions and turn that stove off 'fore y'all burn down the house!" The small kitchen was silent, just as it had been before her parents had invaded Ingrid's breakfast preparation. Now, only the smell of burning bacon and periodic pops of grease filled the room.

Andrew had made it perfectly clear that the actions of the previous night would not be discussed. He figured it would only be a few hours before he would have a similar conversation with the authorities.

Andrew sat down at the table to await his daughter's second attempt at bacon. His seven-year-old grandson, Kyle, ran in the kitchen adorned only in his underwear. The boy jumped on his grandfather's lap and made his announcement.

" Granddaddy , somebody pullin' up in the driveway."

Andrew glanced at his wife, but only for a moment. A second longer would have signaled that Andrew was concerned. He was determined to maintain his composure regardless of what the new arrivals were coming to do to him.

Virginia, however, stared at Andrew for quite some time, then looked out of the window over the sink.

She eyed the backyard and noticed that the grass needed to be cut. Her first thought was who would cut the grass if Andrew were taken away for years, or for the rest of his life? Who would paint the house? Fix the cars? Repair the plumbing? What would she do without her beloved husband?

There was a thunderous, frantic knock on the front door. Ingrid had already begun moving toward the door after Kyle's announcement. She answered it and escorted the visitor. Heavy, thudding footsteps increased in volume across the hardwood floors leading to the kitchen. Virginia kept her eyes on the back yard. She'd seen enough action in one night and couldn't bear much more. Andrew sat sternly awaiting his bacon or the pigs, whichever would come first. Ingrid announced the visitor's presence.

"Daddy, somebody's here to see you."

"M-m-mr. Scales, we bedda g-get down to the office r-r-right away. Somebody d-d-done sh-sh-shot a po-lee-leece-man last night," stuttered Booker, Andrew's employee.

Andrew looked at his wife and she peered back as though his life had just been spared. The grass didn't look so bad anymore.

"Kyle, get yo' clothes. Granddaddy gon' take you down to his office wit' him." Andrew, always a strategist, figured that the appearance of a grandfather and grandson would portray an image of kindness rather than a killer.

C3✥

Upon arrival at the Albany View, the office of the city's only black-owned billboard, Andrew was greeted by his employees' budding questions. He was sole proprietor of the business in addition to owner of several rental houses on the south side of Albany. It was his self-made empire and self-proclaimed kingdom.

"How you doing, Mr. Scales? You done heard what they did to that officer last night? They gon be 'round here huntin' every black person they can get they hands on," Po-Shank announced. Po-Shank was the maintenance man and a part-time freelance writer who divided his time between the Albany Southwest Georgian newspaper, the Albany Herald newspaper, and hanging out at the View. He took the term freelance literally, having never been paid for any of his work.

"Who you thank done it, Mr. Scales?" his secretary, Mayreen, inquired. "Some out-a-towner, I thank. Couldn't be nobody 'round here that stupid, is it, Mr. Scales?"

"Wasn't nobody stupid at all. Mo' than likely it was somebody that was right smart. See, if they had a score to settle with the police, then all they had to do was kill him off and blame it on the black folks. Nobody would ever think of lookin' for anybody else if they found them a right nice scapegoat," Po-Shank offered.

"What makes you say that?" Mayreen asked.

"I keep tryin' to tell you, I'm a journalist and I know people. When the police chief finds out somebody done killed one of his officers, he gon' release the devil himself to try and find out who done did it," Po-Shank replied.

Andrew absorbed all of the information but released none. At this point, he felt it was best to remain silent and learn all he could about the events that would begin unfolding very soon.

"Granddaddy, somebody got killed in here?" Kyle asked.

"No, son. It was an accident that happened last night so everybody tryin' to figure out what happened."

"Wh-what make you think it was an accident, Mr. Scales?" Booker asked, tripping over his own words.

"I'm just speculatin'. I don't really know if it was a accident or not. Frankly speakin', I really don't care," Andrew answered.

Po-Shank was all too familiar with Mr. Scales' every-man-for-himself attitude. Other than his immediate and extended family, Andrew rarely showed much concern for those who weren't helping him make money.

Po-Shank stood with a dropped jaw, "Mr. Scales, you mean to say that you don't care one way or 'nother if a man is dead, why he's dead, or who made him dead? That's cold-blooded."

Andrew formed his rapid rebuttal and readied his response until he caught a glimpse of his innocent grandson. Kyle was staring intently at him.

"Well, I, what I mean is that I, uh, I don't care right now 'cause the facts are cloudy and people gon' be makin' rash decisions and jumpin' to conclusions. Until everybody settle down, I don't care to talk about what might'a happened." Andrew glanced back at his grandson to find Kyle going through desk drawers looking for office toys.

Andrew had already revealed too much about the subject. After all, his intent was to assume the role of an inquisitive citizen trying to find answers like everyone else. He decided to find out what everyone thought they knew around town. No better place to snoop out information than the newspaper widely circulated among the blacks in town—the Albany Southwest Georgian.

The View and Southwest Georgian double-teamed companies seeking advertisement. One of the men would always strongly suggest that a company purchase a second ad from the other's business to attract all potential customers. It was the most lucrative and legitimate business scam in town.

"Kyle, we leavin' again," Andrew commanded. "We need to go down the block for a while. Make 'aste now. Y'all keep a' ear to the ground and call to the house if anything breaks out. Leave a message with Virginia."

Andrew grabbed Kyle's hand and headed for the door just as the phone rang. Mayreen answered and gave her unique greeting.

"Albany View. From headlines to ham hocks, if you see us we'll help people see you. How can I help?" *She gotta change that message*, Andrew thought.

"Yes, he's here, but he's just now leavin'."

Andrew waved off any intention Mayreen may have had of passing him the phone.

"He's actually just walkin' out now. It might be better if I took a message or is there something I can do for you?

Oh, how you doin'? We don't get many calls from yo' office—Today? I don't know if he can make it down there today, but I'll give him the message—No matter what time it is?—Well, what if it's two o'clock in the mornin'?—I know you said any time, but sometimes people don't always mean what they say." Mayreen was an imbecilic interrogator of callers, albeit unintentional. It was her gift.

"Okay, I'll tell him. No matter what time. Okay—all right—I got it—okay, yeah—you, too. Okay, and y'all have a blessed day in the Lord."

Mayreen hung up the phone and began inscribing the message on her pink notepad, mumbling to herself.

"Let's see. While you were out—called at ten thirty—"

"Mayreen!" Andrew exclaimed.

"What! What's wrong? What is it?"

"Who is the message for?"

"It's for you. I'm just jottin' everything down so I can give it to Virginia."

"Mayreen, if you don't give me that message, I swear fo' God I'm gon' hurt somebody.

"All right, all right. That was the police station. They want to see you today at three-thirty, but any time you can make it is fine. But you got to go today and they said it's an emergency."

Suddenly Andrew didn't want the message. He wished Mayreen had never even answered the phone. Panic and fear besieged his spirit and inhabited his entire body. It was a sporadic cancer eating away at his innocence. Andrew could feel the burden of his cold conscience as it became riddled with the permeation of truth and confession.

Inevitably, the seed of Andrew's involvement would be planted. Theories and allegations would sprout names during this day of digging and plowing for answers. The day was slowly aging, but the truth was germinating faster than weeds, choking all that was pure and beautiful in this garden of guilt. There would soon be reaping for sowing.

Three

What You Know Will Hurt You

CS8O

"**A** NDREW SCALES! BOY WE AIN'T SEEN YOU SINCE YOU SEEN us. How you doin?"

"Aw, I'm just fine, D.J. What's been goin' on down here?"

"You know good'n well what's goin' on. These folks down here is about to rip this town apart tryin' to find out who killed that policeman last night. They already been callin' and probin' 'round here. Anybody called over at yo' place yet?" the proprietor inquired.

Andrew was adhering to his self-proclaimed policy of playing stupid. It was time to bring out his tag-along diversion for the day.

"D.J., you ever met my grandson? Kyle, this here is Mr. D.J. Whitley, proprietor of the Albany Southwest Georgian, Albany's second best black-owned place for advertisement." The two friends guffawed as D.J. bent down to swallow Kyle's small hand in his own.

"Nice to meet you Kyle, you can call me Mr. D.J. if you want to."

The inquisitive youngster gave a perplexed look. "Why yo' mama name you Deejay? Did you get in a lot of fights when you was little with a funny name like that?" The small staff in the office snickered at Kyle's inquisition. It was a much-needed breath of freshness on the stale and soon-to-be stormy situation.

"Kyle!" Andrew lashed.

"Andrew, you leave that boy be. You know he don't know no better." He turned to Kyle. "Son, DeeJay is not my name. It's two letters, not one word. The D stands for Damascus and the J stands for Jefferson. Damascus Jefferson Whitley is my whole name."

"Can't you just call yo'self Dumb-ask-us? How you say yo' name again? Why you call yo'self D.J. Whitley?" Kyle probed even further.

"It's Da-mas-cus. And to tell you the truth, young fella, only reason I go by D.J. Whitley is so people'll call me Mister Whitley instead of Damascus. Andrew, that boy there is a natural-born journalist if I ever seen one. Askin' questions and not scared to get to the truth. I think you got somethin' there."

"I got somethin' alright. I got a handful of mischief," Andrew professed staring down at his reflection of generations. He'd lost himself for a brief moment, caught up in the innocence of the small boy. Reality slapped him out of his daydreaming. He realized, the young boy had no clue he was being escorted by a man who'd taken a person's life just one short sunrise ago.

"So, Andrew, you never did say if the Chief had called over to yo' place or not. If I didn't know you betta, I'd think you was hidin' a story from me. Only reason I ain't gon' accuse you of holdin' out on me is 'cause I know you ain't gon' have a new advertiser on your board for another three weeks. They'll have somebody convicted, cooked, and resurrected by that time, whether they guilty or not."

Andrew's facial expression didn't match the jovial ones

of the office staff. His muscles were frozen by D.J.'s sub-liminal prophecy. Andrew couldn't maintain the façade any longer. If he continued dodging the question, someone was certain to get suspicious.

"Tell you the truth D.J., I'm on my way to the police station now. They called me at the office a while ago. I was hopin' that you could fill me in on what you know."

His words cloaked the actual definition of his state-ment, *Tell me if you know how I killed him so I'll know how to lie to the Chief.*

D.J. exchanged his erroneous and far-fetched knowl-edge with Andrew, which was similar to the nonsense be-ing theorized at the View. *It's amazing how stupid people can be when they know everything about absolutely noth-ing*, Andrew thought. If these were the best speculations the town had, Andrew could have walked into the station with a bullet, the dead officer's blood, and a sign that read *For Sale - One Cop Killer* and he could have lied his way to innocence. Andrew announced his departure and tugged his grandson towards the door. D.J. was close behind.

"Andrew," D.J. gently placed his hand on Andrew's back as he reached the door, a gesture signifying that the following words were valuable, or desperate. "Let me know what they talk to you about when you down there. I didn't want to say nothin' in front of everybody, but they called me this morning and they want to see me first thing tomor-row." D.J.'s eyes spoke more fear than his voice.

"No problem. Maybe we'll get together tomorrow for supper and laugh at the foolish questions they was askin' us," Andrew said. D.J. showed no gratitude for the offering, but instead returned a vein-severing grip of Andrew's arm.

"I don't mean call me tomorrow. I want you to call me as soon as you leave that place and get to a phone. You hear me? These fools ain't never seen no killin' like this. In case you ain't noticed by the business the other billboards is gettin', it's an election year."

"I know the mayor's runnin' for—"

"He ain't gon' let a policeman's murder go unsolved for more than two Sunday sermons, even if he got to invent him a killer."

Andrew could smell D.J.'s breath, laced with conviction. His teeth seemed to chatter with concern. His tongue spat innocence onto Andrew which drowned him in guilt.

"People gon' start gettin' real nervous 'round here pretty soon. I don't plan on buying no ticket to da witch hunt. I need to know the questions they ask you, Andrew," D.J. slowly and carefully enunciated each word to his friend—each syllable a dart piercing Andrew's very own conscience.

The two fell silent and Kyle stood gazing up at the giants. He could see the insides of flaring nostrils that hovered above. His grandfather's lips moved, "I'll take care of you, D.J.," Andrew announced then turned to Kyle, preparing to flee once again.

"Let's go Kyle, it's almost three-thirty."

Time was growing older and Andrew was running late for his fate.

Four

Accurate Accusations

––––––––– ⚬ℬ℧ –––––––––

"INGRID, YOU KNOW GOOD'N'WELL, ANDREW DON'T water that garden before sundown. I don't want to hear him fussin' when he get back home," Virginia proclaimed. She continued her fidget-a-thon as she had since Andrew left with Booker that morning. Her typical routine consisted of efficient cleaning and yard work, a bit of sewing and a smidgen of gardening. On this day, she was simply fidget-ing and Ingrid found her noticeably nervous.

"Mama, water is water all day long. It don't matter when you use it," Ingrid said, walking towards her mother. She gently placed the words on Virginia, attempting to smooth the anxiety which had taken possession of her trademark calm demeanor. The gesture offered no relief to the nervous wife. Virginia changed the subject.

"So you gon' let Kyle stay down here for the summer or you gon' be hardheaded again?"

"Mama, I don't know. Three months is a long time for me to be without my baby. You know Angus loves taking him to baseball games when school's out."

"Honey, y'all can come and pick him up one weekend and take him to a doggone baseball game if you want to. That's such a pitiful excuse." Virginia walked over to the living room window again. She'd been watching every action outside since Andrew's departure. "As much as Angus been callin' down here, you'd think you been gone for two weeks instead of two days. That man know he loves his wife. That' sho' is a blessin', chile."

"I know, mama. Angus and Kyle mean the whole world to me. That's why I feel guilty breaking our family apart."

"It's only for the summertime, chile, good Lawd! You act like you ain't gon' never see the boy again. Look a'here, you and Angus might not ever get a chance to travel like this again. You bedda do it while you can."

"It's all just so fast. Angus getting this new job and I get the chance to travel with him in the summer. It's kinda like a dream and I don't know if I'm about to wake up or if it's real. You think Kyle'll understand? He's only seven and it might scar him for life."

"Understand? What he got to understand, baby? He gon' spend the summer wit' his grandparents? He don't care 'bout you gallivantin' up and down the highway with yo' travelin' salesman husband. All he want to know is what you gon' bring him back. You 'bout as silly as a Halloween hen, girl. I swear fo' God." Virginia walked into the laundry room, frustrated with Ingrid's trivial concerns.

Virginia had detrimental deeds to concede. Once in the laundry room, she gathered the clothes she and Andrew had worn the night before. She wanted to wash away the events. Andrew's clothes reeked of stenches she had never smelled. That of fear, anger, and death. The smell of the slain officer's whiskey was on Andrew's collar, sweat of his futile struggles on the sleeve. It was then that Virginia noticed a rip on Andrew's cuff. Examining the other cuff, it was still in tact. Shining like an innocent ray of light was a cufflink. The torn cuff was missing its cufflink, presumably lost during the fight. Virginia thought nothing of it and tossed the clothes into the washer, poured in a generous amount of detergent, and slammed the cover shut. Listening to the rhythmic swaying of fabric and water, she hoped everything would come out clean. Somehow, she knew better.

Ingrid's babbling was barely audible over the commotion of the machine.

"So you think we can do that, mama?" Ingrid finished her soliloquy and Virginia had not heard a single syllable. "Mama!"

"Chile, what is it?"

"Are you even listen' to me?"

"Ingrid, leave that boy down here and come back and get him before school start. Now let that be the end of it. I got to see 'bout ya Daddy's garden."

"Mama, what's wrong with you? I just watered it."

"Let me be, chile. I ain't got—" Virginia was interrupted by a blaring phone ring. It was Po-Shank, still at the View.

"How you doin' Virginia?"

"Fine, Po-Shank. How 'bout yo'self."

"Girl, I'm fine as frog hair split four ways. Havin' a blessed day in the Lord as usual. We just tryin' to keep our heads on straight with this big killin' last night. I guess you know about it."

"What chu' mean I know about it? I didn't do anything, Po-Shank," Virginia replied defensively.

"I know you didn't do nothin', honey. You act like you killed the man yo'self."

"Po-Shank, why you keep sayin' that? I told you I didn't do nothin'. Didn't Andrew tell you?" Virginia's responses were hard and hysterical.

"Tell me what, Virginia? I called to see if he was back from down at the jail, I mean, the police station."

"Jail! Andrew's in jail!" Virginia was panic-stricken.

Ingrid overheard the frightening comment.

"Mama! Daddy's in jail?" Ingrid shouted.

"Oh my God, they got 'em!" Virginia confessed.

"Virginia, wait a minute. He's not in jail. He's at the Chief's office talking about the murder. D.J. got to go down there, too."

"Huh, why they callin D.J.?" Virginia asked. Her emotions were pouring out of her spirit and leaping back in between breaths and pulses. The internal struggle forced her to sit down for the rest of the conversation. Po-Shank explained the inquisition and eventually calmed the tortured wife. Ingrid witnessed the transformation of grief, despair, then relief in her mother's eyes.

The phone conversation ended, as did Virginia's emotional marathon. She looked out the window again, not caring who would pull up in the driveway. The agonizing wife just wanted the ordeal and everything surrounding it to conclude, immediately.

෫෫෮

Andrew arrived at the police station around three forty-five. He feared that a prompt arrival would suggest his need to clear his name as a suspect. An arrival any time after four o'clock would have appeared as though he were eluding the inevitable. Making his way through the front door, a loud squeaking hinge announced his presence. The officers in the room, who were strategizing a manhunt for a suspect they didn't have, turned to face Andrew. Each armed man in the room grazed their hands across their holsters. There was a killer on the loose and it was a killer of the worst kind—a cop killer.

"Little on edge around here, ain't cha, boys?" Andrew offered, pulling Kyle around in front of him. He showed the boy's presence to clear the tense atmosphere of any adult tendencies such as profanity or false accusations made in haste. Kyle stood in front of his grandfather, unknowingly serving as a breast-plate of armor. "This here's my grandson all the way from Atlanta. Tell the officers hi, Kyle."

"Hi," Kyle murmured in an uncomfortable shyness. The setting was strange as were the people standing more than twenty birthdays taller than he was.

The Chief, as if offering a countermove, retrieved a little boy himself. A boy the same height and age as Kyle. A boy who also appeared to be discomforted by the giants and their domain. He was a replica of Kyle, painted of a different hue.

"Andrew, I'd like you to meet my grandson, Joshua. His folks had to make a run and had no choice but to leave him here wit' me. Introduce ya'self son," the Chief suggested. Joshua refused and retreated back behind the desk where he was playing prior to his cameo. "Aw hell, I don't know what's wrong wit' these kids now-days, Andrew. What chu think?"

Andrew was a bit perplexed, yet still wary of his own words. The visit so far was a simple social call. Perhaps it was one of the Chief's cunning attempts at bait and switch. A strategic chess match luring Andrew in closer to the hook before he began reeling in a confession.

"Oh, I don't know, Chief. Thangs changin' so fast now. Don't see why the kids can't change too. So what did y'all want to see me about?" Andrew said, pushing his pawn to the Chief's side. The room was quiet once again and the eyes were adhered to Andrew. He concealed his fear by burying his fingers into Kyle's shoulders. Concern invaded Andrew's cool as he once again became the center of attention.

"Andrew, what's say you and me go downstairs and have a conversation, shall we?"

"Yeah, sure. That's no problem, let's go." Andrew proclaimed, throwing a gauntlet of confidence. "Come on, Kyle."

"No, let's just me and you go. The boys can stay here and play together. You don't mind, do you, Andrew? Josh hardly ever gets to play with boys his own age."

Andrew, the consummate thinker, chose his response carefully. A denial would clearly announce anxiety about the interrogation, but what excuse could he give to satisfy the diplomatic, yet authoritative request. He paused, pondering a bit before he spoke.

"Kyle. I'm gon' go downstairs for a minute. You play with Joshua and come runnin' downstairs if you need somethin', you hear me?" He nodded and ran towards his new partner and the two boys emerged into an ebullient bliss. The guiltless generation began a game of Operation while their grandfathers carried their burdens downstairs.

"You know why you here, don't cha, Andrew?"

"Chief, far as I'm concerned, everybody in town gon' wind up in front of you 'fo' this whole mess is settled."

"If that were true, which it ain't, why you figure you the first one down here now?"

"I 'on't know if you done had people down here or not. Far as I know, you coulda had every black man in the city down in this basement tryin' to interrogate us." Andrew accidentally put up verbal defenses, a slight deviation from his plan.

The Chief altered his original intent and instantly began trying Andrew with eyes of judgment. The authority paused and reevaluated his questioning. Andrew had, in fact, been the first person questioned. There were no suspects, however, Andrew all but volunteered with his defensive remarks.

"You sure are jumpy for a man that's being asked a few simple questions, ain't you?" the Chief inquired, shifting his tone from informative to judgmental. "Is there somethin' you want to tell me, Andrew?"

"Shoot, yeah, it's somethin' I want to say. I want to say that every black man in this town is gon' be jumpy until you get a suspect. Innocent men gon' be runnin' from y'all like a snotty nose coon. I want to say you ain't got no right to pull me in here for no good reason. And unless you got somethin' else, I'm leavin'." Andrew walked towards the door until the Chief grabbed his arm. Again he found himself confronting an aggressive officer of the law.

"Get yo' hands off me! What's wrong with you?" Andrew scolded the Chief. Offended, Andrew trembled from an internal place the Chief couldn't see. Boiling, he held onto the thinnest strands of restraint he had ever known.

"Don't forget where you are, boy!" The Chief's derogatory misnomer fueled Andrew and the small room became an incubator of resentment, instigating violence between the two adversaries.

"Don't you forget who you talkin' to! I ain't no boy!" Andrew bellowed volumes above the Chief. His words bounced against the walls and reverberated through the musty air ducts and landed upstairs in the room where the officers were meeting. A herd of footsteps and jingling utility belts thundered toward the door leading to the basement. The Chief delayed his response to Andrew in order to disperse the parade of officers, presumably, coming to his rescue. After comforting his anxious protegees, he returned to a calmed Andrew. His voice dripped of disdain.

"I'll tell you one thing and you can believe it if you want to. I run this station and everything in it. Try me. Test me if you want to. I can find the reason to make you vanish from this life and nobody'll even think about missing you. You understand me? Now, you know why I called you down here, don't you?"

"Don't threaten me 'cause I—"

"I asked you a question and you'd better well answer it."

"Say what you got to say."

He examined Andrew's attitude closely. His opponent's anger had somewhat subsided. Feeling slightly victorious in the verbal battle, he spoke with civility. "I'll expect you down here tomorrow morning for a press conference, right?"

"If that's how it's gon' happen, I guess so."

"And of course you'll give us a discount seeing that you're a fine citizen and all."

"What?"

"We'll expect a discount for advertisin' a reward on your billboard."

"What billboard?"

"You do still own the billboard near the corner store, don't you?"

"Yeah."

"So we know that you and your people are willing to help us any way possible. If we advertise a one thousand dollar reward on your billboard, people'll know we're serious and might be willing to turn on family and friends for that kinda money."

"Is that what you called me down here for?"

"Yeah, what did you think I wanted? To charge you for murder?" The Chief's rhetorical allegation fell on Andrew like rain on thirsty grass.

"Naw, I just thought that, you know, you needed some help from the community or somethin'."

"You'll be helping us just fine when you give us fifty percent off of the ad?"

"Fifty percent!"

"Do you have a problem with that? I'm sure that Mayor could find a reason to invoke a civil need for the board and we could confiscate it indefinitely."

Andrew retreated from his usual arrogant rebuttal. He now realized no one had a clue of his whereabouts the night of the murder. He was free and would remain that way, or so he suspected. Andrew obliged the request.

"I guess fifty percent is fair considering we all need to pull together and solve this problem." The façade was building.

"Good, I knew you'd see it that way. The press conference'll be at nine o'clock."

"What's the press conference for?"

"We're gonna show everybody how we're pulling together as a community to find this filthy crap-eating coward. A few preachers are gonna be there. Some businessmen, doctors, and, of course, you'll be there representin' the black community leaders."

Andrew's stomach filled with lead-laced guilt. A witch hunt was forming and he suspected the first people dragged in for questioning would be the blacks. It would seem as if he condoned the Chief's actions. Andrew faced a defining moment. Remain quiet and head upstairs to live the never-ending masquerade, or reveal himself and reside in a neighborhood where steel and concrete was the depressive landscape. He headed for the stairs and grabbed Kyle on the way out as his masquerade ensued.

Just as the two walked out of the station, one of the newer officers barged into the office. An overzealous rookie, he had been carefully combing the crime scene all morning.

"Chief, we got something!" he exclaimed, holding a plastic bag high in the air.

The item was placed on the table where the other officers were talking. Andrew and his grandson, still within earshot of the group, overheard the conversation. The Chief walked over and picked up a shiny trinket glimmering through the bag.

"Well, what do we have here?" the Chief said to everyone. Andrew stopped and pretended to tie Kyle's shoe on the steps outside. Kyle had known how to tie his shoes for years now. Andrew turned his head toward the group and listened. The Chief continued, "Seems like while somebody was killing one of my officers, they just so happened to lose a cufflink."

Andrew finished the fake shoe tying and walked briskly to the car.

"There's an inscription on it. What's BBA stand for?" one of the officers asked, glancing over the Chief's shoulder.

The Chief paused, then looked towards the door. His mind was filled with questions he wanted to ask Andrew. Staring calmly at the exit where Andrew had barely escaped, he replied, "...The Black Business Association. It's a group of black so-called businessmen in Albany. And one of 'em just walked out of that door."

Five

The Found Link

────────── ⟳⟲ ──────────

"WHERE MY CUFFLINKS?"

"Why was you down at the jail, Andrew?"

"Virginia, did you hear what I said? Find my cufflinks!"

"Andrew, are you gon' tell me what's goin' on first?"

"I said find them cufflinks, woman!"

Virginia looked at Andrew with burning eyes and fixed her jaws to gather venomous saliva to launch at her disrespectful spouse. She didn't deserve the verbal abuse nor did she tolerate it. The wife of many years was submissive, yet intermittently irascible.

She gave Andrew an immediate about-face and retrieved the requested item. Andrew's concern was slowly evolving as was the recurring theme—intestine-turning fear.

"Where's the other one?"

"I couldn't find the other one. I went to wash all of the mess out of your clothes and I didn't see it."

"Did you look for it?"

"I didn't look for it 'cause I didn't know it was lost."

"Woman, what is wrong wit' chu? You stupid or somethin'? What kinda mess is that, you didn't know it was lost? If you ain't got both of 'em, then one of 'em must be lost."

"Andrew Scales, you bedda tell me what's goin' on, so I'll know why you actin' crazy and talkin' to me like I'm a child. I won't be disrespected and you know that. If it's somethin' that we need to do or somethin' I need to do, you bedda let me know. 'Cause the next time you talk to me like I'm not Virginia Scales, I'm not gon' be Virginia Scales much longer."

Virginia's tenacious words slapped sense into Andrew with each sound. He was irrational, he was wrong, and, finally, he was remorseful.

"Baby, I'm sorry," the humbled husband offered. "I just don't know what's goin' on and I need to find that cufflink because I think the Chief is gon' use it for some kind of evidence."

"Evidence for what, Andrew? What happened down there at the jail?"

"Virginia," Andrew prepared himself to speak of the unfolding events, thereby fully involving her, "somebody found a cufflink at the crime scene, a cufflink like the one that you can't find, I mean, the one that I lost."

"But what that got to do with you?" Andrew's evasion of the truth had infected even Virginia and she was fooled by her own denial.

"It was a BBA cufflink," Andrew replied. Virginia stared at him, still confused. "The Black Business Association? You know the organization that I belong to and a half dozen other black businessmen. Me, D.J., Gus, Mack, Ulysses, and Tyrone. Virginia, you know they gon' try to round us up one by one and line us up for a slaughter, you know that. I ain't gon' let it happen, baby. They can't have me. Please just tell me you got that cufflink somewhere or it might be someplace you didn't look. Just tell me, Virginia. Just let me hear you say it and everything'll be all right."

"Oh, Andrew. Andrew... What we gon'... Why, Jesus, why?"

Andrew raised his shameful eyes and traded glances with Virginia. He peered into his wife's innocent pupils which were drowning in her tears. The liquid blurred her vision and she couldn't see Andrew. A moment later, her eyes cleared, but Virginia still couldn't see her husband. She'd already begun envisioning a life without him.

C3ED

Andrew allowed fear and anxiety to slowly seep out of him during the night. He awoke optimistic, yet still defiant, the following morning. There were details all around him that needed attention. If necessary, he would exclude and include anyone from his plans, even his grandson.

"Good mornin', Kyle."

"Hey, granddaddy."

"What chu watchin'?"

"Superfriends."

"Oh, Superfriends. That's a good cartoon, ain't it?"

"Yep, sho' is."

"Which superhero you like the most?"

"I like Wonderwoman."

"What? You don't like Superman or Aquaman the best?"

"Nope, I like Wonderwoman 'cause she make my ding-a-ling go *boing*!

"Kyle! Watch what you say, boy."

"What you talkin' about?"

Andrew formed his thoughts, but delayed words before he spoke. The boy couldn't be reprimanded for nature's inescapable course.

Observing his grandson look studiously at the tube, he imagined Saturday morning conversations with his grandson by jail visits. Perhaps his grandson would visit him resenting that his convict grandfather had forced him to miss the Saturday morning cartoons. The walls were converging on Andrew's conscience and all he saw was the truth smeared in graffiti.

"Nothin', Kyle. Don't worry about it. When you finish watchin' ya show, I wanna talk to you about somethin'."

"We can talk now, granddaddy. I seen this one already."

Andrew thought he would have more time to prepare his sermon.

"Well, what I want to talk to you about is somethin' very special. Now since you gon' be stayin' with us for the summer, I figure you oughta have somethin' really nice."

"For real? What you gon' give me?" Kyle's eyes glistened eagerly with anticipation, hoping he would receive a Big Wheel or one of the latest toys.

Andrew saw the excitement. Hesitant with his intentions, Andrew's conscience battled his conniving objective and subsequently lost. Why should his grandson have to watch him suffer in a jail cell, Andrew thought. Kyle was a crucial stone in the foundation of a family legacy.

If desired, this young boy would bear a welcomed torch of financial prosperity. Andrew had never done anything for himself. Each effort, every dollar spent, all the contacts made were for his children and their children.

Already assumed to be a wealthy man among the black community, Andrew had quietly become a selfish, self-made millionaire before his grandchildren were even born. He dreamed of Kyle's children becoming billionaires simply by inheritance. It was this forward thinking so many of his friends and associates lacked, never realizing the power of building a secure future for generations. Most people he knew sadly lived for today and saved for rainy days instead of buying stock in umbrellas.

"This is somethin' very special and it's gonna be a special secret between you and me. It's so secret you can't even tell ya mama, daddy, not even grandmama."

Kyle, paralyzed with expectancy, gazed into Andrew's mouth searching for his next words. He'd never shared a secret with a grown-up before.

"I want you to have somethin' that's very special to me. And when I give it to you, put it in a special place where nobody can find it. If you lose it, that's okay. Just make sure you lose it so nobody can find it, alright?"

Kyle motorized his head and nodded it uncontrollably.

"What is it? What is it? Can I have it now!"

"Kyle, this is a very special thing to me and now I am givin' it to you as a pact between us. You know what a pact is?" The motorized head went horizontal this time.

"It means me and you gonna keep a secret from the rest of the world." The internal struggle surfaced again but retreated as Andrew pulled the object from his pocket. "Kyle, I want you to have this, hold this, and keep it. Don't show it to nobody. Don't tell nobody about it. This is between you and granddaddy, okay?"

"Okay."

Andrew opened Kyle's hand and bequeathed to the boy a secret.

"Ooooh, thank you, granddaddy. It's nice." Andrew had constructed such a tower of drama for the small gift that any object would have been impressive to Kyle. He watched the offering roll around in his small innocent palm. It was an insignificant grain of sand nestling in the depths of an oyster, waiting for nourishment and growth before presenting itself to the world a stone, slightly imperfect but valuable.

"Granddaddy, what is this?"

"After this day, never show it and never talk about it. It's yo' future."

Six

Strategies

ANDREW FLED TO THE SATISFYING SOLACE OF HIS GARDEN after the conversation with Kyle. On this morning, he toiled over the tomatoes and tilled soil for more vegetation. His hands eased into the earth, massaging the dirt as a peace-offering for the bad seeds he'd sprinkled. The clumps of soil separated easily, his fingers dividing the minerals like pillars protruding into the ground.

The late morning sun began its ritual of producing sweltering temperatures. Sweat began flowing from Andrew's head. The mixture of perspiration and penetrating heat felt like lukewarm blood running amuck over his face as it found its way to the ground. It seemed as though the garden was being poisoned by his mere presence. The heat could be tolerated, but the frantic feelings were too heavy.

Rising from his knees to return to the house, a virulent vision of a man stared him squarely in the face. He was becoming accustomed to uninvited visitors coming to the house. This figure was familiar, yet his facial expression was foreign. D.J. stood before him, his face contorted with discomfort and a bruise atop his forehead.

"Mornin', D.J. What brings you out this early? You hardly ever come 'way from that newspaper," Andrew said. He knew the visit couldn't possibly be pleasant.

"Thought you was coming back by the office after you left the police station?" D.J.'s tone was malicious.

"Man, Kyle got to carryin' on and was gettin' hungry so I had to bring him back to the house. Boy'd been out wit' me all day long. Figured least I could do was—"

"You said..." D.J. began as he moved closer to Andrew. With no regard for the fruits of Andrew's labor, he trounced through the garden, closing in on who he'd considered an ally. Andrew got a better view of D.J.'s face, unshaven with a fresh bump. "...you was gon' call me no matter what time it was so you could tell me the questions they was askin'."

"D.J., watch where you walkin'. Them's my cucumbers. All they wanted was to advertise a reward on the billboard. I thought since that's all they wanted, he was just gonna ask you to put a' ad in the Southwest Georgian," Andrew replied, looking at his friend's footsteps as he walked closer and pounded more produce. "D.J. watch where you walkin', I done told you, you walkin' in my—"

"Why you ain't call me about the cufflinks!"

Andrew was silent for a moment then realized that a moment longer would have exposed his knowledge of the evidence. When the moments made movements cease and time took too long, Andrew's newly acquired talent for lying surged.

"Wh-what, uh, cufflinks?"

"The BBA cufflinks! The police planted one of our cufflinks at the crime scene and now they tryin' to gather up all the members of the BBA. Andrew, they startin' a witch hunt, you hear me?"

"They did what! How you know they planted the cufflink?"

"How else would it get there, Andrew. You think one of us was out there killin' folks? I knew it was gon' get crazy if they didn't find no suspects soon. But I didn't know they was gonna pull some mess like this. You sho' they didn't say nothin' to you about no cufflinks?"

"I-I-I don't know nothin' about nobody plantin' cufflinks, D.J. I swear." Andrew was evasively telling the truth as well as he could. If the theory amongst the community was that police had planted the evidence, he'd just been given a way out. "Is that how you got that lump on your head?"

"What you think? It's gon' be a whole lot a black folks around here with lumps on they heads 'fore it's all over with. This gon' get worse before it get better."

"D.J., you think we can get the members together this evening for an emergency meetin'? We need to get us a plan together."

"A plan for what?"

"A plan so that we can be united when the heat *really* gets rough."

D.J. devised the notifications in his head. It was the first time he'd had the chance to speak to someone since his visit to the station. "I guess I can get everybody over to the church around 'bout six o'clock this evenin'. What you want me to tell 'em the meetin' is about?"

"Just get 'em there and I'll take care of everything else." D.J. began walking away, this time careful of where he trod. Resolving that Andrew was again an ally, the friend took his trust and began his assignment.

Andrew was steadily adding accessories to his cover up.

౮౩౮౦

Andrew walked wearily into the house. His feet were heavy and dragged the ground where he walked. Virginia was standing in the doorway, fresh from her lip-reading observation of Andrew and D.J.'s conversation. Information was scarce around the house and she wanted to remain abreast.

"What was D.J. talkin' about, Andrew, and was that a bruise I saw on his head?"

"We wasn't talkin' about nothin' in particular. Just some business."

"What kind of business pulled D.J. away from the newspaper? You know he don't leave from 'round there unless it's an emergency."

"Virginia, I can't talk about this right now, baby. I got to get ready for a meetin'."

"What meetin', Andrew? Why won't you let me know what's goin' on? I'm scared just like you are. I need to know that I can help you. Andrew, you not alone. I can help you get through this, but you got to let me see yo' pain so I can rub where it hurts and hold you where it's dark."

Andrew glanced at his wife with retinas of reverence. She was reaching out, running to his rescue. Seemingly, the help he'd wanted had been lying in the bed next to him for half his life. Virginia could pull him from the depths of sin and halt his plummeting descent into the asinine abyss which was consuming his life with each revolution of time. However, Virginia's salvation from the situation was the antitheses of Andrew's aim. Slowly he reached out to his wife and pulled her towards him, resting her head on his chest, intertwining their souls.

"You don't know how much that means to me, Virginia. I don't know why I didn't look for yo' comfort to begin with." Andrew spoke softly to her spirit and disrupted it with the news of Kyle's gift. Virginia catapulted her despondency upon her husband.

"Why would you give that...that evil to that boy, Andrew? You know that ain't right."

"What ain't right about it? I'm just a man givin' his

grandson a family heirloom."

Virginia's face jolted into an expression unlike any Andrew had ever witnessed.

"Is that what you passin' down our bloodline? Lies and deceit? You passin' sin into the family? Andrew Scales, I know sure as the grace that God done placed around your heart and mercy he done showed yo' soul, you not gon' put that burden on Kyle."

"What you talkin' about a burden? I am savin' that boy's life and makin' his future."

"You ain't doin' no such thing 'cause—"

"This what I'm doin' ain't for me. Workin', making a way, savin' money. It ain't for me and it ain't for you. Our time is come and gone, Virginia. I'm tryin' to build this family a foundation."

"Not like this you ain't. It can't be done this way."

"It's gotta be done any way we can make it. Everything can't be good and perfect for us. That's why my grandmama was a sharecropper and her mama was a slave, 'cause it wasn't good and it certainly wasn't right. But they built a small foundation for me and I ain't gon' let it go to waste. I got to build on what they did and make it work for my family after I'm gone."

"Andrew, hear me when I say you got to do right by folks and you got to make this thing right or ain't nobody gone prosper. We got to do right by folks if we—"

"When they gon' do right by us, Virginia! When is it gon' be our time to come out on top! When is it gon' turn out right for us, no matter the circumstance! I'm tired of waitin'! I'm tired of waitin' and shuckin' and jivin' and smilin' and hidin'! My folks and my family is long overdue for a victory and it's gon' start right here. It's gon' start right down there with that billboard that I built for my family. That sign is our sign of the future. That sign is the riches and rewards for Kyle. It's his birthright and I ain't gon' be the one to deny him! You know how many innocent black folk is peppered in this ground for stuff they ain't do and thangs that should've been resolved with 'excuse me' or 'I'm sorry'. Words should have been they justice, not ropes and fire! I can't say I'm sorry no more. It's too late! All I got to say is now it's our time. It's time for me to give Kyle his foundation. It ain't no burden, it's a blessin'! You hear me!"

Virginia looked past the resolute anger in all his twisted justification and saw demise. She relented. Arguing was useless.

"I'm glad you think you right, Andrew. 'Cause if it ain't a blessin', God'll take it from him and curse that boy beyond the vision of his great-grandchildren. And *that* burden will be on *yo'* grave.

Seven

Fighting the Truth

⚮

THE MEMBERS OF THE BBA WERE ALL GATHERED IN THE fellowship hall of Mt. Zion Church. Assembled were Albany's most prominent black businessmen. Andrew and D.J. headed the group. They were in the company of Tyrone, the town barber who was beginning a three-shop franchise in Albany and Macon. Gus, the grocery store owner and an ex-war vet, arrived early still regimented in his military experience. Then there was Ulysses, a used car dealer. He was a skilled negotiator who had begun his business by selling used car parts after high school graduation. Mack, the local mortician, was running late due to a last minute embalming. An unlocked side door awaited his arrival.

Albany's most innovative black minds, all graduates of Albany State, were gathered to derive their defense. Andrew sat at the head of the table where the men perched awaiting the agenda.

"Gentlemen, we have a serious matter ahead of us, and it is vital that we get together on this and be on one accord.

I know y'all used to hearin' from me, but I'm gon' turn my chair over to D.J. this time. I think that he's already had some firsthand experiences with our adversaries, so he might be a little more motivated than me."

Andrew relinquished the authority to D.J. as part of his ongoing strategy. He was becoming frustrated with his own lies, and his conscience was increasing in weight. If D.J. orchestrated the plan, Andrew felt he could interject suggestions when needed and remain clear from suspicion.

"Well, Andrew, I wouldn't say I done had firsthand experiences," D.J. began. "I would say it was more like first nightstick experiences. I was about to turn back and look for Dr. King like we did at the marches, Andrew."

A lofted laugh emoted from the men. Humor at this time was odd, but still appreciated. It relaxed them and eased their minds a tad. "Brothers, businessmen, and friends. As you know, the police have perpetuated an evil deed and linked it to the very roots of this community's harvest. If we allow them to besmirch the name of BBA, there will never be another successful black business in Albany. Ever. This is not about a grocery store, a barbershop, or none of us. It is about the integrity and prosperity that we must salvage for the future," D.J. said.

Andrew was again sinking into the theme his wife had planted—Kyle's future and Kyle's children. His internal trial was in session once again. His heart was the gavel—his soul, the defendant.

"Now, if we don't do something about these fools plantin' evidence at the scene of a crime, we gon' be they footstools forever."

"So what we gon' do?" Gus inquired. He'd been fidgeting all the while. Too much talking, not enough action, the vet thought. "When we up against a trouble, we got to meet it squarely face to face. We in a corner and we got to fight our way out."

"That's true, Gus, but this can't be no war of bodies.

It's got to be a war of words and protests."

"Exactly!" Tyrone yelled. "We need to get every black citizen in this city to line up on the sidewalks in front of city hall with signs and banners. That'll wake 'em up."

"That's a good idea, Tyrone. But remember most folks will think this is about the BBA. They don't realize it's about our whole community," D.J. replied, looking to Andrew for confirmation. Andrew nodded in agreement.

"Let me ask y'all somethin'," Ulysses said. "Where they at?"

The men looked puzzled.

"Don't look at me like I'm crazy. I said where they at?"

Strange looks continued to plague the room.

"Okay, I tell ya what. Y'all gon' act like I'm the only one that's crazy. I'll show you what I'm talkin' about."

The finely dressed negotiator began rolling back the sleeves of his sport coat to reveal his shirtcuffs. Displaying his fists in a battle position, Ulysses stood up and projected his innocence.

Andrew knew exactly what he was asking. It was the inquiry Andrew hoped would be avoided during the meeting. He knew it was an assumed risk and his assumption was correct. Ulysses spoke out, challenging the honesty of each man in the room.

"Where is *y'alls* BBA cufflinks? I got mine right here so I know I didn't do it. Seems to me this the first time evidence been planted as far as I can remember, so what made the police start now?"

This wasn't the agenda, D.J. thought, but the question was valid. "Ulysses, we didn't come here to point no fingers. We here to devise a plan and defend our names."

"Yeah, that's all fine and well unless we gon' burn in Hell. And I for one don't plan on sittin' with Satan. Now, I think before we go sayin' what need to happen to the police, we need to show some proof that it's a reason to stand up for everybody in this room."

"Why you always got to be difficult? Everything got to be a deal with you, don't it?" D.J.'s authority was being usurped and his motion disregarded. The disrespect cloaked the importance of Ulysses' question.

"This ain't about no deal, D.J.! You the one talkin' about everybody on one accord. How we gon' be on the same accord if everybody ain't got the proof? I'll stand up and take a blow for each one of y'all long as I know everybody done right by me. Until then, y'all just some regular old knuckleheads on the street."

"You selfish fool!" D.J. retaliated. "How easy you think it is for the police to make a copy of these cufflinks? They can do whatever they want to! You understand that? You think this about how much money you can keep makin'? If you'd get yo' hands out yo' pocket for a minute, you'd realize that we already in this together whether you like it or not!"

"'Case you ain't noticed, D.J., my hands ain't in my pockets. They high in the air with my cufflinks on. Tell you what I have noticed. I noticed that you the only one puttin' up a fight about showin' yo' cufflinks. You got something to hide? Did you make a contribution to the FOP last year?"

"What you say!" D.J. began walking towards Ulysses. "Who you think you talkin' to? I ain't no punk off the street that you hustle for one of them broke-down cars! You gon' talk to me like you got some sense!"

"You come over here old man, you bedda have some cufflinks or a stick 'cause I ain't playin' with you."

"Boy, I'll whip yo' a—"

Andrew interrupted D.J.'s motions and his profanity. The meeting was losing control and tension was taking over the room.

"You just show me the cufflinks!" Ulysses blurted out, unmoved.

"I ain't got my cufflinks!" The walls absorbed the

swelling animosity as everyone turned to D.J.

"And why not?" Ulysses probed.

"'Cause they at home in my drawer. Only time I wear 'em is for functions and what not."

"That's fine wit' me. We'll wait here 'til you run home and get 'em. What y'all say? Everybody else don't mind goin' home to get theirs, do you?" Some men shrugged shoulders while others blinked in bewilderment. Not only had the authority and agenda changed, but the room was now a dartboard.

"That ain't gon' prove nothin', Ulysses," said Andrew.

Everyone turned to Andrew who still had one hand on D.J. to restrain him. "If we all go home and bring back the cufflinks, that means we gon' lose hours of plannin'. We gon' be right back here where we was before the meeting began, and Mack ain't here. We just gon' assume he guilty when everybody else bring they cufflinks back? This is crazy, Ulysses. We all know each other.

"Business is based on trust. We all businessmen and if we didn't trust each other, how would we have made it this far?"

Andrew was proactive in saving himself from exposure. Each person pondered the rational speech. They looked down at the floor, perhaps lowering their heads in shame or in search for an answer.

Ulysses announced a resolution that continued to fuel the tension.

"Since Mack ain't here, I guess we can go ahead and think of some plans. Next time we meet, everybody need to bring those links or they can keep walkin' right on to the police station. If Mack was here, he'd be on my side 'cause I know for a *fact*, Mack don't go *nowhere* without a pair of cufflinks. So y'all can thank Mack next time you see him 'cause—"

The loquacious salesman was interrupted by a knock on the side door. Andrew sank into his chair at the resounding thuds. It was the sound of fists pounding upon the chambers of fate, splintering each knuckle, shredding the skin, and exposing the blood-saturated truth.

Ulysses walked towards the door and changed his mind in mid-stride.

"Well, fellas, look like y'all gon' have to make trip home after all. Come on in here, Mack. Some of our *friends* got some explainin' to do."

As he opened the door, Ulysses was disturbed, frightened, and then angered. Through the door walked eyes of fury and hands of vengeance.

"Well, well, well. Did you think I was gonna miss the meeting?" There, bulging through the door, was the Police Chief accompanied by four officers.

Eight

Searching for Suspects

ᘓᘔ

THE CHIEF'S STOUT DEMEANOR DAMNED ANDREW BE-
yond his most horrific visions. Andrew could sense the
Chief's intuition about who had committed the murder.
Dancing and deviating from the authorities' direct line of
sight, he positioned himself on the opposite side of the table behind the other soldiers in the room. A battle was
brewing.

"What the hell y'all want?" D.J. offered.

"Well now, D.J.," the Chief replied. "What kinda man
would use profanity in the Lord's house? My mama always
said if you swear, you'll lie. If you lie, you'll steal. If you
steal, you'll kill. Kill anybody lately, D.J.?"

"Seems like you should have listened to yo' own mama
there, Chief. Wonder what she'd say about you plantin' that
evidence?"

"What did you say, boy?" a haughty young officer responded. You don't accuse the Chief of no such charge.
This man reigns over this city with trust and integrity. He
did not come down here to be slandered by the likes of you
crooks and killers. We gon' shut down this organized crime
ring of BBA or whatever the hell you call it. The whole

bunch of you ain't nothin' but money launderers and pimps."

"Who you think you talkin' to, little young punk?" Gus, the war vet, bellowed. "You crooked cops ought to bleed *mud*, you so dirty. Get out of this church! This is a private meetin'!"

"We ain't goin' to do nothin' of the sort," the Chief interrupted. "We will stay here as long as it takes to get some answers." His glance engulfed Andrew again.

Pausing to allow the silence to swallow any lingering comfort, he walked over to the offended men, his officers a few feet behind as they moved to different quadrants of the verbal battle zone. Above them was an exposed air duct. The flow of air bending and blowing was symphonic with the vibrations of the air's corridors. The mistaken music was a sheet of stealth for the repetitious strikes penetrating inside the men's chests.

Everyone was imprisoned by the Chief's instant deliberations. Eyes still on Andrew, he spoke. "Seems like to me we have a slight dilemma, which can easily be solved. In fact, it will be resolved in this very room on this very night. The way I see it, the solution to my problem is living and breathing among us right now." His feet were moving back and forth, but his words were searing darts, poking Andrew with each joust. "I need you gentleman, and I use the term lightly, to take a moment and show me a small accessory which you may own. Now I realize that some of you aren't very professional, therefore you don't always dress professionally." The Chief blended insult with his forthcoming accusations. The recipe was much too bitter for the members of the BBA.

"Chief, let me tell you somethin'," D.J. interrupted. "We don't appreciate you bargin' in here talkin' to us like we some ignorant morons. You are talkin' to—"

"Are you confessin' to the crime, D.J.?" the Chief asked in a smooth infectious tone. His words were hypnotic to D.J.'s brash interruption. "'Cause that's all I'm prepared to listen to right now. I don't want any proclamations, no revelations, no outcries of injustice, nothing. I want you all to show me one by one *both* of your BBA cufflinks. And if you don't have them, tell me where they are and what time you'll be at police station tomorrow to show them to me or my men."

Once again, the airflow through the ducts was the supreme sound amid the silence.

"Here go mine right here, Chief!" Ulysses exclaimed. The car salesman was an impulsive dealmaker and this deal included a commission of freedom. Presenting himself in this manner dismantled their consorted effort of a planned protest. "Yes sir, here my cufflinks are right here, Chief. I was tellin' my colleagues just a few moments ago that if they didn't have they cufflinks then I didn't want nothin' to do with no protest about no planted evidence. So I'm gon' head on to the house now if y'all don't mind. When y'all get through here, just call—"

"You'll do no such thing, Ulysses," the Chief announced, removing his hat. He pulled a chair away from the table and parked himself, talking all the while. "We'll all stay here until we finish questioning everybody. You see, Ulysses, if we don't get the right answers, then we'll have to take the whole lot of you down to the station for accessory or obstruction of justice, whichever you prefer. It don't really matter to me. So you can sit your expensive cufflinks down right next to your cheap suit."

The Chief relaxed, swiveled his head back around, and turned to his suspect du jour, Andrew. He had hoped to bait him until his erroneous innocence juiced out, exposing Andrew to his friends and colleagues.

"Where are your cufflinks, Gus?" the Chief asked.

"None of yo' business!"

The Chief turned away from Andrew and motioned over to his officers. "Cuff him."

"Wait, wait. What is this?" Gus backed up and braced himself between his friends. The room shuffled with the anticipation of bodies being thrown about.

"Hold it! Stop! Hold it!" The Chief's voice rang out, halting the commotion. "If there is anyone here tonight that does not know the whereabouts of his cufflinks, or refuses to tell us, you will be arrested as a prime suspect for this case." He was calm for the moment. "So please, let's not waste time and let's not be stupid here. If you are not cooperative, life as you know it will be over." A fevered evil possessed the Chief's tone. "My officer's blood was shed on the highway and someone must pay! You will pay with your life! You will pay with your family! You will pay dearly! You'll pay a price so steep your children's great grandchildren will NEVER, NEVER be able to pay your evil demonic debt!"

Salivating with hate and vengeance spewing from his heart, the being which consumed him subsided and the evil left him instantly. He turned once more to Andrew and spoke peacefully like the reciprocal of a two-faced human. "Now, Gus. Once again, where are your cufflinks?"

Gus looked around. He searched for support from the members. There was none, only fear and desperation.

"My cufflinks are," he swallowed, "at my niece's house in Jacksonville. I let her husband use them for a banquet. I swear that's the God's truth, Chief. You can call her if you—"

"No need," the Chief calmly replied. "Man like you ought to be able to make that drive and back with no problem. Make sure you have those cufflinks at the station by tomorrow mornin'."

"But Chief, that's a four hundred mile drive, round trip. Can't you just call and—" Gus' rebuttal was stopped by a fiery glance. "Okay, I'll have 'em there by nine."

"I know you will. I wouldn't expect any less from you," the Chief patronized Gus before he moved on to the next man. "So what about you, Tyrone? Where 'bouts might your cufflinks be, my friend?"

"You ain't never been nor will you ever be no friend of mine. Doubt if a' evil thang like you even got friends. How you just gon' walk up in the Lord's house and—"

"Let me stop you and everybody else for the last time, Tyrone. This is the last time that I'll ask about the cufflinks and somebody shoots off at the mouth about the weather, Jesus' house, or the neckbone buffet down at Carter's. Next time I ask and don't get the response I'm looking for, you're gonna get dragged down to the station. And I *do* mean dragged."

Nostrils were burning with resentment. The grown men despised being threatened like disobedient children. They had been falsely accused, insulted, humiliated, and now threatened. There were no more verbal or mental subjections—only the physical remained.

"They down at the barber shop in the back room with my tuxedo."

"Woo wee. A coon dressed like a penguin. I can't wait to see—" A young officer's racial slur was cut short by the notepad the Chief hurled through the air—its target: the officer's forehead.

"All right. I'll see you at nine as well. And what about you, Mr. Meeting Conductor D.J. Whitley? Where pray tell are your fine accessories?" The Chief was spreading an extra layer of sarcasm, baiting him to defy his freshly made threat.

D.J. formulated a nasty reply, *They're in yo' wife's jewelry box. I left 'em there as payment for her skunk stanky sex. And I want my change back.* The Chief looked at D.J., waiting to drag him to the station. D.J.'s slanderous insult would have to wait until another time. The angered man tamed himself and responded, "They're at the newspaper office in my desk drawer right next to my revolver and my checkbook."

"Leave the revolver, but bring the cufflinks and check-book tomorrow morning. You never know when the spirit of giving will inspire you to make a donation to the Police Little League Baseball Association. That takes care of everybody except, uh, one Lone Ranger. Andrew Scales. I presume I'll see you tomorrow morning," the Chief said, rising from his seat and inching towards Andrew "or is there something you'd like to tell us? Where are your cufflinks, or should I say where is your cuff link?"

The cool air from the unit was futilely blowing by Andrew. Sweat danced down his face and soaked his shirt. He was terrified and visibly nervous. His emotion directly contrasted the other men. Disdain and anger possessed their faces, but Andrew clung to an unfiltered fear. Terror took over his tongue and he babbled the residue of his deceit.

"At home," Andrew murmured, realizing there were no more detours of deception. The moment of truth had announced its arrival when the officers knocked on the door. He would tell the occupants of the room what really happened and hoped they would understand and have mercy. He even announced a reward for information about the shooting on his own billboard. An ironic generation of revenue, he could collect on his own bounty and write off the cost of materials needed for advertising his own capture. D.J. was assaulted, and now there was a manhunt amongst his friends. There couldn't possibly be a grain of grace for Andrew. Perhaps the Chief could drag him away in a wild whisk, then he wouldn't have to live with the looks of the other men in the room who'd once embraced him, but would now assuredly condemn him. Trembling, he awaited the unfolding of his fate.

"What you say, Andrew?"

"At home."

"At home? Is that it? No specific location? It's not at home, near the 8-track, next to the phonograph? Your buddies told me where theirs were so I could practically go over and pick them up myself. And you say 'at home'?"

The other accused men smothered Andrew with suspicious looks. Ulysses sucked his teeth with satisfaction because the Chief was proving his initial theory.

"Yeah, at home."

"What's at home? Your cufflinks or your cufflink? I'll see you tomorrow 'cause you've got nothing to hide, right?"

Andrew stared at the floor trying to will himself through it, hoping some omniscient osmosis would transport him to a place of innocence. He realized the hesitation had been too long, a second more and silence would have become confession. Between that millisecond of guilt and innocence, he spoke, "Nope."

"No, what? No you won't be at the station tomorrow, or no you have nothing to hide? Say it Andrew! I dare you to say it before your friends, the authorities of this city, and God almighty!" The evil had reappeared. "I command you to say 'I don't have my cufflink' or 'I don't plan on coming to the station tomorrow because I will confess to the murder of an officer'! You say it! Say it right now!"

Andrew, defeated with frustration, yelled, "To hell with you! Damn you to hell! So what I—"

"Get out of here! You ain't welcome and you ain't invited! You are condemned from this place! I will run you out of this town if I have to. If you won't leave I'll bury you here 'cause I'll kill you! I won't stand for this no more!" It was Mack marauding through the door just as Andrew began his confession. His untimely interruption turned the attention away from Andrew and descended upon his rambunctious rhetoric. There was only one statement in Mack's attacking arsenal, the rest was physical confrontation.

He walked to the youngest officer and bumped into him, challenging the man not far removed from puberty. The officer transfused into a beet-colored boy. He looked to the Chief for an answer, the question covered his face, *can I kill him*? The Chief darted over towards Mack who was now in the center of the room. Even the Chief was too stunned to reach for a weapon. He was unsure how to regain control of the meeting.

"Hold on, Mack. Don't come in here takin' my authority. We are discussin' evidence from a crime scene and you can't come in here—"

"I said get out! To hell and back in a dead man's Cadillac!" Mack saturated the Chief's nose with breath drowned in whiskey. He was drunk—dangerously drunk. "I'll tell you about the scene of the crime. You crackas went down to the jewelers and made a BBA cufflink! You lookin' for the cufflink? You don't need to be askin' nobody from the BBA. You need to ask yo' own men, these cowards you call cops," Mack yelled, stumbling and then bumping into the same officer again. He put his hand on his revolver this time as Mack continued his sermon.

"Don't ask us about no cufflinks! Ain't that right, D.J.?"

"I got my cuff link. So speak for yo'self, Mack," Ulysses announced, holding up his sparkling sleeves once again.

"Shut up, Ulysses! This ain't about us. It's about them. It shol ain't about me 'cause I ain't got my cufflinks and can't tell you where they are and the last time I had 'em". The men's eyes shot towards Mack as they realized he didn't know what he had done. Andrew's sweat dried and he stopped trembling. It was another open door of evasion and he shamelessly walked right through it, allowing Mack to continue.

"What did you just say, Mack? Are you tryin' to tell me that you don't have the only piece of evidence that exonerates you from being a prime suspect in this case?" The Chief stood directly in Mack's face while retrieving his handcuffs.

"What I said was to hell with you! Now get out of our

meeting and get out of our church before I get crazy!"

The Chief nodded to the other officers to move in closer. One by one they encircled Mack as the Chief spoke, "Mack, I'm placing you under arrest for the murder of Officer McCord. You have the right to remain silent. Anything you say can and will be—"

Mack reached back and cracked his knuckles, recoiled his forearm, and split the air with blinding velocity as he delivered a cavity-crushing rock to the once perfectly structured cheek of the Chief. Bones were dismantled in the man's face and Mack felt the shattering impact of his hand and wrist as he pushed his shoulder through the blow. The Chief was pummeled by the hit and stricken by Mack's courage and stupidity. An officer reached for Mack, but was rejected by the mortician's footprint now embedded in his chest by a powerful kick. The officer's breath fled his lungs, leaving him temporarily paralyzed from the diaphragm up.

Each member of the BBA merged glances then thoughts. Should they hold him back or fight the officers? Instinct gave way to reason when another officer hurled his nightstick over his head toward Mack. D.J. had seen too many sticks lately. He intercepted the weapon just before it would have splashed Mack's blood onto the floor. D.J. tackled the officer, slamming both of their bodies against a wall. The force shook the walls up to the clanking air conditioner. The unit stopped and the room ignited with the heat of battling enemies.

Some men chose opponents while others retreated to spectator seats. Tyrone chose a partner as though it were a violent square dance.

Ulysses and his cufflinks moved towards the door, cowardly placing one foot outside in case the war raged too close to him.

Andrew, strategizing once again, stayed close to the middle of the room. He'd decided he would allow the fight to go on without his assistance, and then offer his aid for breaking up the mayhem. If no one was watching, he'd slip in a couple of blows.

Mack went for the lung-frozen officer and clamped his hands around his throat. What little breath the officer hadn't lost was now being cut off from his brain. Mack had no idea how much control he had over the officer's life.

The Chief regained his balance and ferociously slammed a chair into Gus' right side. Gus fell with the force of the strike, but was stopped by a table. He turned to retaliate, but found no strength in his arm—only agonizing pain. The same neurons that delivered the message of pain to his arm, delivered the realization that his limb was broken. He shifted positions and attacked the Chief with his left arm. A powerful black burly fist penetrated the air, but nothing else. The Chief dodged the intent and buried his own fist deep into Gus' stomach, forcing him to the floor. Mercilessly, he shifted his weight backward and followed through with a swift kick to the fallen man's head. Gus' body flinched and went limp. He was unconscious.

The suffocating officer was no match for the man who dealt in death every day. His face contrasted in the life-taking hands of Mack. A blue and black mosaic was slowly becoming an abstract for the officer's life. Realizing he could not free himself from Mack's grasped, he possumed until Mack released him, dropping his head to the floor.

Tyrone was tirelessly exchanging shots with his man until he landed a sneaky jab directly into the officer's nose. Tyrone fractured the man's shin with his steel-toed boots. The officer was wounded, upper and lower body. Bleeding from the nose and limping badly, he retreated, shriveling into a protective fetal formation.

Ulysses placed more of himself out the door as the Chief walked towards Mack.

This was Andrew's chance to play peacemaker. Mack had just defeated his man, as did the Chief and Tyrone. If he could control the chaos while the Chief was outnumbered, it would show favor when the storm exhausted and more questions were raised.

"Hold it! That's enough! Everybody hold it where you are!" Andrew yelled.

"Andrew, you get out my way. I'll kill you just to get to that cracker so I can kill him!"

Mack looked beyond Andrew and saw death as he had daily. It was there looking at him, transparent to walls and ceiling and floors. The structure was invisible as were the men in the room—except the Chief. Mack could feel the smell of death pricking the membranes in his nose. It was here in this room and death was coming for someone.

Mack's victim rose from his possum state, his face full of color again—the color of determination—determined to prevent Mack from stealing the breath from anybody ever again. His hands were clasped around vengeful steel loaded with malicious lead.

"No! Don't—" the Chief began as he watched Mack jerk toward him from the force of bullets opening six holes in his back. Death had come and gone.

Nine

Early Departure

——— ⚙ ———

AFTER LEARNING THE DETAILS OF MACK'S DEATH, HIS family faced rarely asked questions. Who would bury the city's black mortician? Who would serve as escorts for the funeral procession? Normally, the police force provided the service for mourners of the dearly departed. They wanted nothing the police had to offer. They'd considered using a local motorcycle club, but learned, of course, they had no authority to stop traffic as the need existed. The surrounding cities' police forces were advised not to cross into the turbulent times which were slowly swallowing Albany, Georgia.

Mack's wife announced her decision; the bereaved would block traffic themselves. Not by conventional means of hand waving or traffic lights. They would use their mere presence by walking the entire route of the funeral procession. A route from Mt. Zion to the Oakview cemetery was long, but bearable.

She'd made it known that before the interment everyone would leave from the church. From there, able bodies would walk down the sidewalk hand in hand, detouring downtown in front of the police station and then to the cemetery. The five-mile march would seem longer by the feet of shuffling mourners.

☙❧

It was a somber Saturday. Saturated by a simple sun, the temperature was predicted to reach a hundred and one.

This day—normally reserved for lounging and relentless recreations—had a melancholy task to complete. Today was a premature home-going service, the enrollment of a new saint amongst the heavens. Friends and well-wishers arrived promptly, a few even a half hour early. Strong-willed women and masculine men all shed their protective skin, succumbing to sorrow the instant they moved through the church doors. Weeping eyes gazed from the woeful people dispersed throughout the sanctuary. Those anxious to arrive and offer their support were jolted with a heavy sadness upon the unsightly image of Mack's home-going vessel. The reality was disheartening. A successful businessman, a friend, a neighbor had been slaughtered—in God's house. A widow left alone in her bed, drowning her pillows with tears. Children only allowed to remember the word that once flowed easily from their lips. Now the word had become a memory—Daddy.

Soft comforting notes of gospel tunes camouflaged their way into the atmosphere, bringing glimpses of peace. Seconds of relief. The ushers, who were once stout columns of strength for the attendees, lowered their heads, refusing to observe the depressing scene and hiding their own faces washed with the salty release of overflowing tear ducts.

A pastor began the order of service, his words direct and comforting. He spoke on the weeping of night and the joy of morning. Eloquently, he foretold of the meek and humble inheriting the earth. Combining syllables with inflections and phrases with pauses, he soothed the troubled souls of the saddened while blessing Mack's spirit as he ascended homeward.

Upon completion, he relinquished his position to a lone soloist, Mack's brother, Marcus. A golf caddy who'd refused to help run the family funeral business, the crying brother presented himself before the congregation in his best attire; an old gray pen-striped suit sprinkled with patched holes over the knee and elbows. He'd long ago lost the two ties that were the anomalies of his wardrobe. Today his dress shirt was fashioned by a paisley imprinted bathrobe belt, of necktie width. Only he and God knew the secret. Shoes that once belonged to the fortunate found their way to his closet through the town's thrift shop. The frugal man harbored his money for golf equipment and lavish golf trips.

A musician flirted with the keyboard, trying to find a suitable pitch for the ill-dressed man. Marcus waved off the organist, signaling that his effort would be a cappella. Clearing his throat and bellowing out the first note, he released a deep, scratchy, yet soothing sound. His voice brushed the air as though they were strokes of abstract hues, painting images of angels about the church. Marcus sang the first line,

Soooon I will be done with the troubles of this world...

He held on to the last note, strangling the words with quivering vibrato. The bereaved looked past his shabby threads and inhaled the melodic masterpiece he concocted like a pot boiling over with blessings. When the meal was too much, the family members began screaming out for their loved one's early departure. The song's sounds, the words, the meaning, squeezed their hearts, forcing them to run out of the sanctuary. They scurried out and seemed to move so fast, they floated with the angels in the image of the man's melodic brush strokes. His music was comforting, but confusing.

Recipients of the song's offering battled with the acceptance of the words as praise for Mack's endeavors while at the same time supplying sorrow for his infinite absence in their physical lives. Marcus continued to sooth and torture.

...Nooo more weepin' and a wailin'...

Reaching towards the coffin that consumed his sibling, he was now serenading only his brother. Perhaps professing to him emotions he'd never taken the time to express while he was still here with him in the flesh. The physical manifestation of the brothers' love had now become exchanges of gestures between heaven and earth. Marcus concluded the solo, wishing he'd sang for his brother years earlier. The last lines of the song were cloaked in cries, screams, and commotion of people running from sorrow and yelling at pain.

Upon the song's finale, the church was half-empty and the courtyard outside was half full. People were outside, waiting, grieving, holding on.

...I'm goin' home to live with God.

Andrew remained in the sanctuary next to his wife. Tears were escaping her eyes and her husband was immovable in his seat, paralyzed and drowning in his own guilt. Virginia made an effort to turn towards Andrew. Not able to look in his eyes, she struggled with a soft, stern, shaking inflection.

"Andrew Scales, this seed you done planted is startin' to fester. And this burden is makin' a stench so bad I can't hardly breathe no more. As I sit before God in his house right now at this very minute, I swear you bedda get this weight off of us." Pausing, she painfully turned to look at his face and continued, "'Cause if you don't, I will."

Ten

Valuable Time

 началась

WEEPING AND WAILING SIGNALED THE DESCENT OF Mack's
spiritless body into the earth. The men who had witnessed
the atrocity stood over the sinking coffin. Each of them
reached in their pockets to retrieve the source of the as-
sault—their cuff links. They had all agreed to bury the
cufflinks with Mack's body, even Ulysses. They hoped it
would end the era they all wanted to erase. Tossing the
shining trinkets into the hole, the grown men quickly turned
to walk away. Andrew hoped the men wouldn't notice that
his pair of cufflinks didn't match the ones they'd all thrown
in.

началась

Virginia, disgusted with death and deceit, caught a ride
home after the symbolic march, leaving Kyle and Andrew
to drive back home from the church on their own.

" Granddaddy , what was that y'all threw in the grave?"

"Oh, that was just some stuff that was important to us.
Mack was a good friend and we all belonged to the same
group."

"The stuff you threw, was from the group?"

"That's right, Kyle."

"What was it?"

"Just some old jewelry. Nothing much."

"I thought it was special."

"Well, not really. It was—"

"Cufflinks not special?"

"How you know we threw cufflinks in the grave?" Andrew was afraid Kyle had been talking to someone.

"I walked over there and looked in when everybody was gone. They looked like the special gift you gave me."

Andrew pulled the car over to the curb and slammed the gearshift in park.

"Kyle, you remember what Granddaddy told you about that gift I gave you."

"Uh-huh."

"What did I say?"

"Don't never tell nobody about it and don't ever show it to nobody cause it's our special gift."

"That's right and if you tell somebody they might get jealous. Then I'll have to go and buy them one. That present cost a whole lot of money. If I do that, I won't have money to buy you Christmas presents and birthday presents and ice cream!"

"We goin' to get some ice cream?"

"We shol' can, but you got to promise that you won't never talk to nobody about this."

"Okay, I won't say nothin'. I'm gon' get a triple scoop from the ice cream shop!" Kyle said, turning his attention to the delectable treat awaiting him. Andrew wasn't sure if he'd understood the importance of his request or if he was being motivated by the ice cream.

It was a mistake, Andrew realized, hiding the evidence this way. Had he known the BBA would dispose of the evidence in a manner safe from all but grave robbers, he would have waited. But he wasn't living within logic at the time. Each tick was a second of torment and each hour was a haunting. Logical thinking couldn't have survived in that frame of life. Andrew relented in a cloak of confidence that the secret was dying in an infinite trial of trust.

Heading out again, Andrew redirected the car toward to the ice cream shop.

"What did you think about the funeral today, Kyle?"

"It was funny 'cause all them grown people was cryin'."

"Ain't nothin' funny about people cryin', Kyle. Why would you say somethin' like that?"

"I thought only kids and babies was supposed to cry. I ain't never seen my daddy cry."

"Everybody got tears. Just 'cause you ain't seen yo' daddy cry don't mean he don't do it. People cry when they happy, cry when they sad, and cry when they hurt. Those people at the funeral today was hurtin' and ain't nothin' funny about hurtin'."

"How'd they get hurt?"

"Well, you know what it feels like when you fall down and scrape your knee, right?"

"Yeah."

"This is a different kinda hurt. This is the hurt you can't feel on the outside, but it aches you really bad on the inside. It's the feeling that something is gone when you want to have with you. Understand?"

Kyle glanced over at his elder and then out the window, watching for the ice cream shop to appear.

"Not really."

"You remember when you had that dog named Pete and we let it stay here in Albany while you was in Atlanta?"

The small boy darted his eyes at Andrew, angry that he had brought up a ghost from the not-so-distant past.

"You mean the dog that grandmama let run away after he ran through the house and chewed up her girdle!"

"Now that's between you and ya grandmama. I ain't getting' in that one. But it hurt when that dog was gone didn't it?"

"Yeah, shol did! Huuh."

"Now, imagine that dog being ya mama or ya daddy, or ya friend or—"

Said Kyle with a humbled hush, "Or you granddaddy?"

"Yeah, or maybe even me. Think how bad it would hurt if we had to leave...forever." Andrew paused, allowing his words to swim in the silence of his explanation. Kyle pulled himself away from the anticipated vision outside of the car. He looked down at the floor mats. For a few stolen seconds, the young boy envisioned a world without people whom he loved and cared about. Reflecting back on the funeral, his impressionable emotions could feel the heavy pain from the tears he'd described earlier as, funny. Now releasing his own drops of pain down young cheeks, he spoke to Andrew.

"Granddaddy. Don't leave me, okay? I don't want you to go nowhere, okay." Rushing as many loving words as he could, Kyle moved from his side of the car and placed himself against Andrew, laying his arms over the grandfather's stomach. It was the best hug he could give. "Granddaddy, I love you, just don't leave, or go nowhere, or die, or run away, okay? I won't tell nobody about my present, I promise. Just don't leave me. Stay here for the rest of my life, okay?" Kyle rested his head on Andrew, sobbing as he thought of a world without his favorite old person.

"I can't stay here for too long," Andrew offered, as he cut the engine from the car.

"Why not, Granddaddy!" Kyle asked, his voice dripping with regret.

"Cause I got to go in there and get you a triple scoop," Andrew replied, wearing a devilish smile as he pointed at the ice cream shop.

Kyle looked outside to confirm the gesture and turned back toward Andrew, smothering him with every bit of love a seven-year-old could give his grandparent.

Eleven

Preparation

ᚳᚣᛒᚷ

WEEKS AFTER THE FUNERAL, MACK'S BROTHER AND WIFE, unable to sustain the business, turned to Andrew for help. The city had found its scapegoat in Mack. Since he'd professed that he didn't know where his cufflinks were, officials placed the blame solely on his dead shoulders. It was the quickest resolution to what would been a slowly solved case. Aside from the Chief, those seeking a conviction accepted the events as justice. Apparently, Mack's alleged guilt in the murder, prompted businesses to rid themselves of association with the funeral home.

Most of the black families continued to patronize the business, but the resources used by the home were pulling out. A bank refused to honor the terms of its loan and demanded full payment or threatened foreclosure. None of the other banks would give the business credit since its sole proprietor was deceased.

Embalming chemicals and tools couldn't be replenished; therefore, bodies couldn't be processed, which would generate the much-needed income. All of the bodies in waiting were days away from decomposing and one had even begun the first stages of stench. The only choice was to bequeath them to other funeral parlors.

Friends from the community tried to take up collections and solicit donations from organizations. Any crumpled cash scraped up during the effort was dissolved in past due bills. Andrew was the final hope of Mack's legacy.

"Andrew, I shol 'preciate ya seein' me like this. I just don't know where else to turn," Mack's brother said. Adorned in his typical golf attire, Marcus held the hand of Mack's wife, Emma. She could barely hold her own body together, let alone her spirit.

"I ain't never know nothin' but golf courses, so this funeral thing is kinda new to me. One thing I do know about is debt and it seem like we done took on quite a bit of it since the bank folded on us and all."

"That ain't right! That ain't right at all!" Andrew exclaimed, prolonging the inevitable request for money. "I don't see how they can do that to y'all. I'm sure Mack had a contract on the loan and if you find a good lawyer, he might be able to get that loan back. There's a lawyer I met that lives up in Decatur. He'll—"

"That's a good idea, Andrew but, we need money to pay a lawyer, which is why I'm here. Emma says that yo' business is doin' real good and you and Mack was in this business group, so I thought you might be able to help with a nice size loan. Maybe you and your other business buddies can help out, too?" Marcus massaged the words into Andrew, his eyes searching for favor.

Andrew rose from his seat and walked over to the window staring at his garden, speculating about rain. "What kinda loan you and Emma lookin' for?" Andrew asked, rubbing his stubble-infested chin.

"We was hopin' that y'all could get together and between the whole group, you could come up with the entire amount," Marcus replied.

"For all the money the bank want on demand?"

"Yeah. That plus a little to get us over until we get some steady business comin' in."

"How much we talkin' about exactly, Marcus?" Andrew looked down at Emma, still paralyzed with pain.

"All together, if you could get the group to see your way with lettin' us borrow ninety thousand, we should be all right."

"Dollars!"

"Yeah. What you think I was talkin' about, shoes?"

"I don't know. That's a whole lotta money. Even for the whole group."

"How much do you think you and the business group could loan us?"

"You ain't got to go through the group," Virginia interjected, appearing in the doorway.

"Hey, Virginia. It's good to see you. How you been doin'?" said Marcus.

Virginia's presence would not be cordial, but cold and direct.

"I'm fine, but it ain't me that's got the problem. Emma, Marcus, don't worry 'bout goin' to the Black Business Association for help 'cause—"

"Yeah, that's what it's called, the BBA," Marcus said.

"You don't have to go through them 'cause Andrew is gon' make this whole thing right," Virginia whipped a glance at her husband. "Ain't you, Andrew? And if he don't, I know somebody that will."

Virginia's threats were becoming more frequent now. He returned the daring stare his wife gave with humility and respect.

"I'll do what I can to help. Y'all know that," Andrew relented.

"That's a great, man. We shol' appreciate that. We knew you'd come through."

"Why don't you stop by the office tomorrow about nine and I'll write a check."

Virginia kept her eyes glued to Andrew. She knew he'd suggested the office so she wouldn't find out how much money he would be giving.

"Man, I can't thank you enough. Let's go, Emma." Marcus and the woman rose wearing smiles of relief they'd lost between the funeral and the Scales' sofa. Andrew's decision was a transformation of their emotions, restoring their optimism.

Andrew escorted the couple out and headed for the back door to toil in his garden. Virginia stood in his path blocking the back door.

"Don't you play with this thing, Andrew Scales."

"I'm gettin' real tired of this, Virginia."

"Well, I'm tired, too, Andrew. You know why? Cause it's buildin' and it's spreadin'. This thing is bigger than you now. And if you don't kill it, it's gonna sprout into a thousand souls."

"What thing is this you keep talkin' about? You sound like a witch doctor always talkin' about souls and burden and sins. Can't you find somethin' else to talk about? Say something else for once," Andrew said, changing his intention of going out. Instead, he remained in the kitchen and poured a glass of sweet tea.

"Andrew, I can't say nothin' else because that man is dead in the ground for something he didn't do. Do you understand what that means for those who labor in his death and those that dwell here on the earth mournin'? I can' say nothing else because it's crushin' my lungs. It's stranglin' my breath just to think about it at night."

"I done already had this talk with you once and I don't plan on havin' it again."

"Didn't nothin' come outta the first talk except for lies and deceit."

"I'm not havin' this talk again, I said."

"We gon' have this talk again and we gon' keep on havin' it until you fix this thing."

Andrew drew himself directly in front of Virginia. He whispered aggressively, "It ain't nothin' to fix 'cause it's done already fixed itself."

"Have you lost yo' mind? Is this what you call fixin'? A man's business about to fall apart for somethin' he didn't do? A widow, that could have been me, crippled in her own misery. A town split by the races? This is how things get fixed in yo' eyes?"

"What you want me to do, woman? Why I got to do more damage than what's already been done?"

"'Cause you know why all this has happened. You know how it coulda been stopped. I love you more than anything that's got life in it, but I love you so much that I can let you go so that what's right can be done. Do you understand that?"

"Right is gonna be done. It might not happen today, but years from now, right is gon' make its way to the front. And if somebody got to hurt for the sake of right, then that's what got to happen sometime."

"You know that's wrong."

"It ain't no more wrong than all other things that ain't good."

"It ain't right, Andrew," Virginia proclaimed, moving away from him. He walked toward her, forcing his disposition.

"Why you keep sayin' that? I done already told—"

"Two bodies have left this earth 'cause of us! That blood is runnin' through this house! Do you hear me, Andrew? That blood is like a river of pain. I can feel the waves crashin' against my mind every night. It ain't right for them two men to be dead and us not tell somebody what we—"

"Who else dead, grandmama?" Kyle poked his head around the corner, awakening from an afternoon nap. All three stood in the awkward moment.

"People die all the time, Kyle," Andrew began. "Presidents die. Movie stars die—"

"Policemen die," Kyle added. Virginia headed for her bedroom with haste. Each word made her feel like an accomplice to the spreading virus.

"Well, yeah. That's true, son. So we got to make sure that we make the most out of life while we're alive, okay."

"Okay, granddaddy. I was just comin' downstairs 'cause I thought you was gon' be in the garden."

"As a matter of fact, I am. You know ya mama and daddy gon' be here in a little while to take you back to Atlanta?"

"I know," Kyle answered with disappointment. "Can we go in the garden one last time, please? I hate when summer time is over. I wanna stay with you and grandmama."

"Come on boy. Let's check on the garden one last time 'fore you head back up the interstate." Andrew retrieved his sweet tea, gulped down the soothing cool liquid, and headed outside with Kyle.

Surveying his vegetables and checking for insects, he noticed Kyle walking behind him, imitating his every step and trait. The shadowing boy began his interview.

"Can't I go to school in Albany and stay here with y'all?"

"Naw, you don't need to do that. You got to get back home to your friends. Ya mama and daddy need you at home."

"But we ain't got no garden at home and we—"

"If you stay here, you got to go to bed early on school nights and get up early in the morning."

"For real?"

"Shoot, yeah. Watch where you steppin' now. Don't get on my tomatoes."

"I'm sorry," Kyle offered, correcting his steps. "I may as well go back home then."

Andrew chuckled. "I guess that's the best thing for you,

but you know what?"

"What?"

"I'm gon' try to get yo' mama 'nem and aunt and some other folks down here for Christmas."

"For real!"

"Sho' 'nuff. We can all stay at the house and ya'll can go to bed together and when y'all wake up—"

"Santa can come to yo' house!"

"Yep, and we can all have us a good old time. Then you can come back down next summer."

"Thank you, granddaddy. Albany is the best place in the whole world. I'm gon' live here when I get big," Kyle said. His ebullience spilled over into his feet, which tromped the tomatoes again. "Sorry," he admitted, looking up at his Grandfather with guilt.

"If you don't learn how to walk right in my dirt, you ain't gon' be down here too many mo' times," Andrew replied, allowing a smile to escape.

"You mean right like how grandmama talkin'?"

"Ya grandmama has a lot on her mind lately."

"She still sad 'cause them two men died? Do you know why they dead?"

Hesitating, Andrew wanted so badly for his daughter to pull up in the driveway and take Kyle away from more false explanations.

"Granddaddy wants to explain somethin' to you. Everybody, no matter who you are—black, white, man woman—we all do bad things or we get in trouble. But what makes it okay is the good stuff we do. If you do enough good, then the bad stuff really don't count."

"What do you mean?"

"Listen. If you act up in school, like you talk too much or you forget to do your lesson, when you a good student, your teacher might not care that you did somethin' bad."

"For real!"

"Yeah, but only if you done a whole lotta good stuff.

Because when you do, if people say bad stuff about you, it won't even matter. The reason why is because you'll be such a good person, understand?"

"A little bit."

"One day you might find out that somebody is saying bad things about me."

Kyle showed his concern by projecting eyes of sadness at the mere mention of someone slandering his grandfather.

"What they gon' say?"

"Well, I don't know. Different people might say I did somethin' or they might call me names."

"Why?"

"I ain't proud of everything I done. But like I said, the bad stuff we do ain't much if we do good things all the time."

"You do good stuff with me all the time."

'That's right and I want you to always remember that. If somebody says somethin' bad about me, you remember all the good, okay?"

"If somebody say somethin' bad about you, I'm gon' kick they butt like the Incredible Hulk!"

Andrew released a laugh for his grandson and a sigh of relief for himself. The session was complete. Laughter was interrupted by a single car door slamming in the driveway. It was time for Kyle to conclude what would become many summer sessions with his favorite elder. An unwarranted visitor, however, would prolong this session. Expecting to see his daughter and son-in-law, the bulging figure of the police Chief ripped his stomach with knots.

Extending and accepting his own invitation through the driveway and around back to the garden, the Chief approached Andrew. He resumed the cold stare he'd begun in the basement of the police station. The Chief patted Kyle on the head as a symbol of truce, while at the same time showing there were no boundaries of who could be touched if need be.

"Hi, Kyle. You remember me?" the Chief asked. Kyle shook his head. He was now on the defensive about anyone coming to defame his grandfather. "That's okay. I remember you. My grandson talks about you all the time. He wants to know when you can come over and play with his race cars."

"You mean, Joshua?" Kyle asked, warming up at the mention of toys.

"Yeah, that's him. You remember now, don't you?" Kyle nodded his head with enthusiasm. "I thought you would. You remember that day you came to the jail don't you, Andrew." The Chief completed his sentence in Andrew's space.

"Is there something I can help you with? I'd suspect you wouldn't want to be showin' yo' face on this side of town for a while."

"Oh really. And why is that?" the Chief asked, crossing his arms, awaiting a response. He was setting Andrew up as he had in the basement.

"Seein' how the police have killed a member of our community recently, one would think you're not welcome over here."

"Well, if that's the case, you shouldn't show your face on this side of town either, since we're talking about killing people." The two men froze each other with challenging looks.

"Kyle, go in the house and wait for ya mama," Andrew instructed, eyes still on his adversary. After he heard the door close, he smiled a bit and walked out of his garden.

"You got somethin' you want to say to me, Chief?" Andrew asked, his voice soft and threatening.

"You got somethin' you want to say to me, Andrew?"

"I sho' do."

"Say it, then."

"Get the hell out of my yard."

"Anything else?"

"Don't come back," Andrew snarled. "Stay away. Get out. Hit the road. You ain't welcome here. Take the stank you brought with you. You get the picture?"

"I got it, Andrew. Now I got something to say. It sure is a coincidence that you got all hot and bothered that day in the basement before you knew what I wanted. Even more so a coincidence that the minute you left, one of my officers came in and told me about the cufflinks." The Chief walked in a small circle, staring at the ground. "Then, if that wasn't enough, I couldn't help but recall the coincidence of the night Mack was killed. I couldn't help but recall how on that night, everybody talked about the whereabouts of their cufflinks." he halted his movement and strangled Andrew with anticipation. "That is everybody except you."

The gauntlet was on the ground now. Both men, opposing each other, walked a few steps closer and Andrew responded, "You accusin' me of somethin', Chief?"

"You confessin' to something, boy?" the Chief replied, hoping to incite Andrew.

It seemed the two had gone back in time to the same standoff they'd had once before. Andrew, boiling with the anger of death, had less to lose now with the advantage of hindsight.

"If you tryin' to imply that I didn't have my cufflinks, I'll have you know that I placed mine in the grave with the body of my dear friend along with the rest of my associates. If you don't believe me, why don't you go and dig him up? You think things is hot around here now, you go over to that cemetery with a shovel and see if you don't stay in there forever."

"Don't threaten me, Andrew Scales. I'm not a second-rate officer that drinks on duty and pulls people over without callin' it in first."

And that was it. In one sentence, the Chief had summarized the genesis of Albany's bloodspot: an officer, liquor, and a temper. Andrew fought with all he had not to take his eyes off the Chief, which would have been the single admittance of his guilt.

The Chief kept twisting the shank of suppression deeper into Andrew's gut.

The staring continued. Not one grimace. Not a flinch. There was barely a breath. Andrew could feel his fingers tingling as the clinching of his fist-strangled blood cells escaping to his aorta. He was about to smash a blow of lightning against the Chief's temple and cease his existence in one second. As the thoughts instructed the muscles and the muscles initiated the bones, and the arm began to cock backwards, a horn blew in the driveway. Ingrid and her husband pulled up to retrieve their son. The summer was over, as was the battle.

The Chief looked in the direction of the car and gave one last strike before leaving, "If no one else knows, Andrew Scales, I know. Maybe not now or maybe not later, but there will be justice." He smiled the gentle, conniving smile that made ordinary men confess even to long-past boyhood crimes.

The blood was seeping into the ground of Albany, Georgia, infesting the fruit. Andrew looked up at a motionless sky, wishing it would rain and wash it all away.

As quickly as the Chief left the backyard, Ingrid and her husband appeared on the back porch. Ingrid's face was covered with concern and a bit of suspicion. Her father had not been the same person since the night he and Virginia returned home late at summer's inception.

His actions, coupled with the town talk, prompted her to ask the questions Andrew had become so skilled at dodging. Angus dared not wander off into the turbulent waves of his father-in-law's personal matters. He was a passive cosigner in the presence of Andrew.

"Garden lookin' good, pops," Angus said.

"Thank ya, son. I always knew I liked you. Right from

the start."

Andrew wanted this conversation brief and uneventful. Angus grinned, knowing that he had made the right remark again.

"Daddy, why are the police over here?" Ingrid said, imposing.

"You know them fools is still actin' crazy after what happened to Mack. I guess he still tryin' to mess with folks."

"But why is he over *here* messin' with folks? Why is he messin' with you?"

"I don't know. You got to ask him if you want to know."

Angus retreated into the house, smelling the brew of friction. He didn't want to be in a position where he would be forced to take sides.

Ingrid moved closer to address her father face to face. Andrew was growing frustrated with the recent barrage of personal face time. His daughter whom he had punished, then admonished, for years, was now asserting herself in an effort to press her father for answers. She folded her arms and spoke, "Daddy, did you have somethin' to do with what happened to that policeman and Mack?"

Andrew shook his head. "Girl, naw, why you ask me somethin' like?" he responded, walking away from Ingrid and avoiding eye contact.

"Look at me, Daddy! I am serious. You been actin' strange ever since you and mama—"

"I don't know who you think you talkin' to, but I ain't Kyle! You don't come in my house speakin' nothin' about death to me! What's wrong wit' chu? Bedda act like you got some respect!"

Retreating from her father's fury, Ingrid was instantly reminded of his scorn when she was a child. The booming resonance had once rolled through the house as it was now in her adult ears, painting childhood images of discipline.

She could not respond although she wanted to. There was an urge to accuse him of hiding secrets so deep they were falling from the soles of his feet and she could see the truth where he walked. For an instant, she had the inclination to ask why he and Virginia were as far apart as she'd ever seen them. His spewing words drowned anything she had left to say.

Turning to walk into the house and retrieve her son from this place that was now an odd structure with strange people, she glanced at her father to tell him with her eyes that she knew something was awry.

Twelve

Shallow Pockets

AFTER TELEPHONING FELLOW MEMBERS OF THE BBA, the only donation Andrew could solicit was good wishes and condolences. Each man cited financial strongholds on their respective businesses. White advertisers were encouraged to pull ads from D.J.'s newspaper. The other members were feeling the suffocation from banks which had loaned them money.

Andrew, feeling ever more fragile with the blood now drying his soul from the inside out, gave of himself. There was a lone safe deposit box, unknown to workers inhabiting the bank. If there was ever a time to become reacquainted with the treasure, it was now. It was his obligation, a gesture for the family who knew not the depths of Andrew's involvement.

He entered the bank, sauntering with an arrogant stride, briefcase clasped in his right hand. Daring anyone to question his presence or not render to him immediate service. Andrew's demeanor commanded the attention of a bank employee. A red-haired woman decorated in lavender garments with clashing blue eye shadow, made eye contact with him. Holding his hand in the air, he summoned her with a twitch of his fingers to walk towards him.

When she arrived at the vault, Andrew informed her that he wanted to retrieve items from his safe deposit box. The woman laid her eyes on Andrew from shoes to crown as if to ask, *you have a safe deposit box?* Nevertheless, she retrieved a key to oblige.

Alone in the vault, Andrew opened the box, exposing the small hidden fortune. Packed tightly inside the box was an assortment of large bills. Some were as crisp as freshly minted notes, others had ragged edges, curled and torn. Andrew kept his personal supply of cash here, making deposits every two years. It gave him enough time for bank employment turnover to lose track of his visits. Having maintained the practice since his early twenties, Andrew had amassed in this box, unbeknownst to most, over three hundred and fifty thousand dollars. His bank account was a measly thirteen thousand. Each time he visited the box or thought about it, or even remembered that it existed, he thought of his grandson.

He envisioned Kyle walking into car dealerships and buying showroom cars in cash. Thoughts of the boy buying a home with one check beamed a smile upon his face. The hoarding of money was never for himself, but for future generations.

On this visit, he'd come to extract the savings as he emptied the diverse notes into the briefcase, leaving only the titles to his cars and nine hundred sixteen dollars. A joke for the bank if they came snooping.

Andrew closed the brief case, fastened the shining locks near the handle, and headed for the home of Mack's widow.

CঙৎO

"Three thousand dollars! Is that all y'all could come up

with?" Marcus exploded at Andrew's token.

"Marcus, Emma, times is tough. The banks' tryin' to squeeze us and right now folks' businesses just ain't that strong," Andrew replied, alternating eye contact between the two.

"Man, I thought y'all was runnin' this town. Ain't y'all suppose to be the top business mans in the city?"

"Yeah, but even good businesses have bad times."

"Bad times? Three thousand dollars ain't bad times! That's no times! I can make this in a year carryin' golf bags."

"I didn't get you that money in a year. I got it in a day." Andrew said, then paused as he got up from his chair and walked to the window. "Besides, couldn't nobody contribute but me no way."

"What you say?" Marcus asked.

"Everybody else kinda tapped out right now, so I had to go in my own stash and scrape up what I could."

"Andrew Scales," Emma began. "That's a noble thing you done and I'm sure Mack would thank you for it."

"I appreciate you sayin' that Emma 'cause—"

"Andrew," she paused, allowing both men to wallow in her unspoken words for a moment. Andrew sat waiting for the inevitable accusation. "You know good and well that three thousand dollars ain't even gon' keep that place runnin' for one week. We got bills to pay and families we need to try and get back. How we gon' do that with these table scraps you done brought up in this house?"

"I appreciate it more than you know. But you walk outta here and try to tell them men to reach down where they can't see and come up with somethin' to help preserve my husband's legacy. If not, we gon' either sell it or file for bankruptcy. Either way we gon' lose it."

"Unless we sell it to somebody we know and use it sort of like an investment loan or somethin' like that," Marcus suggested, thinking with desperation.

"Sell it to who and for how much?" Emma asked.

"If we need ninety thousand to get us on our feet, we could sell it for two hundred thousand. If we kept runnin' the place and gave the buyer return on they investment plus interest for about five years, we could keep it."

"You think so? If we do that, you really think we could keep my husband's business?"

"It's a long shot, but it might work," Marcus replied.

"What you think, Andrew?"

"Emma, I got to be honest wit' cha. I don't know anybody 'round here with that kinda money to spare,"

"But you know some people up in Atlanta, don't you? Some black folks with that kind of money, right?" asked Emma.

"I know a few people. The best thing I could do is get you in touch with 'em and let you go from there. It'd be best if you talked to the people, seein' how the business is in yo' family."

"You right. If you get me the names, I'll call every one of 'em. We can drive up and meet 'em, can't we, Marcus?" Emma immediately found strength in her hope. Plans and ideas were running rampant through her mind.

"Yeah, I guess so. We ain't got nothin' else to do."

Emma lifted herself from the chair. Her husband's legacy was breathing again, or so she thought. She walked over to Andrew and embraced him.

⊂੪⊃

While Andrew's employees at the Albany View slithered through the strange atmosphere that had become their work environment, an electrical problem shorted a wire in one of the lighting fixtures and covered a small portion of the office with a nocturnal gloom. The repair costs of the wiring equaled that of a small remodeling project. Andrew

99

decided against the repair, opting instead for a small lamp in the corner.

Band-aid repairs infected the office now. A cracked window on the side of the building, stricken with pieces of duct tape, was camouflaged by cardboard.

Peeling white letters on the front door were brushed over with bottles of liquid paper. The new paint was yet another unfulfilled promise by Andrew. Employees fanned with fury at lunch each day around one forty-five. It was at this time, for some strange reason, that the air conditioning failed. A city utility representative informed the office that a new generator was being installed on their electrical grid. Each day a power test was performed, initiating an electrical surge through the grid. This pull of electricity overloaded the antiquated circuits in the office, which controlled power to the air conditioning unit. The test lasted for one hour and the circuit breaker tripped, disabling the unit and possessing the office with strangling heat.

Had Andrew requested to be connected to another grid when the worker announced the installation, the city could have performed the service at minimal cost. Delinquent in his request, Andrew lost the opportunity and instead purchased fans for his employees—fans that circulated hot, empty air in the office.

Despite the dilapidation, the Albany View was successful beyond its means. The billboard had clients lined up for the remainder of the year and well into the following year. When Andrew visited Atlanta, he drove around the city gazing at the growing billboards in the downtown area. He researched and followed the names inconspicuously resting at the bottom of the giant pictures. Turner. That was his goal, to be a Turner or Carnegie, or at least give his grandson the resources to live in a financial destiny. Therefore, he had no concern for trivial repairs to an office which his clients rarely saw. It was, in his eyes, a diamond hibernating in the rough while his employees simply viewed it as a rough hibernation.

"Is Mr. Scales c-c-coming in t-t-today?" Booker stuttered to Mayreen.

"He called and said he had some things he needed to get done, so he'll be in around one or two. Why you ask?"

"'Cause w-we need s-s-some toilet paper and I gotta g-g-get another r-r-rat trap."

"A rat trap! We got rats in here now? I swear before Moses' walking stick, if this place don't get straightened up, I'm gon' quit and go work down at the river sellin' bait. This don't make a bit a sense. Do you know the handle fell off the toilet last week? I got to stick my hand down in the back to flush it. This place is gettin' filthy."

"You ain't gon' do no such a thang," Po-Shank yelled from the back of the office. "Who you think gon' buy bait from you when people can get that from just about anywhere? You ought to stop talking crazy, talkin' about quittin'."

"Don't tempt me, Po-Shank. I ain't but about two tablespoons from walking out of here and leavin' y'all. Then what you gon' do?"

"Have some peace and quiet, that's what we gon do," Po-Shank replied, as Booker confirmed with a laugh. Mayreen huffed and returned to her work.

"Booker, why you wanna know if Mr. Scales is comin' in today? You don't never ask no other time."

"We-w-we need t-to cover up that m-mouse hole. It's getting' b-b-bigger all the time."

"Mr. Scales ain't worryin' about the mouse hole. He got more important things to worry about than some old stupid mouse."

"Like why I got to jiggle that broken toilet."

"Mayreen—"

"And gettin' the window fixed."

"Mayreen—"

"And fixin' the air conditioner."

"Mayreen!"

"And fixin' the icebox so my salmon croquettes won't spoil before lunch time."

"Mayreen!"

"What is it, Po-Shank?"

"Is you finished?"

"Somebody need to fix the curb outside, too. The door on my El Dorado gettin' scratched up."

"Is that it?"

"I need a new chair 'cause by the end of the day my bloomers be all up in my crack."

"You done yet? I need to get ready for the contractors to put up a new sign and if I stand here all day and wait till you finish yappin', Jesus'll come back before you get done."

"I ain't thinkin' about you or those contractors. This place is fallin' apart and I ain't gon' work in this."

Mayreen's proclamation was interrupted by Andrew's entrance through the squeaking door with ailing letters. The problems of the office were cheap paintings to him now. They existed, but he didn't notice them anymore.

Booker started in right away with his emergency of the day, "M-m-mr. Scales, that r-r-rathole gettin'—"

"Not now, Booker. Po-Shank, what time the contractors gettin' here?"

"Should be pullin' up any minute now. I got everything ready for 'em outside."

"How you been doin', Mr. Scales? I ain't seen Virginia at prayer meetin' in a while."

Andrew glanced over at Mayreen, daring her to continue her questions about his personal life. She sensed the displeasure and swiveled back around in her bloomer-compromising chair.

"I'm fine, Mayreen. You finished that file like I asked you to yesterday?"

Abashed by Andrew's harsh tone, Mayreen opened the

bottom file cabinet to retrieve the requested work.

"That r-rathole k-k-keep gettin' bigger every day, M-m-mr. Scales."

"Booker, I told you we got other stuff to be worryin' about," Po-Shank interjected, banishing a response from Andrew. In the midst of the scolding, Mayreen began shattering the walls of the office with ear-bending screams. Shrieking and shaking, Mayreen leaped atop her chair and sprung to the desktop. Blazing her terror with immense volume, she kicked papers and utensils in the direction of the situation's source.

"It's a rat! It's a rat in my desk!" Orchestrating a duel dance, Mayreen stomped towards the desk drawers where the vermin was enjoying her unrefrigerated salmon croquettes. Unscathed by the woman's amateur attack, the rodent crawled from the drawer and sprung to the chair, perhaps in defense of its own life. Mayreen could see the long pink tail stretching six inches in length. Its dull, turbid grey body clung to the chair as it looked up at Mayreen and projected high pitched squeaks.

Under attack now by the miniature menace, Mayreen stomped with ferocity. She screamed, grabbing her skirt and unknowingly heaving it above her waistline, exposing her silk leopard patterned bloomers and suffocating crack.

Booker, in direct view of the silky scene, stared at the commotion and spoke without stutter or hesitation, "I guess she wasn't lyin'. That chair does make her booty eat them drawers."

Mayreen began varying her steps and shouting for her savior.

"Oooh, Merciful Father, the Blood of Jesus! Ooooh, Merciful Father, the Blood Of Jesus!"

Mayreen syncopated her chants with the shouts, carrying out an impromptu dance routine high atop her work area. The rat, still squeaking in the swivel chair, searched for an escape route.

Suddenly there was a swift and quelling blow. Andrew had grabbed a broom during the commotion and moved up behind the rat. Mayreen shrilled and the rat squealed at the commencement of the hit. Stunned by the force, the creature fell from the chair to the floor and onto its back. Andrew struck the intruder again, this time initiating the swing with his hand far behind his head as would a member of a chain gang before crushing a stone. With the power of ten, he hit the thing again, leaving it only to squirm with the smallest amount of energy left in its body. Death would surely take over the small rodent in a matter of minutes. That was too long for Andrew. He smite another blow to the rat, bringing about its certain end. Mayreen shielded herself from the act by clinging hands to her bosom. Stillness held the room hostage, but Andrew knew death too well now. He struck the rat again and again. A broom, ordinarily used to whisk away all that was dirty, made way for a cleansing. It was cracked and snapped in two.

Andrew took half of the weapon and attempted to flatten the lifeless being beneath him. As though the pounding repetition would make the thing vanish, he kept hitting the rodent now issuing grunts and moans. He was working. Working to rid matters that were not to his liking. It had become his pastime.

Fatigue invaded his plight. He had but one blow left in his arm. Gasping for breath from exhaustion, Andrew noticed the other piece of the broom lying near him. He grabbed the splintered wood, clasped it tightly and drew it back. Upon the spear's descent, Andrew yelled and his crescendo came about at the puncture of the rat's side, spewing its tainted blood on himself and on Mayreen's belongings.

The office occupants gazed in shock at the incident. Mayreen stood paralyzed on the desk. Drops of blood were infecting her personal items and work area. Booker was speechless and dared not even think about asking Andrew why'd he acted in such a way. Po-Shank stood near the door, visualizing Andrew turning the broom onto larger beings. He readied himself for a quick exit. The contractors had arrived and were sitting in their vehicles. If something happened, he could signal them for help or open the door and scream the situation.

Andrew rose from the slaying, examined the faces of his employees, looked down at his conquered victim, then walked toward the door and spoke as if nothing had just happened, "Po-Shank, look like the contractors just pulled up outside. You got everything ready?"

Mayreen was awakened from her shock by the cold comment of her boss. She was overwhelmed by Andrew's dismissal of what he had done. Now calm and confident in her demeanor, Mayreen made her way down from the desktop. She gathered the few clean items she had left and grabbed her purse. Slamming drawers and ruffling papers, she caused a stir which provoked the men to pay attention.

"You goin' somewhere, Mayreen ?" Po-Shank asked, exercising his self-proclaimed authority.

"I'm not workin' in this evil. You won't see me around here no more. Sir," she said, addressing Andrew with a rare formal title. "I don't know who you are or what you did to get here, but you ain't the Andrew Scales I know and work for. And before I type another letter or fetch one more file, I would rather starve to death. Y'all need to do somethin' about this place. Somethin' ain't right in here."

She ended her brief proclamation and walked towards the door, keeping her stare fixed on Andrew the whole time. The men looked at her, then at each other. Booker was waddling between Mayreen's common sense and his loyalty to Andrew. Never turning her back to him, she walked out into the hot Albany sun and reveled in what felt like cool freshness.

Thirteen

Discomfort Zone

―――――― ⊂ℰℰ⊃ ――――――

"I'M GON' NEED YOU TO COME DOWN TO THE OFFICE
and help out a little bit," Andrew told his wife with an insinuating command. Virginia was sitting on the front porch
shelling black-eyed peas when he made the foreign request.
The sanctity of her life was contained within the house.
Virginia was a homemaker. It was her joy and passion, the
sustaining of lives as they entered and exited the doors of
her world. Other than tutoring, she had known no other oc-
cupation, nor did she need one.

Andrew was the best provider her family had ever
known. Virginia had never wanted for anything. She never
wanted to work at anything except keeping a home. Virginia had always nurtured their children, several nieces and
nephews, friends of the family, neighborhood children and
even a few stray cats. A person's life was better because
Virginia had touched it, if only for a moment. Now she was
being asked to leave that and be something else—someone
else.

"So you lost Mayreen today, huh?"

"How'd you know that?" Andrew asked, surprised that

his wife was so informed.

"She called over here a little while ago. I knew somethin' was wrong when she asked me why I wasn't at prayer meetin'. She ain't never called to ask why I wasn't at church."

"That woman always was a little nosy. A slight bit crazy, too." Andrew relaxed at the superficial break in tension.

"Crazy, huh? That's exactly what she said about you when you was killin' that rat."

"Aw, Virginia, I don't know why she gotta make a big deal over somethin' so small. All I did was—"

"Small? Andrew, she said you was actin' like a mad man. And you got blood on her. That woman was so upset it took her a good twenty minutes to tell the whole story. And then you let her walk out without even apologizin'. What's gotten into you?"

Virginia placed the vegetables in a pot on the porch and turned her body to Andrew. "Or should I say what's still in you?"

"Don't start, Virginia."

"Well, when you gon' finish?"

"Lord have mercy. All I did was kill a rat."

"She said you kept beatin' the thing long after it was dead, like you had the devil in you."

"Ain't nobody had no devil."

"She said you broke the broom on the thing."

"Hell, it was just a rat, woman!"

"Who you think you talkin' to?" Virginia asked with raised eyebrows.

Pausing in his disrespectful tone, Andrew fled from his verbal rebuttals.

"Virginia, we gettin' a lotta new business down at the office and I'm gon' need some help. That's all I'm askin'," Andrew said humbly.

"And all I'm askin' is that you start cleanin' up this

mess before the dirt chokes us to death. I thought you were gonna do somethin' for Emma and Marcus?"

"I'll have you know that I took Emma and 'nem some money to help get 'em on they feet."

Virginia looked pleasantly surprised. A rush of relief spread throughout her body. She felt a cleansing circulating in her spirit and restoring her soul. Virginia could feel a slight elevation of the burden. Sheltering her enthusiasm, she gave her husband a contained acknowledgement for his actions.

"At least that's a start. You still got a long way to go, Andrew Scales. And time is running out."

"Look, are you gon' come down to the office and help out or not?"

"Andrew, I can't just come down there and stop what I'm doin' here."

"What you got to do here but clean the house? You can do that when you leave the office."

"Excuse me? Keepin' this house together ain't as easy you think. You ought to try it one day."

"I wish all I had to do was to keep the house straight."

"Watch what you say, Andrew."

"Look, I need some help at the office. You gon' help out or not?"

"Andrew, the way I see it, you got two options. You can call Mayreen, apologize, and beg her to come back. Or you can hire somebody else to help out. I'm not a' office person."

"Okay, that's all fine and good, but I need somebody to help out for the rest of the week and then I'll get somebody new or I'll get back in Mayreen's good graces."

Virginia walked over to her shelled peas and ran her fingers through the podless objects. She continued her work as though it would always go undisturbed. Who would shell peas, sweep the floors, tend to stray cats while she was away working out of her comfort zone? One week out of her environment was a lifetime without substance. Now she would be working for someone else and doing someone else's work.

"Andrew Scales, I'll do this thing until the end of the week and not a second longer. You gotta promise that you'll find somebody else to do this work 'cause it ain't me and you know it. You need to call Mayreen and tell her you sorry, too. Po' lady cryin' and hollerin' in the phone. Need to be ashamed of yo'self."

"Okay, baby. Don't worry about it. I intend to make everything right," Andrew replied, strolling over to his wife and meshing his lips to her cheek.

Andrew had plenty of intentions, none of which included the broken promises he'd given to his wife.

Fourteen

Yuletide Discontent

―――――― ೞ ――――――

IT WAS CHRISTMAS TIME IN ALBANY; A CONFUSING climate for visitors. The city's Floridian relation intertwined with its Georgian atmosphere. With temperatures wavering in the fifties and sixties, children often frolicked about the city wearing springtime garments. The common child's concern was for Santa's discomfort in the warm weather because of his North Pole wardrobe.

Where other cities' surfaces were laced with newly fallen snow or frost-covered lawns, Albany was punctuated with crisp St. Augustine grass. The blades were trampled by Northern refugees fleeing winters above the Mason-Dixon. Palm trees stood tall as they did in the fall, then weathering winter's gentle tease.

The Scales' household was a blur of children. Andrew and Virginia had invited people from near and far. Carpet was covered with kids aging from one to eleven. The older children dispersed headlocks and noogies before parents stepped in to officiate, then ceased the miniature wrestling matches.

Each tick of the clock initiated another small disaster. A

smashed finger, a stepped-on toe, a pulled braid, and then the worst of them all—a loose tooth accidentally extracted due to an airborne baby doll.

Upon the sight of the tiny ivory object lying on the floor, the child flexed her lung capacity and bellowed out for the entire house to hear. Screaming with all of her toothless might, she sent people scampering. Children ran away from her, escaping accusation for the disengaged tooth while adults ran to her, ascertaining her screams of terror.

The frightened girl was comforted with blankets of *'po' baby'* and *'it's okay'* and, finally, *'shhhh'*. As the crying subsided and reoccurred like a psychotic siren, a force made his way toward the girl. Andrew parted the adults, scooped the child up in his arms and gently commanded her to stop crying.

"Baby child," said Andrew. "I want you to stop cryin'. I done lost my teeth just like you. Everybody lose teeth, you hear me? It's gon' be alright 'cause when you stop cryin', ya mama and daddy'll take that tooth and wrap it up. If you put that tooth under yo' pillow before you go to bed, the tooth fairy gon' come and put some money under there. But you got to stop cryin'," Andrew affirmed.

The little girl whimpered and sniffed as leftover tears tried desperately to release themselves despite Andrew's authority. With the girl lying in the hammock of the elder's grasp, Andrew shouted to the heads peeping around the corner.

"The rest of y'all get in here right now! If I hear one mo' voice that's louder than dead dust, somebody goin' out to the switch tree! Don't make no sense for y'all to carry on like moon monkeys." The children were terrified and their parents were snickering.

"Ain't nothin' funny! Y'all just as bad 'cause you can't control yo' kids." The snickering terminated as the adults looked in other directions, slightly offended and embarrassed.

"Let me tell you what's about to happen. Every single one of you kids gon' sit right here in this living room on the floor and not move one muscle. You know why?" Andrew halted his speech, allowing suspicion to swarm the room.

The children looked towards their parents for salvation from this baneful man. The younger children's eyes swelled with tears. One child's lip was trembling as though the punishment had already been inflicted. Virginia entered the room and stood in the doorway, disturbed by Andrew's scorn.

When the suspicion yielded more silence, Andrew continued, "Because I'm gonna tell you the best story you ever heard in your whole life." Andrew's stretched smile signaled that his disdain had been a façade. "It's story time! And then we can go out and play in the garden! How about that?"

The children danced and rejoiced with glee. Adults laughed in relief, thankful that Andrew hadn't gone completely mad. Virginia shook her head at his antics and returned to the kitchen. The adults reveled while reminiscing about the wonderfully colorful stories he'd told when they were children. His stories were as magical as the feelings flying through the room during his production.

"Are you gonna tell us the story now?" the little girl still in his arms asked.

"Baby child, we'll have storytime as soon as—"

"Hey, everybody!" Ingrid announced, bursting through the door with her husband and Kyle in tow. The last family to arrive was showered with hugs and kisses. The full cheer of the season had now been bestowed upon the house.

Andrew forced his way through the small crowd again. Without hesitation, he rolled the small girl out of his arms and into the unprepared hands of another adult. Not expecting the package, the parent almost dropped the pampered girl. Rushing to Kyle, he blurted out for all to hear,

"There's my favorite little boy in the whole world!"

"Hey granddaddy!" Kyle yelled, with a smile running off of his face. The pair embraced unlike any other two-some had that entire day. Their kinship was special and no-ticeably different. All of the other children were envious of the hug, yet ambitious to receive the same affection from Andrew.

Releasing themselves from one another's embrace, Andrew called out to the others, "Okay, everybody, we can start the story now. Kyle is here. Everybody come on and have a seat."

"Daddy!" Ingrid said, exhorting such blatant preferen-tial treatment. "The other kids are gonna be jealous," she said just above a whisper.

"Ain't nobody gon' get jealous, girl. Sit down some-where," he replied, then turned towards the kids. "Scoot over. Make some room so Kyle can sit in the middle." Now that the favorite was amongst the ranks, Andrew had little regard for the others gathered.

"Sit right here, Kyle," said one of the children. Being next to Kyle, the child quickly realized, was the same as being next to Andrew. Kyle obliged his cousin's request which placed him exactly in the middle of the crowd. Beaming at his grandfather, Kyle was happy to be back in Albany.

The time away from his grandfather seemed like two eternities. Here, Kyle was a star, a prince sitting next to the throne of his king grandfather.

The love Kyle had for his own father was made whole by their relationship. Spending time in Albany taught Kyle how to admire and appreciate an older male figure in his life. While at home, Kyle and his father were bonded be-cause of the conditioning he was exposed to in Albany. Kyle was conditioned to love heroes and his heroes were right there in his family.

Andrew's love for the young boy was unconditional. So

unconditional that Andrew was forsaking the truth that would test their relationship and banish their family name.

"Who likes goin' down to the Flint River and skippin' rocks in the summertime?" Andrew asked the attentive audience. Children perched on the floor ejected their hand high.

"Me, me, me," they all cried out in one voice.

"Who knows that there's a wizard in the water?" Andrew probed, as the intrigued faces waited for the next morsel of words. Virginia, familiar with another version of the story, turned her boiling pots to a simmer. The story she'd heard wasn't fit for children. Andrew was on center stage now and the curtain had been drawn. Whispering, forcing everyone to listen closely, he began,

It's a wizard in the water.
Sleepin' deep below the pebbles and the fish.
If you skip a rock twelve times,
he'll give you anything you wish.

The children visualized the number of times their rocks had waltzed on the water, some even calculating on their fingers. Andrew continued, inflecting his voice to a normal, yet deceptive, tone.

The wizard is tall and the wizard is long.
He uses the water to make things go wrong.
For kids that are good and act like they should,
The wizard brings toys to their neighborhood.
But for kids who act bad and don't tell the truth,
He'll fill yo' house with water, right up to the roof.

Ending the dramatic introduction, Andrew abandoned the rhyme scheme and crafted the prose of his story.

"You see, the wizard in the water is older than the whole city of Albany. Before there was boats on the river and train tracks on the ground, the wizard was in the water.

Way back when Indians lived on the river, the Indians was called Creeks. They used the river to survive, fishing and hunting and making arrowheads. The Flint was all they

had, but the Indians used to call the Flint River Thronateeska! And in Indian language, that meant the place where
the Flint was picked up. But the wizard had another meaning for Thronateeska. To the wizard in the water, Thronateeska meant the place where white men left us."

"Andrew—" Virginia interjected, hinting that the story
wasn't appropriate for the young listeners. Andrew took
heed to the implied warning, but showed no intentions of
stopping.

"One day, when the Creeks was working on the river,
white settlers came and took over the Indians' land. They
burned the place where Indians lived and killed all of their
animals. Suddenly, the Chief Indian of the Chehaw village
walked out in front of the settlers. He stood proud and tall,
reached in a pouch, and pulled out some colored powders.

"The Chief took a blue powder and rubbed it across his
face. He took a white powder and wiped it on his tongue.
He took a red powder and slapped it across his chest. Then
he took a deep black powder, rubbed it in both of his hands,
looked up at the sky, and slapped one of the settlers in the
face!

"There was fighting and everybody was runnin' and
pushin', hittin' and shootin', killin', but nobody was
lookin' at the river. The water was turnin' and spinnin'. It
looked like a big tornado coming out of the water. Then the
water shot up into the sky like a rocket to the moon! It was
the wizard in the water.

"The wizard looked down at the people fightin' and
reached down with his wet hands and splashed everybody
and everything. The wizard pushed everybody away 'cept
for the Chief and the settler with the black powder on his
face. He grabbed the two men who was covered in the different color powders from the fightin' and pushed them
deep, deep, deep into the river. And nobody would ever see
them again.

"The wizard held out his arms made of water and

shouted for all the people to hear. He was as loud as a giant waterfall.

This is my river and different colors must work together! If different colors cannot work together, I will drown you all one day! The Indians looked up at the wizard because they wanted to work together with everybody. But the settlers jumped on their horses and rode as far away from the river as they could. They stayed way up north 'cause they didn't want to share the land with anybody and they didn't want to work with all colors.

"Andrew!" Virginia shouted. The kids were swinging on the branches of Andrew's story. The smallest ran to his mother, frightened. Others waited for the conclusion.

Adhering to his wife's wishes now, Andrew concluded the story with warm grace.

"And since everybody wouldn't work together, the water wizard wouldn't let anybody stay there for very long. People have to work together if they want to live a long time. People came with steamboats and tried to work on the river, but the water wizard put sand bars in the river and put some of the water deep in his water pockets so that the water was too low for steamboats and they had to use trains. And now, nobody can't do anything in the river except fish and skip rocks. In hot summer days, if you look real close you can see the top of the river shining with different colors. That's that old water wizard reminding us that until we work together, he gon' come back one day and it ain't gon' be nice. The next time y'all go down to the river, pay yo' respects to the wizard and if you skip that rock twelve times, make a wish so the water wizard won't come back."

The children's necks were locked upward as they stared at the storyteller. The tale that had first been sweet, then dynamic, then scary, then provoking, was no more. It was now a subliminal moment, which would ride their small minds until the day it meant more than a story from an old man. Or until it had become a mental picture shattered by the boulder of time.

Kyle sponged the words, absorbed the lessons, and took heed to his grandfather's wisdom. Though mentally immature compared to the adults, Kyle heard something else in the story, perhaps a lesson Andrew had just taught himself.

C08O

The families eventually opened presents, indulged in gluttony, and retreated home. Kyle, of course, begged to stay a few days longer with his grandfather—and grandmother since she lived there as well. There were no objections in that it provided a vacation for one household and a pause in monotony for another.

Left with only three changes of clothes and his shining new bicycle, Kyle relished in his extended vacation. Bedtime was procrastinated by more of Andrew's concocted storytelling. Morning merged into lazy afternoons at the hands of Speed Buggy and Hong Kong Fooey cartoons. The two friends, separated by decades, shared the minutes that composed the day.

"Granddaddy, can I ride my bike down the street and back?"

"I thought you wanted to help with the seeds out back?"

"We can do that later. When I get back to Atlanta, we gon' be racin' and I need to practice."

Andrew absorbed the excitement in the boy's eyes and it squelched his own disappointment.

"Go ahead on then. I can't have you goin' back to Atlanta losin' no races."

Kyle disappeared from the living room and raced into the carport to retrieve his bike. Andrew chuckled at his grandson's enthusiasm as he watched the credits flash on the last moments of the cartoon.

"That boy know he loves his granddaddy," Virginia said, startling her husband.

"Whew! You sacred the hot mess out of me woman," Andrew replied, sharing a laugh with his wife. "Yep, that's my favorite one right there. That's gonna be the heir to my throne."

"Speakin' of thrones, when are you gonna get another servant to take over my job. It's been five months now and you still got me workin' down there part-time."

"Aw, Virginia, are we gonna start this again?"

"Andrew, it's been five months! Look at this house. It's fallin' apart. Let me show you somethin'."

Virginia dashed into the kitchen and returned holding a loaf of bread. The package was tattered near the end and pieces of the loaf were protruding through a hole.

"Do you see this?"

"Yeah. What about it? It's a loaf of bread."

"It's a loaf of bread that a mouse done got into!"

"What!"

"You heard me. It's mice in here. Andrew, you know we ain't never had no mice or anything in this house. It's dirty in here, Andrew, and I ain't got time to do all that mess at the office and keep house, too." Virginia stumbled in her resolve, tired of asking and demanding actions from her husband. Instead she approached him this time with civility and love.

"Baby, I know you got a lot goin' on down at the office. I want to help you and I think you know by now that I will do just about anything for you."

Walking closer to Andrew and locking their eyes she said, "Even when I know it's not right. Andrew, you need to get somebody else to help at the office so I can help us get our house in order. If the house falls apart, then we can't weather the storm when it comes. "

"Virginia, if you could just hold on for—"

Andrew's plea was cut short by the irritating and fearful sound of rubber fighting asphalt. A car had come to an abrupt stop outside. An instant passed as Andrew tried to reconnect his statement, then in another flash he connected three thoughts. The car. The screeching tires. His grandson outside on a bike.

He ran through the door in time to hear the sounds of an adult voice scolding a child.

"Watch where you're ridin' that bike, boy! If you can't ride a bike, then you don't need to be crossin' the street!"

Four houses down, Andrew saw a police car. Thinking the police had been in the area and stopped to help out with the accident, he began to jog toward the scene. He then realized there were no other cars near the police vehicle. Andrew saw Kyle's bike lying near the curb. The vibration in his chest increased when he saw an officer bent over looking at a small body. Now Andrew was sprinting the remaining distance to the scene.

The officer continued yelling, "If I see you tryin' to ride across the street one more time—"

Andrew bumped into the officer unintentionally, but not really. He was trying to view the body that the officer was scolding. Andrew knelt down to the black asphalt which had caught his grandson and kept him there. Unharmed. Regret and fright ran from his body as his chest began to heave more slowly.

"Are you okay, Kyle? Are you hurt, son? Is everything okay? Anything broke?" The concerned elder covered Kyle with questions. Kyle was fine, frightened, but fine.

"I'm waitin'," a bitter voice called out from over Andrew's shoulder.

'Waitin' for what, a butt kickin'?' Andrew wanted to reply, but instead offered, "What you waitin' for?"

"I'm waitin' for you to say excuse me. Unless, of course, you prefer that I read you your rights. In case you didn't notice, you almost knocked over a uniformed officer tryin' to get to that little monkey that can't ride a—"

Andrew's motions snapped the officer's sentence. He jumped from the ground and positioned himself a few feet from the opposition. Familiar territory.

"What did you say?" Andrew asked with a psychotic softness. A small crowd was sprouting into a larger one.

"You need to teach that boy to stay off the street if he can't ride a bike," he replied, evading the question.

"Did you say something about a monkey, you redneck fool?"

"Who do you think I am? What do you think this badge means?"

"I know what it don't mean. It don't mean you can talk to me or my grandson like some second-class citizens. It don't mean you can cuss and shout at a little boy who's scared to death cause you coulda killed him!"

Andrew and the officer were so close, they were exchanging breath now. The crowd retreated a few steps, sensing the two men would need space for this event.

"Don't you raise your voice at me! I'm not drunk and the death'll be on the other side of the law if you try that mess on me, boy!"

"What you say!" Andrew threw back both of his arms, intending to smite the officer's skull with a crushing impact. "You muthafu-"

"ANDREW! ANDAAYYY!" Virginia screamed from behind the crowd. Her voice, straining to be heard, cried out to be obeyed and slammed against Andrew's ears. "Don't you do it again! I done had enough death around this house! Don't you do this again!" She was jogging towards the people, parting them as though they were beings of weightless flesh.

She reached the two opposing men and looked at them both, giving Andrew more eyes than she had the officer. Kyle, still confused about the occurrence high above him, watched his grandmother defy her aging bones as she knelt down to retrieve him.

Swooping him up, erasing his fear, she smothered his head in her loving grasp. Kyle was refreshed in the security of Virginia's arms. Having been wrapped here only a few times, Kyle could only cry. He released all the fright his own shock had postponed. Virginia squeezed the boy, perhaps trying to comfort him by ringing the tears from his eyes as she would a favorite dish towel.

Virginia carried him back towards the house and Kyle rested, breathing the scrumptious smells which inhabited her apron. The screeching sound on tires vanished as he recalled the scent of biscuits. Tumbling from his bike was forgotten in the smell of ham. The violent conversation of two angry men was lost against a sticky stain of jelly colliding with one of his tears, making this place a salty, sweet rescue.

Kyle had never loved his grandmother more than he did now during these paces which would eventually end at the house. If the asphalt of Albany had just pushed him away, his grandmother's gentle hold had just pulled him back in.

Watching the couple saunter away, the crowd later turned their attention back toward the battle which had begun before Virginia's intervention. Andrew and the officer gnarled at each other again. With Virginia's words still reverberating in Andrew's ear, he conceded the staring contest. The officer looked around at the germinating crowd and then how far he'd have to run to his car for a backup call. His anger quickly curbed.

"Did you hit that little boy?" someone yelled from the crowd.

A rush of saliva pushed down the officer's throat and his neck was invaded by a hue of red.

"You bedda get back in that car before you get hurt!" a cry came from the crowd.

Maintaining his composure, still resting in his authority, the officer tried to take control of the situation.

"Now y'all don't want to do something you'll regret later, now do you?" The officer moved to take one step back, then realized a gesture of retreat would have projected his fear.

"What you say?" a large man asked walking toward the officer. "We'll drive this car into the river and nobody'll ever find you or yo' red neck 'cause we'll put 'em in two different places."

Women with children standing by, covered their faces from the fusing hate and anger. Realizing witnesses would be accomplices, they began walking the children back to their respective homes as to clear the coliseum for lions. The officer's rush of red was rising to his cheeks now and the crowd could see him being painted before their eyes. There was only one shade darker, his own blood. He watched as the innocence of children and the protection of women fled the area.

Suddenly, a bottle was broken against the curb. The neck of the makeshift weapon was clutched in the hand of someone willing to take the first brush stroke on the canvas of the officer's face. A man flaring malt liquor from his breath charged toward the officer. He would cut the officer and the gathering would become a massacre and, finally, a slaying.

"Put that bottle down, boy. What's wrong wit' you?" Andrew asked. His tone was calm, though demanding. "What's wrong wit all y'all? Ain't this town got enough blood runnin' through it already. Kids got to play out here. You want them to play after we done kicked a man's head in on the same spot where they play kickball? You wanna explain to the little girls why they hopscotch chalk won't cover up the red spots on the sidewalk? I don't plan on explainin' death no more so y'all go on back 'bout ya business," Andrew said, not realizing his slipped confession.

People in the crowd had heard Virginia cry out, *'Don't you do this again'* and there were questions among the sharp-minded. With Andrew's slip and the officer's threats, people were interrogating Andrew in their heads.

The officer didn't wait to be excused. As soon as Andrew intervened, he'd made small, inconspicuous steps towards his cruiser. In the worst case, he could yell his location and the problem before the beatings began and back-up would arrive in time to catch a few fleeing violators.

But there would be no call. There would be no back-up. There would be no violence. Today there would be peace. Andrew had brought civility back to the very crisis he'd created. A few threats and name calling in the officer's direction ended the scene as he drove off, admitting only to himself that Andrew had saved his life.

Walking back toward his own house, Andrew derived the words that he would speak to Kyle. He was thinking how he would explain his actions. Andrew hoped that his loving grandson would not view him as a monster dwelling in a man's body. The first attempt would be an apology and then questions about his injuries. Then he would explain to Kyle about his uncontrollable anger. More apologies would follow and then, if he'd allow him, he'd take Kyle to the ice cream store for root beer floats. After filling him with carbonation and cream, they could spend some time tilling the garden and planting seeds. That was his formula for easing his grandson's pain. He would walk into the house and bend down to meet him face to face. Rehearsing his line of forgiveness, Andrew was interrupted by a push on his shoulder, urging him to turn around.

It was two of the young boys thirsty for the officer's blood back at the gathering.

"Mr. Scales, so what's this about you havin' to explain death once before? Is there somethin' we don't know about?"

Fifteen

The Dumb-namic Duo

—— ⊗ ——

"RAY-RAY, BOONE, WHAT KINDA NONSENSE Y'ALL talkin' about now?"

"Mr. Scales," Ray-Ray began. "We couldn't help but hear you say somethin' about explainin' death. Now, to me that sounds like you been around death before or close to somebody that got killed."

Boone, the speed–talker, yelled in less than two seconds, "And you 'on't even work at no funeral home!"

The twosome standing before Andrew composed Albany's small population of vagabonds. Each day they wandered the city looking for trouble. The two goofs walked in shoes made of trouble. Each step was a journey closer to mischief.

A plight initiated in the seventh grade, Ray-Ray and Boone were destined for Hell's Heathen Hall of Fame. The two had made weekly trips to the blind school and put talcum powder into Braille textbooks. Waiting outside in the bushes, they watched for students exiting with white streaks on their faces. The reoccurrence of laughter in the bushes eventually led to their conviction at the hands of a scolding principal.

As they matured, so did their antics. By the tenth grade, the two had become shake makers at the ice cream shop. On a normal blazing summer day, customers migrated to the shop in search of heat relief at the remedy of chocolate shakes. Those customers later fled to the restroom after consuming the laxative-laced concoctions blended by the duo. Had it not been for their snickering at the line of people standing outside the bathroom door twisting their stomachs and gritting their teeth, the two would have pulled off the caper.

Word spread that people who had eaten at the ice cream shop stayed in bed the following day with stomach viruses. The shop owner recalled the cackling cabal of boys and deduced that there must have been a connection. Not only was there a connection, but there was also thirteen packages of laxatives underneath the counter where Ray-Ray and Boone worked. The two were heathens of the most absurd kind.

Now their endeavors were geared towards petty crimes and scams. They'd planned to live on the beach near Sapelo Island, Georgia with the huge dividends of their next big heist—whatever it might be. Andrew and his comments had peaked their conniving interest.

"I'm gon' ask you again," Andrew asserted. "What kinda nonsense are y'all talkin' about now?"

"Mr. Scales, it shol is funny that you said you done explained death already—"

Boone blurted in full-speed, "And you 'on't even work at no funeral home."

"Boone, shut-up," Ray-Ray snapped. "It's funny that you said that, and the policeman had said that he wasn't drunk and death gon' be on the other side of the law. What he mean by that Mr. Scales?"

"Yeah, what he talkin' 'bout?" the fast-talking comrade added.

"I don't know what he was talkin' about, but I can call him and ask if you want me to. I'm sure he wouldn't mind talkin' about them dead chickens people been findin' in the river, too. What y'all know about that, chicken-killers?" Andrew said.

Boone mouthed off, unknowingly confessing to the crime, "Man, we ain't killed no chickens in the river. We killed 'em in the truck and then threw 'em in the river. The cops can't blame us for killin' no chickens in the river."

"Shut up, Boone!" Ray-Ray exclaimed. He lunged toward his friend, silencing him, then turned back to Andrew. "If you don't know what he was talkin' about, then what was yo' wife talkin' about when she said don't do it again and she had seen enough death around this house. Sounds to me like you done had a fight with a cop before."

Ray-Ray moved closer to Andrew and dropped the quiet accusation. "Even sound like you done killed one before."

"Let me tell you somethin', boy. We ain't got nothin' but life around this house. Look around back and you'll see a garden waitin' for the warm growin' time. Look inside my house and you'll see a little boy that grows everyday. It's a lot of life in here. But I tell you one thing. We can get some death on this front porch right now if you don't get the hell off my property. I'll let you smell death. I'll let you see it. I'll even let you hold it in your arm like a baby and then, I'll let death rock you to sleep. If either one of you want to stay awake in this life, you'll forget what you heard on that corner."

Andrew's speech had ended, but his intimidation was still lingering. He stood in the presence of the two, his lip beginning to quiver, his fists pulsating from their grasps around his anger. Andrew still had a tenacious residue left over from the officer on the corner. After he'd soaked the suspicious young men with contempt, he turned to enter the house. One thought was swimming in his mind. If two morons had caught his own slip, the officer's accusation and his wife's confession, what were the other witnesses thinking?

He entered the house and saw Kyle watching television as though nothing had happened. Virginia, however, was pacing on the back porch. After searching, he found her there praying.

"What you askin' for?" Andrew inquired.

"You know what I'm askin' for. I'm askin' for it all to end. I know you mad that I confessed what you did to all those people out there, but I told you to get this thing off of us. And I'm not sure that me yellin' it in front of all those people is enough."

"Virginia," Andrew started, paused, and sighed. "What is it that you want me to do?"

"It ain't about what I want you to do no more, but what you need to do. You need to let people know how that officer died and you need to let people know that Mack had nothin' to do with it. I done my part. I said it so enough people will want to know and—"

"Ain't it enough that I helped Mack's family get back on they feet? Virginia, I done told you for the last time that it's been done to us and ain't nothing wrong with us doin' it to them."

"And I done told you for the last time that until you clean up this filth and I mean all of it. I mean every piece of trash, every crumb of nasty, and every speck of dust. If you don't clean it up, they'll be puttin' this dirt on yo' grave. I said something in front of that crowd. I got it off of me. Now it's *all* on you.

CRRO

Ray-Ray and Boone had been disregarded and disrespected. If they were ever to gain notoriety in town as real criminals, they would have to pull off an unprecedented caper. A feat, for which men like Andrew, would fear them.

After Andrew demanded they leave his property, the two jumped into their primer-colored Ford Pinto. The primer was an upgrade from the purple spray paint they'd tarnished the car with after high school. Each man entered the car from the driver's side. The passenger's side was held closed with Boone's belt—another of their schemes gone wrong.

Once in the car, the radio was set to full volume. Sounds screamed from the only operable speaker on their mono-stereo. The boisterous music was not intended to invade the city streets. It was, however, camouflage for the knocking engine-rod that dubbed their car as the town chitty-chitty bang bang. When people heard the metallic battle underneath the car's hood, they knew it wouldn't be long before their appearance. Not far away was an unsightly vehicle with the tasteless hood ornament the two had super glued to the car—a red high heel shoe they'd stolen from a stripper in Atlanta. Another caper gone awry. They'd meant to steal her bra.

"Ray-ray, where we goin'? This ain't the way to the rib shack."

"We ain't goin' to the rib shack, Boone."

"But they got the all-you-can-eat neckbone special tonight."

"Boone, after we pull off this score, we gon' be eatin' shrimps, steaks, lobsters, and anything we want every night."

"Oh, man, that sounds good. I love me some scrimps. You know what I want. Some of them real fancy steaks. The kinds that's real small and round. Suppose to be the best cut of meat you can get. They call 'em filit mig-none."

"Filit mig-none? You mean filet mignon, fool!"

"Is that a good piece, too? I'll take both of 'em."

"I swear sometimes I don't know why I fool wit' you."

"So where we gon' get all the money to eat scrimps?" Boone asked. Ray-Ray took a sharp left turn, throwing Boone into the driver's seat.

The passenger's seat had come unbolted during their first getaway while trying to rob a delivery truck. Thinking the truck was filled with radios, the dumb desperados ended up stealing three cases of breast pumps.

"Get off me!" Ray-Ray yelled. "Didn't I tell you to put that seat belt on?" Boone reached down between his seat and the inoperable door. A chain rattled as Boone prepared to tie down his makeshift seat belt. He routed the chain through a bracket underneath his seat, inside a hole they'd cut in the floor, across his lap, and through the handle of the door—the inoperable door.

"Now," Boone said, finally settled. "Where we gon' get the money for all this good eatin'?"

"We gon' get it from one of the richest men in Albany, Andrew Scales," Ray-Ray answered, as he killed the clanking sound of the car by putting it in park and turning off the ignition. "Come on. We're here."

"Aw, man! I just put my seat belt on."

"Well, just take it off."

Boone obliged, unrolling the chain through its route. He exited the car through the driver's side and followed his partner, into the police station.

Sixteen

A Switch for Snitches

―――――――――――― ⚜ ――――――――――――

"WOULD YOU MIND REPEATING THAT, RAYSHAUN?" THE Chief asked, sitting behind his desk.

"I told you. My name is Ray-Ray and you heard me the first time. Andrew Scales killed the policeman out there on the interstate. We suspect there's a nice reward about information like that."

"Bartholomew, you're with Rayshaun, er Run-Run or whatever you call yourself now. You're in on this, too?"

"He don't even work at no funeral home," Boone blurted out again. "Don't be callin' me Bartholomew either. My name Boone."

The Chief was displeased at the interruption, but now they had his attention.

"So you boys got any evidence to prove this?" The Chief, offering no concurrence with the allegations, wanted to hear more unfolding details.

"Yeah we got evidence! His wife said he did it and he said he did it, too," replied Ray-Ray.

The Chief was baited by his own eagerness to prove what he'd known all the time. Reality begged the question.

How did these two buffoons garner a confession from Andrew and his wife?

"Let me get this straight. Are you tellin' me that Andrew and Virginia Scales confessed to the both of you that Andrew Scales killed the police officer that a deceased man allegedly murdered?"

"And he don't even work at no funeral home."

The Chief and Ray-Ray exclaimed in unison, "Shut up!"

"Well, they didn't say it in those exact words, but they said it. She was saying somethin' like, 'don't do this again' and they was talkin' about 'explainin' death' and all that stuff."

"When did all of this happen?"

"This afternoon when one of your officers almost killed Mr. Scales' grandson."

"What!" the Chief yelled, rising from his desk. People outside the office heard the outburst and turned their attention to the meeting. "Somebody almost killed his grandson, Kyle? My officers?" The Chief shouted at the mention of the only joy he and Andrew shared, the love of their grandsons. The boys were symbols of their legacies and the gateways to the doors of their families' future generations.

"Yeah, one of 'em almost killed that boy. Just about crushed him while he was riding his bike. In fact—" Ray-Ray scanned the station for the culprit. An officer at the water cooler, avoiding eye contact, tried to walk out of the room when he realized Ray-Ray's eyes were like searchlights. "That's him right there."

The Chief sprang from his office, rattling the blinds on his door, "Jenkins! Get in here!"

As the officer discarded his drinking cup, he walked towards the office still swallowing, though the water was a memory now. He entered the office and the Chief slammed the door, reenacting the rattling blinds' dance of anger. The Chief, careful not to disrespect his officer in the presence of the wanna-be hoodlums, constructed his conversation.

"There's an incident involving a young boy on a bike I want to talk to you about later. But for now, these two—" the Chief struggled with the description "—gentlemen say you overheard a confession to murder by Andrew Scales and his wife."

Jenkins giggled after looking at the two and then parked himself in a seat near his boss.

"To tell you the truth, Chief, there was a lot of commotion goin' on and yes I did hear something about don't do this again or there's been enough death, or somethin' like that. I can't rightly say what it was. I wasn't payin' too much attention after a while because I was tryin' to figure out how I could get back to my car and keep my life."

"What are you sayin'? Am I hearing that you were in a riot situation?"

"No, not quite a riot, it could have been. There were a few angry folks out there and I was well outnumbered. People started cussin' and walkin' closer, surrounding me like vultures."

Ray-Ray began fidgeting because the officer was walking down the path that would eventually be the crossroads of their own involvement. He tried to derail the officer.

"Chief, you heard him. He said she was talkin' about death. And then—"

"As a matter of fact, one of the things I do remember real clearly was somebody breakin' a bottle and gettin' ready to use it like a knife. And if I'm not mistaken, it was these two."

Jenkins let his statements drip in the room, filling the office with suspense. Each man wondered what the next would say. Ray-Ray and Boone felt the tingling warmth of trouble cover their skin. Jenkins waited for an order. The Chief tried to determine how he could further his own accusations with the corroding confession the two had just heralded.

Finally the Chief pressed on by asking, "Now, how did you manage to get out of this situation if you were outnumbered by all of these folks, and where did all of this happen? I hope you're plannin' on filling out a report."

"It was over on Mercer, a few houses down from Scales'. I was patrollin' his neighborhood just like you had asked us to start doin' and—"

"Go on, go on," said the Chief, cloaking his latest attempt to harass Andrew.

"And, I swear, if it hadn't been for Andrew, I mean Mr. Scales, I might not see my family tonight."

"How do you mean?"

"I mean he was the one that told the crowd to break up and leave me alone. Chief, I stared death in the mouth and my name was on its tongue. Just before it spoke my name ending my time here, Andrew Scales reached down its throat and yanked out its tonsils. I jumped in the car and drove off. Don't know if I ever seen a man with that much respect and authority over people and not have a gun or a badge."

"Jenkins, don't get all sappy on me. Are you tryin' to tell me that Andrew Scales helped you out of this predicament?"

"No, sir. No Chief, I'm not tryin' to tell you that at all. I am tellin' you that Mr. Scales saved my life."

Their plan had gone all wrong and the snitches needed to react.

"That don't change the fact that his own wife came runnin' down the street screamin' *no more death*. Don't you know what that means? It means Mr. Scales done killed somebody before!" Ray-Ray was irate. His position was being severely compromised.

"Chief," Jenkins began. "I don't know what happened out there on the highway that night, but I do know one thing. Mr. Scales had a chance to hurt me, but instead he protected me. I don't know why he did it, but that man helped me when I needed it most."

"I hear ya, I hear ya," the Chief said. He swiveled around in his chair, facing the window. He'd begun keeping score as Andrew had gained points on the side of righteousness. Andrew's grandson was a scorekeeper, balancing his wrongs with his good intentions. The Chief needed a break. A decision had to be made: keep the unrelenting offense or relax and apply a passive defense? Andrew had come onto the Chief's playing field and helped one of his own players, the ultimate sacrifice of graceful sportsmanship.

Again the office swam in silence. The swivel chair seemed indecisive about revolving and showing the Chief's expression.

"Jenkins, I'll expect a full report on my desk by morning. I want to know every detail, every word and every witness that was there," the Chief said, turning around to face his officer. "You understand me?"

"Yes sir."

"That'll be all, Jenkins." The Chief buried himself in the paperwork that the interruption had ended.

"Yes, sir. What about these two?"

The Chief glanced up. He lowered his head less than a thought later and replied while continuing his work, "You boys are under arrest for intent to harm an officer of the law."

Jenkins grinned as he unbelted his handcuffs and read the two tattletales their rights.

C3&O

In the basement jail where the Chief and Andrew had experienced their first altercation, the two failed criminals were boiling in their own contempt. Ray-Ray had visions of taking Andrew's life while Boone sat complaining that he'd missed the neckbone buffet.

"Man, this ain't right! I could'a been eatin' them neck-bones right now. Soppin' them jokers in hot sauce and eve-rything. Now we gotta stay down here just 'cause that little knucklehead almost got hit on that bike."

Ray-Ray emerged from contemplating when he was struck by the revelation of Boone's gluttony and ignorance.

"Boone, sometimes you stupid, but sometimes you a genius and don't even know it."

"What, you like hot sauce on yo' neckbones, too?"

"Naw, fool. You know why we in here again?"

"'Cause you tried to snitch on old man Scales and we parked the car out in front of the police station and it's probably towed by now so when we get out, we got to call my mama to get another advance on my allowance so we can—"

"Boone."

"Yeah?"

"Shut up before I smack you so hard yo' grandmama's nose start bleedin'. The reason we in here is because of Kyle, Mr. Scales' grandson. If he hadn't fell of that bike, none of this would've happened. Sho' is funny how Mr. Scales came runnin' out the house all worried about his grandson."

"Sho' is. I fell off my bike one time and my granddaddy came runnin' down the street and said if I got back on it, he was gon' slap the fool out of me."

"Boone, we gon' get famous off of Mr. Andrew *every-body respect me* Scales. When we get outta here, we gon' get more money that this rat hole police station could have ever gave us."

"Yeah, that's what I'm talkin' about. Get paid! What we gon' do? Get a job working for Mr. Scales and steal his money?"

"Naw, that's too easy. We gon' get the big payback on

that old fool," Ray-Ray announced, stretching out on the cell's cot to contrive the details of his plan.

"What we gon' do, Ray-Ray?"

"Boone, when we get out this cell, we gon' make a plan."

"A plan to do what?"

The baneful Boone replied, "To kidnap his grandson."

Seventeen

Butt Shot

SPRING BREAK FOUND KYLE ONCE AGAIN LOOKING OUT of the car window at the Albany welcome signs—pecan trees. Moments and miles would pass in the car and his parents would drop him off at the tranquility of Mercer Avenue. There he would lavish in seven days of love as he had become accustomed.

He spent birthdays in Albany despite his popularity in his West End Atlanta neighborhood. *If they want to come to my party, they can come to Albany,* Kyle told his parents regarding his young decision. If there were special moments in his life, he wanted to share them with his grandfather, the elder he cherished more than any other.

Upon arrival, after the affection, salutations and reminiscing, Kyle and Andrew hurried out to the garden to witness the seasonal miracles in the backyard. The seeds they'd planted were sprouting and the barren soil was giving birth to new chances for the earth's nutrients.

At other times Kyle tagged along with his grandfather as he conducted business of the Albany View. The billboard was getting more attention and more inquiries by advertisers.

While driving through the city, Andrew imparted vitamins of business knowledge upon Kyle's impressionable mind. Andrew hoped that by allowing Kyle to see his activities and take part in conversations, he would become excited about being a part of the Albany View.

What little time he had left was spent playing with the water wizard. He'd pedal down to the riverbanks or catch a ride with friends who fished. Of course he had two bikes now—one for home and one for this, his other home. Kyle spent hours searching for the flattest rocks near the river. He spent only a few moments skipping all of them away, trying to reach the elusive twelve skimmers across the liquid layer.

He took special care while skipping a final stone. It was shale rock, a dark, sleek and flat mineral unlike the others he'd tried. Clamping the rock with vice-like strength and caliper accuracy, his tongue poked from the corner of his mouth, a sure sign of determination and focus. His upper body bent to maximize his launch angle and he cocked his arm back like a tight trigger. Reaching back as far as he knew how, Kyle flung the rock out away from him, stumbling along with the momentum. He watched as it slapped the water and rose again. The black object was dancing and running on its own steeplechase, leaving streams of ripples in different stages and different sizes. Kyle counted as the rock neared its submersion. "Seven, eight, nine!"

It was his personal best. *Nine skips! It must be the rock,* he thought. Three more skips and not only would he have street bragging rights, but he'd get the impossible wish from the Water Wizard.

Until now it had been a fallacy, a well-constructed story from the talents of his grandfather. But with three skips left to make, the story had transformed into a theory.

Kyle darted off into the woods to look for more prized shale. He couldn't remember the branches or the trees he'd seen before he'd found the first one. He had no concern with landmarks. Kyle was thinking of the flattest launch angle, his most powerful thrust, and the wish he would make.

He'd wish that his parents would move to Albany and live in the same house as his grandfather. This was the wish he would make and it would last forever. Atlanta would be only a memory and this place would be a magical land that had happy endings every day, no matter the problems between the sun's rising and setting.

Where did I see that rock, he kept thinking until he finally saw it. A piece of shale even flatter than the one he'd just whirled out onto river's dance floor. It was smaller so he could throw it further. He reached down to retrieve it. As Kyle tried to stand erect again, he was forced back down.

A jolting blow smacked against his head, dazing him a bit. A push on his backside laid him out and Kyle found himself lying on his stomach, face down along the floor of branches and rocks.

"Get up, little punk," a voice commanded.

"Little punk. That's all you is. A little pissy-tailed punk," another voice chimed with velocity.

Hesitant to see the source of his pain and fear, Kyle rolled over onto his back and was surprised to see two strange faces. Their identities were disguised with Spanish Moss they found near the entrance of the wooded area.

It was the dumb duo, Ray-Ray and Boone. Boone had forgotten to pick up the masks and didn't realize it until Ray-Ray asked for them as they exited the crap-mobile. With no openings for their eyes, they either blew an opening in the air plant or pulled open a small section as though their faces had curtains.

They'd been following Kyle on his trips to the river. Until now he'd always been within an earshot of adults, but his rock expedition had taken him out of SOS range this time.

"Where that old grandpa of yours at now, huh? Can't help you now, can he? Call him. Go ahead!" Ray-Ray yelled.

"You can't call him 'cause it ain't no phone out here," Boone said. He was overcome with an outbreak of laughter, causing his Spanish Moss to slip off a bit. He caught it and inhaled a whirlwind as the plant was sucked into his mouth. Boone coughed and gagged while Ray-Ray remained poised and ready to execute the plan.

"Stand up to yo' feet, boy," Ray-Ray commanded when Kyle was slow to move. He smacked the boy, unleashing his vengeance for embarrassment and jail time at the hands of the boy's elder.

Kyle rose to his knees and Ray-Ray jerked him up by the collar. He began dragging the boy across the abstract floor of organic items. Questions raced through Kyle's mind. Who were these men? Why were they doing this? Would he die today?

"Sto-o-op," Kyle managed.

Ray-Ray stopped towing the boy for a moment and knelt down to meet his face.

"You shut up, boy! You hear me? We'll stop when we good 'n' ready. When yo' grandpa sends us the money, then we'll stop. Until then, you shut up if you wanna keep livin'."

"Yeah, we gon' be eating the neckbone buffet every day after we get that money," Boone added.

"Leave me alone! Let me go!"

Ray-Ray was offended by the rebellious disrespect. Wrenching the boy's shirt in one hand, the angered man reached back and torqued his arm beyond its limit. He swirled his hand around and down against the defenseless boy's face. The collision of cheek and hand echoed through the woods and Kyle was knocked to the ground.

Boone stood shocked at his partner's brutality. Ray-Ray

wiggled his hand, shaking off the pain the blow had caused even him. He pulled Kyle to his feet once again. Fearing another vicious smack, Kyle stood erect and readied himself to obey every command. Ray-Ray pulled the boy in the intended direction and the three were off walking to the next stages of the caper.

Boone walked alongside Ray-Ray and whispered, "You shol' did smack that boy somethin' awful. I thought we wasn't gon' hurt him."

"Sometimes you got to make changes. That's just how it is when you pullin' off somethin' this big."

"I see. Yeah, you right. Maybe when we get to the car I— Ou-ou-ouch!"

Boone shouted with pain, grabbing his leg. Ray-Ray stopped and watched his partner's instant agony. Boone jumped up and down on his good leg shouting, "Whew, Lawd! Lawdy, lawdy, lawdy. Mmm, mmm, mmm."

"Boone, what's wrong wit' you?"

"Man, somethin' bit my leg. Must have been a wasp or—Ow-w-w!"

This time, the affliction hit Boone in the butt. Now the man was hopping on one leg, holding his right butt cheek, and wondering where the insects were coming from.

Suddenly Ray-Ray was inflicted by the pain as well.

"Ouch! What is this stuff? Woooo!" The piercing thrusts were painfully discomforting, yet bearable after a few moments. Another sting, shot into Ray-Ray's shoulder and he released Kyle.

Kyle thought about running, but was scared he might run into the swarm of whatever was torturing his apprehenders. He stood there witnessing the spectacle.

Ray-Ray took another shot to his leg, which forced him to the ground. Boone began slapping his back and rubbing his legs, certain that the bugs were in his clothes. He moved like a robot with defective windshield wipers for arms. Ray-Ray was stung once more. The hits were coming faster now, but not one of them touched Kyle.

"Leave him alone!" a voice shouted. All three were quiet looking around for a body to match the voice. There was no disturbance of leaves or the rumbling of sticks, only quiet. In the elevated distance, they heard a mechanical crank, another silence and then the instant depressurization of air.

An instant later, Boone was pushed back with a bite to his face. The pain was shocking and he couldn't utter a word until he touched a scratch on his face. There was a tiny streak of blood on his hand.

"Ray-Ray, somebody shootin' at us!" Boone, the more clueless of the two, had solved the puzzle. It was the only reason he could think of that might explain why Kyle had not been inflicted.

"What? From where? Why we ain't dead yet?" Ray-Ray asked.

The elevated voice rang out again, "Get away from him!" Again came the mechanical crank and the depressurization, then the pain.

"Ow! Stop! Okay, okay! We movin', we movin'!" Ray-Ray yelled.

Kyle peered into the woods toward the voice and saw a slight movement in a tree twenty yards away. The tree seemed to have a moving trunk near the top, then the trunk sprouted branches which looked surprisingly like legs.

It was a miniature man heavily camouflaged in hunting clothes. The person finally descended to the ground, carrying a pellet rifle pointed at the wounded prey. The hunter-hero was no bigger than Kyle.

Slowly, the armed person walked over to him. Kyle backed away several steps, not sure of the hunter's intentions. His face was also camouflaged by a mask, a real mask, unlike the moss the wounded were barely wearing now.

Pulling the mask from his face, the hunter revealed

himself as he asked Kyle, "You all right?"

Relieved by the appearance of a familiar face, Kyle smiled and placed his hand on the shoulder of Joshua, the Chief's grandson. He greeted him with the same enthusiasm he had that day at the police station when they'd shared a good time and a toy.

"I was just out here huntin' squirrel, and I saw them slap you. They lucky I didn't have my deer rifle. I'd a killed 'em both. That's why I was up in the tree. I'm practicing for deer season. What you want to do with 'em? This is only a pellet gun, but if I get close enough, I can take 'em out."

Ray-Ray, angered that he'd been attacked by a boy, made a slight advance towards the two.

Joshua cranked the gun, took aim, and launched a pellet into Ray-Ray's foot.

"Agggggghhh! I'm gon' kill him."

"What did you say?" Joshua asked, cranking the gun again.

"Nothin'. Nothin'. I didn't say nothin'."

Joshua lowered his weapon and turned to Kyle, "So what you wanna do with 'em?"

Kyle pondered the question, remembering the pain he'd briefly suffered.

"We can walk 'em down to the station and lock 'em up or," he paused, "you can let me kill 'em." Joshua smiled and winked for only Kyle to see.

Kyle smiled and winked back then said, "Naw, just shoot 'em in the booty and let's go home."

"If that's what you want, partner." Joshua directed his aim until Kyle interjected.

"Wait. Hold on a minute." Kyle walked over to Ray-Ray, grabbed his collar and blistered the man's face with the same powerful slap he'd received. "Now you can shoot 'em in the booty."

Joshua commanded the two to turn over and take their

medicine. He delivered the request, one shot for each cheek. Afterwards, the two ran off through the woods and continued their kinship.

ॐ

Ticks of the clock eventually introduced evening. Virginia had retreated to the solace of her home where she'd been all day. Andrew had hired a student from Albany State to work at the office, and there was bit of peace at the Scales' house again. As Virginia indulged in a much-deserved break, she merged with a rocking chair on the front porch. Kept company by plastic cups, a pitcher of sweet tea, and lemons fighting buoyancy halfway up the pitcher. The burden of working at the office, at home, and the residue of death still lingering in her conscience were taking their toll.

Mercer Avenue was quiet and happy again. Its brief engagement with hate had been made a memory by days on a calendar. Cars occasionally passed by, drivers all waving, some blowing. Virginia greeted them all with a hand of kindness. She began waving by default upon hearing vehicles coming her way. She'd already begun waving when an unwelcome car came down the street and eventually invaded their driveway. The infrequent visitor was again inviting himself for what could only be an unpleasant conversation.

"Evenin', Mrs. Scales," said the Chief.

"Fine, and you," she replied coldly, insinuating that she'd rather not dally about in small talk.

"Your husband around?"

The Chief knew the answer. He wanted to make sure they would be alone while he probed. The Chief had taken over patrolling this neighborhood after learning of the bicycle incident. He could never catch her at home alone because she was always working at the office. Until he saw her on the porch, the Chief hadn't realized she was at home during the day once again. Andrew was at work, he hoped, and she was on the front porch away from the phone, so she couldn't call him. It was time to strike.

"Do you see his car in the driveway?"

"No, ma'am. I can't say that I do."

"If you're lookin' for him, he's down at the View. I'll go call him and let him know you're on your way," Virginia said, attempting to rise from her resting spot.

"No, no, that won't be necessary, Mrs. Scales. I really wanted to talk to you for a while. You see, I heard about Kyle's accident and I've been so busy I didn't have a chance to stop by and check on him. I've got a grandson that age, you know."

"That was Christmas! That was four months ago, Chief."

"Like I said, I've been really busy."

Virginia cut her eyes away from the Chief and landed a glance on the pitcher. She noticed condensation running down the container the same way she wanted to run from the Chief.

"So?" the Chief began.

"So what?"

"So how's Kyle doin'? I imagine he's back up in Atlanta now?"

"He's fine and he's down at the river playin'. Kyle always spends Spring Break with us. In fact, he's down here just about whenever he's not in school."

"Is that a fact? I wish I would have known that. Joshua, my grandson, is always over at our house. They could have been playin' with each other."

"Mm-hmm. I guess so," Virginia replied.

"You know, Mrs. Scales, there's something that bothered me about that whole incident. A short time afterward, people came to me sayin' that you were there shoutin'. They said you were shoutin' somethin' about death or 'I can't take no more killing'. Is that right?"

Virginia, never having tasted a lie, replied, "I may have said something along those lines. Like I said, that was three months ago."

"But you do remember sayin' it?"

"I suppose so. Why?"

"What do you think you could have meant by that? 'No more killing'?"

"This city done had enough death. That's what I meant."

"Yes, it has," the Chief agreed, rubbing his chin. "But did you also say something to your husband like, *'don't do this again'*?"

"I may have, yes. What's this about, Chief?" Virginia's frustration was festering. She stood up, preparing for the verbal challenge.

"So what did all of that mean?" the Chief enunciated slowly 'Don't do this *again*. No *more* killing.'"

"You got somethin' specific to ask me, Chief?"

"I've already asked you three questions and I still don't have a clear answer." Snide crept its way into the conversation.

"You got a specific question to ask me, I said!"

The Chief couldn't hold back. He forced the accusation upon the woman, "I think your husband killed my officer. And I think you know whether he did it our not. Do you? That's my question!"

"You can't ask me that."

"I can very well ask you anything I want to because—"

"You can't ask me that! Don't ask me that!"

"Why not? Don't you know the answer?"

"You can't ask! I won't hear it again! Leave this house right now, you hear me!"

"I will ask whatever I want to. Don't you tell me what—"

"You cannot ask me something that I can't lie about!"

Virginia dropped back into the chair.

Mercer was quiet. The entire city seemed silent. For one brief moment, the world did not appear to utter a sound. Virginia sat paralyzed by the darkness that had consumed her family's innocence that night on the highway. The Chief stood dumbfounded because he had not questioned this woman of candor long before now.

The truth resided in the soul of someone who knew only honesty. Her truth was an overdue fetus suffocating in the pain of lies, crushed in a womb of deception. It wanted to know life so that life could know the truth.

"Mrs. Scales, what did you say? Can you tell me what you know?" Virginia shook her head, not as an answer but as a weapon. She was fighting herself. Fighting to lose her husband or keep her sanity. The hurting woman clutched the arms of her chair. She wanted to lie. She tried to imagine the taste of dishonesty, but it didn't know her pallet. She wanted to tell the truth, wanted to give birth to it, let its purity refresh this place and heal the wounds that continued to bleed. This feeling hurt. It hurt in her brain and migrated its way to her chest. Virginia hadn't known this pain before, but as she sealed her vision, shielding her eyes for all things in her sight, her pain manifested in a physical form.

Relieved briefly by the interjection of a screaming phone inside the house, Virginia left the chair to flee this porch where deceit and honesty were fighting. Her movements seemed slower than before, and walking was a battle for her body.

"Mrs. Scales, what—" the Chief tried to hang on to this time to what would finally be his victory.

Virginia struggled to speak. "Chief, pour yourself some tea. I need to get the phone."

"You need any help?" The Chief noticed her awkward movements into the house. He wanted to offer himself as much as possible. With kindness and nurturing, he knew the truth would finally spit itself out. He looked out at the street, watching for Andrew's arrival.

The phone's siren was silenced when Virginia answered it. She dropped the phone's receiver as though it were fighting her hand. Virginia's body seemed to reject normality. Something was wrong.

"Helloorh?" She sat on the couch. Her speech strange.

"Virginia, that you?" Emma asked.

"Mm-hmm." Moans were easier to produce than words.

"Just wanted to leave a message for Andrew. Let him know that we called all those folks up in Atlanta. Couldn't nobody help us with the funeral home. They all liked the idea, but didn't wanna take the risk. I guess we'll be closing up for good and the bank'll come and take hold of it."

Virginia was confused by Emma's statement. Andrew never mentioned anyone in Atlanta helping Mack's widow. He'd only told her that he'd given them money to help out. Until now Virginia thought the business was back to normal. She wanted Emma to explain, but was frightened at the sound of the foreign phrases possessing her mouth.

Virginia concentrated and kept her speech short, "Andrew said he gave you money to make everything work ouurt?" The last syllables slipped away from her and the speech was again slurred. She clasped the phone now with gelatin strength.

"Virginia, we appreciate what Andrew did, but he said y'all was in a tight spot and all he gave us was nine thousand dollars. Now I know that ain't nothin to sneeze at, but we need almost five times that much."

"He said everything was all right becasurse—"

"Honey, if he told you everything was fine, he wasn't bein' honest. That's why he told us to call them people in Atlanta."

"He said he was gonnar make it r-right." Virginia couldn't control her speech now and her body tried to reject this crippling invasion. She tried to stand so the gravity could heal the distorted blood flow. Emma kept talking.

"And since we're talkin' about honesty, what's this I hear about you tellin' Andrew not to kill nobody again? People been talkin' about somethin' that happened when Kyle almost got run over. Said you was screamin' about death or somethin'.""

Virgina's speaking ability was completely destroyed by Emma's last statement. Standing was impossible. The same gravity she'd sought to cure the ailment brought her crashing down against an end table and a fragile lamp shattered as it fell victim to this curse that festered in her house and now plagued her body. The lamp shattered as the light bulb gave way to a dim room and to darkness in her mind. Virginia's body destroyed the table and sent a shocking sound throughout the house and onto the porch.

Kyle and Josh had just walked up and were explaining the adventure to the Chief when they heard the crash. All three ran into the house and found the motionless body of Virginia. The Chief ran to the car and radioed for an ambulance, then asked the dispatcher to get a message to Andrew urging him to rush to the hospital. Kyle hovered over his grandmother, offering the same comfort she'd given him after his fall from the bicycle.

"Wake up, grandmama. Wake up, grandmama. It's gonna be okay." The loving boy cradled his grandmother's head, never realizing that his arms had just become her home-going vessel. The burden had been too great and her stroke too severe.

Eighteen

Lay The Burden Down

⫷❦⫸

KYLE WITNESSED A SHOW AT THE HOSPITAL. HE watched this movie of life with no sound. His parents arrived three hours after the phone receiver was dropped on the floor. Back in Atlanta, a receiver lay dangling waiting for better news to prompt its reunion with the hook. Kyle's mother walked the hallway sobbing for her own mother.

Andrew stood by the side of his wife's body, his tears oblivious to joy that would come some morning far away for someone else. Sadness was the infectious disease in this wing of the hospital. Slowly it took over and consumed the untimely consolers. They were too late to pray and too early for the funeral. Others poured in and joined the consoling, the comforting, but inevitably the crying.

Virginia's life was a blessing to them all. Her wisdom was cloaked beneath her unassuming fluffy gray hairs until called upon by a trivial question. Kyle once quizzed her about her knowledge of buckeyes and she postponed the lesson for another day. Then, during a summer road trip to Watertown, Tennessee, Virginia held class from the passenger's seat, showing him a living example of a buckeye tree. When Kyle quizzed again about how she knew so much, her reply was always the same humble reply, 'I just read a lot.' It was good enough for him.

And now, only his grandfather was good enough. Kyle needed Andrew to talk to him and tell him everything would be okay. Tell him that his grandmother was flying around with angels and would watch him plant in the garden.

Kyle wanted to hear that his grandfather was happy because Virginia would see God before him. So he kept watching the silent movie in the hallway, the movie that showed people several lives taller than he open their mouths and shake their heads while nothing came out but the look of pain.

He'd never seen so many grown-ups cry at the same time outside of church. Kyle was worried about his grandfather. Removing himself from the seat for consolers in waiting, Kyle crept by the adults and the medical staff, entering the room where his grandfather stood.

Gently, he reached up and tugged at Andrew's pants. The sobbing man could not respond to touch or any feeling other than that washing his cheeks. Ignored, Kyle walked to the corner and sat unnoticed.

There was so much crying outside no one cared that the Chief had joined them. He approached Andrew. The sound of the Chief's voice dried his tears. Andrew wanted to kill this man before him, the last to stand in the presence of his wife. What he had said to her was irrelevant at this point. Andrew wanted him to stop breathing, have no pulse, and cease to exist.

"Andrew, you have my condolences. Your wife was an honest and—"

"Die." said Andrew. "Please. Just stop livin' right here in this very place. Ain't nothin' in my life good 'cause of yo' breathin'. If the devil is willin', may he have the souls of my great-grandchildren if he'll give me yo' heartbeat at this very second!" Andrew's voice trembled with hatred and regret for the extremities he spewed. He meant none of them, and then all of them. "I know what you said to her. I know what you must've been talkin' about. You ain't had no business talkin' to her. She ain't got nothin' to do with this."

The Chief stood petrified. Perhaps the devil was yielding to the evil request. He'd never heard this voice of hatred before.

Andrew spoke in a crazed calm, "If I had the strength in my body, I'd kill you. I'd kill you deep. I'll kill you so bad yo' ancestors would die again. And I'd go spit on the graves of they forefathers. This thing ain't had nothin' to do wit' Virginia. Just 'cause you think I was in the wrong don't mean you can bring my family in this. *I* was the one that k—" Restraint and deception knew him even in his bottomless depth of hurt.

The Chief would not have touched the matter here had it not been for the hate Andrew had laced in his mind. He retaliated, even now. His voice low, he said to Andrew, "I came by here to try and be human during this time. But you won't let me. I *am* sorry about your wife whether you believe me or not and that is the truth. And the truth, Mr. Andrew Scales, is something I would suggest you become familiar with and soon, I mean right now. Put down this lie because it is a dagger in your hand. A dagger of death for people other than yourself, people not even born yet."

Andrew lowered his head at the mention of truth. He turned from the lecturer and caught sight of Kyle sitting in the corner. His knees were pressed against his chest. Andrew wondered if he had been listening to the foul words that would undoubtedly harm his young ears. Was the boy there at all or was he merely sitting, awaiting rescue with a firm hug?

Kyle exchanged a look with his grandfather, a look that confirmed he had heard every word, but was unclear about the malicious intent. The look transposed into a question, *'Are you coming to pick me up and tell me it's all right now that you're done talking?'*

The answer came swift and cold as Andrew turned to the Chief. He looked again at Kyle, met his asking eyes, then lowered his head and began slow solemn movements away from his grandson. His wife's death had just begun to weigh his body and drag his soul. For the first time in his life, Kyle watched as Andrew began to weaken.

The grandfather evaded the truth and exited the room— alone. By doing so, he condemned generations to come.

PART II
Kyle's Crucible
1994

♋⚬♋

Nineteen

The Nouveau South

─────────── ◌ঙ৪ৎ ───────────

Seventeen years prior, the pecan trees along
highway 257—now named the Georgia-Florida Parkway—had served as a sign for Kyle. Upon seeing the trees
as a young boy, he knew Albany was less than three radio
songs away. The twenty-four-year-old MBA was making a
permanent residence in Albany, and the trees were once
again his welcome home sign.

The groves of fruitful figures stood on both sides of the
road like an army of stout, static giants. Seasons changed
their uniforms, disguising them to visitors. Winter robbed
the foliage and persuaded them to take on the look of
American Elms. Branches originating midway up the trunk
aided the façade. Bare limbs pointed directions with no
purpose or structure. Parasitic mistletoe plagued small portions near the top, appearing to be small explosions of premature blossoms.

Spring resolved the unsightly confusion with lush green
leaves that harbored the tree's fruit. The sweet reward of
pecan was shielded among its own breakable armor. Some
shaken from their base while the others matured and

dropped to the ground which allowed for simple reaping by the young and old.

Driving between the welcoming soldiers on both sides of the highway, Kyle reveled in amazement of the symmetrical strength of each tree. Rows of repetition paralleled one another as far back as he could see and continued along the road for miles as the groves angled towards the highway. Kyle was forced to look ahead of the car and out to the right in order to witness the precision of each row.

As he drove past, he turned to watch the line of trees. It seemed as though they were taking cover in the beauty of their own origin. The trees were hiding in their own humility.

Perhaps these were the ancestors of the pecans Kyle and Andrew snacked on during porch conversations. With nutcracker in hand and a paper bag full of pecans, Kyle loved the brown fruit. He watched in amazement as his grandfather trapped pecans in the meat of his palms and destroyed the shell with pectoral power and heavy hands. The crumbled treat was given to Kyle and he completed the task of digging out the fruit. Occasionally, he smashed the shells weakened by his grandfather, which made Kyle feel as mighty as his older hero.

Those times were distant memories he longed to rekindle. Kyle had attended Howard University in Washington, D.C. where he developed a keen sense for business. Howard was a wonderful, though trying time in his life. He was exposed to new people and new cultures, but was many miles away from the Albany he had come to love in his early youth.

As spring breaks and holidays afforded him road trips with his friends, he rarely visited his grandfather. They'd written each other letters since his freshman year, but they gradually ended as the writing from Andrew became increasingly shorter and more difficult to decipher. The last letter was all but a plea for Kyle not to expect any more writing from Andrew. The composition was much too arduous now.

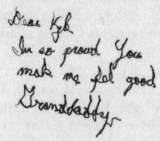

Dear Kyl
I'm so proud You
make me fel good
Granddaddy

Punctuation and spelling were time-consuming formalities Andrew could live without when conserving energy was his first priority. Kyle was forced to watch his grandfather grow old through letters and infrequent phone calls consumed with brevity.

Just as his letters had changed, so, too, did Andrew's voice. The booming resonance that once dripped in soulful slang was now soft rhetoric interspersed with babble and stuttering.

Holiday breaks back home to Atlanta yielded a mere one-day trip to Albany, hardly enough time to show love with any significance. Kyle and Andrew's kindred relationship survived this way during Kyle's undergraduate and graduate studies at Howard. During one of the city's warm Christmases, Kyle had driven down to Albany alone. The man he found leaning against the rails to remain erect was hardly his grandfather. Andrew's broad shoulders were slumping and caved like wilted spring flowers. His fingernails were long and saturated with dirt underneath. The lonely man struggled to care for himself. That Christmas was the first of Andrew's dilapidation. It saddened Kyle to see his grandfather in this light. This magical man that, as a young boy, Kyle thought would live forever.

His only connection to Albany was a lovely girl he'd met during junior year. Her name was Camilla and, to Kyle's surprise, she was from Bainbridge, Georgia. A town twice as far south as Albany and twice as small. She re-

minded him of all things Albany, especially his grandmother. They'd often spoke of marriage and getting en-
gaged. All the more reason for him to settle in Albany. This
summer he would drop to his knees and ask her to become
the flesh of his flesh.

It was the pain of visualizing his decrepit grandfather
that led him back to Albany. He was to take over the Albany View. Kyle's father had considered the job, however,
the industry was picking up and his commissions were increasing each financial quarter. He couldn't break free to
help Andrew.

Kyle's mother, Ingrid, refused to work at the same office that helped take her mother's life. She believed that if
Virginia had stayed home and never worked at the View,
the pressure would not have been so detrimental.

Trust had been restored in the banks and Andrew
opened an account for his bulging business. The View had
grown to eight billboards and was generating one point two
million dollars a year in revenue, most of which was being
diverted into other bank accounts unbeknownst to Andrew.
An accountant bearing the title of friend turned out to be
anything but.

Refusing six-figure offers from the east coast's most
prestigious companies, Kyle packed his bags, loaded his
MBA, and headed for southwest Georgia. His plight was
simple, albeit ambitious. Take care of his grandfather, audit
the View, acquire three more billboards, and eventually
land the Mecca of southern advertising—a billboard located in downtown Atlanta.

The pecan trees were long behind him now as he entered the city limits and traded the pecan army for pines,
oak, and whatever potpourri of trees lined the roads. As he
passed the secluded Miller Brewing plant, he wondered
how he could get in and solicit the company for billboard
space. His conscious gave way to capitalism as he contem-
plated advertising more liquor in the city's south side.

Kyle reminisced at every stoplight. Each store held meaning to his childhood. The ice cream shop he and Andrew frequented. A movie theater where they'd seen Herbie the Luv Bug. His face was overcome with smiles just before his rearview mirror was overcome with flashing lights. Kyle had inadvertently run a red light during his nostalgia.

Crap, he thought. Kyle was well aware of the historical tension amongst races in Albany. There was an extra pinch of displeasure added to the recipe of resentment with the authorities.

Though he was still an amateur businessman, Kyle realized the value of cohesiveness with authorities. It simply made sense to have favor of local politicians, police officers, and men of the clergy. With everyone on his side, no one could be against him. Kyle would be a shrewd persuasive entrepreneur. It's the only way he figured the Atlanta billboard could be attained.

Pulling over into a grocery store parking lot, Kyle retrieved his license and tuned up his tolerance. He wasn't expecting a pleasant experience. A tall officer with a boyish face approached the car with a black pad in his hand.

"May I see your license and registration, please?"

"Yeah, sure," Kyle replied. There was kindness in the officer's voice and the cordial question was surprising.

"Sir, do you realize that you ran a red light back there?"

"Yes, I know. This may sound crazy, but I was remembering all the good times I use to have when I grew up here and I—"

"Your license plate says Washington D.C. That's a long way from Albany."

"Uh, well, yes. I know. I went to school at Howard University and I'm moving down here so I—"

"You're moving from Washington D.C. to Albany?"

"But I'm originally from Atlanta. I've just recently graduated and I've come to help my grandfather run his business. He owns the Albany View. It's only a few billboards around town. Hopefully—"

"Shut up!" The officer demanded with a strange smirk riding his face. Kyle could be tolerable, but he would not be disrespected. He was, after all, Andrew's grandson.

"Excuse me?"

"Are you tryin' to tell me that Mr. Andrew Scales is your grandfather? Your name is Kyle."

"Yeah, I suppose you know of him?"

"Know *him*. I know you. You know me! I mean we know each other. Kyle, it's me Joshua! Remember, the chief of police's grandson?"

"You gotta be kiddin' me! Joshua, man what's up? You're a cop. Had to be like your granddad, huh?" Kyle climbed out of the car.

"Look who's talkin'. You're movin' down here to take over the View."

"I heard that you could use a few black millionaires down here, so why not me?"

The two exchanged laughs and a boyhood hug. From a distance the action seemed inappropriate. It appeared as though there was a confrontation between the two. The confusing scene prompted screeching tires from an under-cover officer passing by.

A plain-clothed officer maneuvered his way from the vehicle. His motion was slow and heavy. If the men had been fighting, they would have reached the twelfth round before the old man made his way to the ring.

"Hold it right there. Put your hands above your head. Get on the ground now!" An aged Chief, protective of his grandson, drew his weapon and pointed it towards Kyle.

"Whoa, whoa, whoa, grandpa. Everything's fine. This is Kyle, Mr. Scales' grandson, remember? He's movin' down here to take over the View."

"Kyle. Is that you?"

"Yes, sir. It's me all right. You're not gonna shoot me, are you?"

"What the hell you two doin' out here fightin' in the parkin' lot?"

"Aw grandpa, we wasn't fightin'. Can't two old friends hug each other without somebody callin' the White Citizens Council?"

Kyle and Joshua shared a giggle, while the Chief attempted to decipher the joke or insult.

"Besides," Joshua added. "Aren't you supposed to be campaignin' down at the civic center?

"I was on my way until I saw you two gropin' all over each other."

"Are you running for mayor, Chief?" Kyle asked, realizing the business advantages of knowing the mayor personally.

"State Representative," Joshua answered as the Chief began the task of getting back into his car.

Some squirms and squeezes later, the Chief was behind the wheel and buckled up.

"I sure could use your vote and any friends you make, seeing how you're gonna be an Albany resident now." The Chief knew he was fighting a losing battle running for office in a district which was sixty-five percent black.

"We'll see what we can do, Chief. I'm sure there are few things I can use your help with down at the View, so we'll work somethin' out."

"Not in town fifteen minutes and you're already runnin' things. You're just like your granddaddy, son. How is he, by the way?" the Chief asked, hoping the answer would be 'on his death bed'.

"He's alive and kickin'. Not too high though. Last time I heard from him, he's getting weaker and weaker, you know?"

"I imagine so," the Chief offered, turning the ignition in his car. He made a comment over the revving engine, "That's what happens when you run from the truth." His words were barely audible just as he had intended.

"What'd you say, Chief?"

"Give him my regards, will ya?"

"Sure, no problem," Kyle responded as he watched the car pull out of parking lot and into the traffic. "Still patrolling the streets, huh? He's gotta be late seventies early eighties doesn't he?"

"Yeah he's up there. Kept in good shape all these years, though. That's all he knows how to do. He'll probably die with his badge on."

"It's funny how things turn out," said Kyle.

"You got that right. So they teach you how to swing a golf club up there in Washington D.C.?"

"I was a business major. It was practically a required course."

"We'll see what you got. I know this great course here. We gotta hook up and play there."

"You mean the country club?"

"No way. There's a fat cat up in Atlanta that owns his own private course down here. Most folks don't know about it. I can get us on, though."

"Cool," Kyle replied, thinking of the transactions he could make on an elite golf course. "I love meetin' new people."

"Oh, really? Then we gotta go quail huttin' because—"

"Excuse me? Black folks don't spend time in trees shootin' animals."

"No, this is quail huntin'. We hunt on a plantation used especially for growin' quails."

"Did you say, a plantation?"

"It's not a *real* plantation. Just a huge plot of land owned by someone that raises quail."

"That's crazy. You mean to tell me that you shoot birds in somebody's backyard?"

"It's hardly a backyard. We're talking about fifteen hundred acres of land."

"What! Somebody owns fifteen hundred acres and all

they do is hunt on it?"

"Well, yeah," Joshua replied. He was shocked that the fact was not common knowledge.

"You're kiddin'."

"No, I'm serious. It's the Pinefield Plantation . I'll take you over there one day."

"So you mean to tell me that some guy has his own private golf course here and some other guy has enough land to build a suburb?"

"Never quite thought about it like that, but yeah I guess so."

Kyle was drowning in the grandeur that would propel his lucrative ambitions.

"I think it's about time Albany got some young black millionaires. After all, this the new south, right?"

"It's still the south, and some parts are new, but others still remain the same."

"Like what?"

"Like gettin' a ticket for runnin' a red light." Joshua chuckled and signed the ticket, ripping it from his pad. "Have a nice day, sir. Oh, by the way, welcome to Albany."

Twenty

Dilapidation and Downsizing

─────── ☙☙☙ ───────

Finally arriving at the childhood resort of his grandfather's house, Kyle witnessed death dueling with life. Things living were doing so with no control. Things dying had done so, many times over.

The front lawn sprouted blades of grass and weeds choking each other for positions of prominence. A lawnmower's blade would have strangled in this horticultural horror as the yard now required harvesting instead of trimming.

Dandelions contrasted the yard's appearance the way mustard brightens a lone frank. It was a sympathetic weed, yet very abundant.

A single screw in the door of the mailbox was its last hope to defy gravity. The post upon which it stood succumbed closer to falling each day.

Grass grew through the seams of the sidewalk while the graveled driveway hid beneath more vegetation. Newspapers surviving in cracked rubber bands huddled at the entrance of the carport. News had no purpose in this place. The shiny paint job of Andrew's El Dorado was ruined by the adhesion of pollen, rain, and time. Pine needles and a haphazard recipe of leaves camouflaged the peeling vinyl roof.

Pots served as coffins for plants long dried out on the front porch. Where plants once reciprocated oxygen with people, dirt traded nothing with no one. An empty mason jar provided a home to a brown ring stain on the inside, perhaps the last sweet tea consumed in the summer's heat.

The antiquation of the house was foreign to the only new structure; a ramp for wheelchairs, or a walker, or whatever device aided whoever needed it.

Adult vision had wiped away childhood days, the way windshield wipers cleared drops of inconvenient rain. It was then that the passenger could see what was truly on the road ahead. And what Kyle saw was a larger task than the role of town mogul. He would first have to become a fixer-upper of all things.

Suddenly he remembered that his grand entrances were not through the front door. He'd always bounced around the side of the house and ran in the backyard where his grandfather was usually working in the garden.

After his brief epiphany, Kyle marched around the side of the house. The space seemed much wider years ago and the distance was a football field longer. He was quickly learning that time distorted perception.

Nearing the corner of the house, before he saw the backyard utopia, he imagined his grandfather waiting at the back steps with a bushel of tomatoes or green peppers. Andrew would say to him, *'Boy, you too late for the harvest. Gotta wait till next year'* or *'There's my favorite grandson right there.'*

Kyle inhaled beyond his lungs' abilities and stepped out to his long lost playground. Waste greeted him. Wasted space, wasted dreams. Even the breath before the last was wasted. Each breath was a waste because the air was stale here. Air that plants and flowers could never refresh. Air that was just as dormant as that in the front yard where this nightmare had begun. This was not his grandfather's house.

This was not his Albany. This was not his childhood. This was somewhere he had never existed, in his life nor in his most melancholy thoughts.

Lying before him, deserted and dried out was his grandfather's garden. The place where he had grown and helped things grow, was barren. The vegetables grown out of habit and cameos of rain had been snacked on by small rodents leaving signature bite marks. Ground once nurtured until minerals leaped from its soil had become as hard as galvanized gold.

Leaves carpeted the yard having never been raked the autumn prior, nor the previous autumn. Kyle walked around the yard, swishing leaves with each step, creating a crushing melody as a result of the interchanging seasons. He watched the leaves as they elevated and fell at his feet. The grown man was searching for a bit of his youth beneath the overdue raking. The leaves were too thick and time had been too long. This was a yard in which Kyle had never played, a garden he had never seen. Not like this.

Against the back fence he spotted a shiny object, the fender on a bicycle. It was the very one on which he'd barely escaped death. Now rusted and ragged, it was confirmation that happiness and youth had escaped. The inevitable was tapping Kyle on the shoulder, telling him to prepare for what could only be worse—the inside of the house.

CR80

"Granddaddy? Granddaddy, it's Kyle. I'm here."

"Who dat, Kyle? Hey, come on back here," a raspy voice called from what seemed like a dungeon.

The house was deplorable. Curtains were drawn and a dark drab consumed the house. This structure was hurting from the inside out. The outer appearance was merely a glimpse of its interior disgust. A heavy feeling seeped into

Kyle as he walked through the kitchen. He could feel the saturation of grease on his skin. Pots and pans used for frying were piled in the sink, caked with the solid white residue of good eating and bad cleaning. The roaches seemed to enjoy it. Even the linoleum was slippery with the unmopped remains of meal preparation. He took short strides to prevent himself from falling.

Empty mouse bait boxes were tucked in the corners of the floor. The mice had moved on to the treats in the garden.

Walls seemed to swell with pain and dark gloom. The filth made Kyle's head throb instantly. He entered the living room and became light-headed. It wasn't the filth or the lighting. He felt so far removed from this room it was almost as if he had never been here. Strength was fighting fear and anguish fought hope. All things good were losing and the winners were telling Kyle to leave or fall to the floor, fall to the floor in the very same room in which Virginia had collapsed. He thought of returning to the kitchen for a glass of water, but recalled the condition of the dishes. Kyle shook his head ferociously, claiming victory of his mental stability, and continued his trek.

The scent of mothballs permeated the house. A common practice of mythical beliefs passed down from families before, the round spherical garment protectors were a mainstay in many of the old houses. It was a confusing odor. The bitter smell triggered senses of protected clothes but antiquated thinking.

Furniture had tears in the fabric, broken legs, and busted arm rests. Company didn't stop by much, which negated upkeep of the sitting items. The fireplace used for the few cold nights was home to paper and trash from the house. Collecting firewood was yet another unconquerable feat here.

"Kyle, I'm back here, son," the weak raspy voice called out.

Kyle entered the hallway which led toward Andrew's voice and was smacked in the face by the smell of urine. Old urine, saturating whatever held its residue. A few steps more and the odor's presence grew stronger. More unwrapped newspapers lined the hall. Mouse bait along the wall here was completely eaten by the hungry pests.

The dizzy spell returned as he finally entered the lair of regret.

"There's my favorite grandson right there!" Andrew announced, coughing when breaths should have been taken.

Kyle had never seen his grandfather this way. He'd never seen anyone like this. The ingrained pictures of the two playing in the garden, buying ice cream and story time; vanished more with each blink.

Andrew was in the type of bed used in hospitals. The protective rails were lowered to allow escape. He wore a gown; pants were too cumbersome, more tasks, more problems. As he rolled over to try and hug his grandson, he exposed himself and Kyle saw the adult diaper his grandfather wore. The man whom Kyle had watched control everything around him, except the wind, could not control his own bladder. Here was the source of the unbearable stench. Andrew had missed the bedpan and that which did not miss hadn't been emptied in days. His own feces soiled the sheets on which he slept. Andrew was, no doubt, dodging the diseases that swam in his own waste.

He managed to dangle his legs from the edge of the bed. Atrophy had captured his muscles, withering them away. The limbs hanging from the bed looked like bone-dead branches in late fall.

Kyle wanted to be sick, but he'd much rather simply stop living, or have his eyes gouged out—anything not to bear witness to the sight of his grandfather. He stooped down to hug him, but carefully this time. The strong playful hugs of old were impossible now. He may have very well broken Andrew had he squeezed hard enough. There would be no physical affection anymore. The two were forced to touch each other with their words.

"Boy, it shol' is good to put my eyes on yo' face."

"Granddaddy, it's good to see you, too. Mama said you had a nurse to help out around here. Where—"

"I run her off!" Andrew traded his coughing for breathing again. "Told her I didn't need her help no more."

"Granddaddy, you need somethin'. This place is nast— it needs to be cleaned up a little bit."

"I know. I ain't worth a wooden nickel in a fire these days. If Virginia was here, she'd be right by my side takin' good care of…. Dammit, I miss her every day she gone! I can't take it no mo'!" Andrew transposed his normal conversation into a frightful panic, then he brought himself back to a strange calm. It was an outburst of sorrow and tears to refresh him.

"But I'm glad you here, Kyle. I always knew you would take care of me."

"That's right. I'll take care of you and I'll take of our business."

"That's my boy right there!" A long coughing spell ensued this time and Andrew appeared to be choking on life itself.

"You all right? You need some water?" Kyle thought once again about the dishes of disgust and realized he would soon be a dishwasher.

"No, I'm fine. Every time I think about the View, I get sick to my stomach. Them fools down there is stealin' my money."

"Who? Mayreen and Booka 'nem?" Kyle's anger caused him to abandon his formal education and he slipped into slang.

"No. Mayreen and 'nem ain't worked down there for a while. I had some volunteers come down there to help and they did such a good job I hired all of 'em. The first one I hired was some old accountant and he brought his friends on wit' him. I know exactly how much money I had in the bank. My family saved and I had rental properties for as long as I can remember. I ain't no dummy. You hear me?"

"Is that right?" asked Kyle.

"I got a bank statement in the mail sayin' half my money was taken out of my account in less than three months. They tryin' to rob me slow so I won't miss it." A fierce cough raged through Andrew's chest and filled his throat with mucus. Andrew didn't know sanitation anymore so he spat it into the urine. Kyle grimaced and almost lost his last meal. The acid and saliva mixing in Kyle's jaws shot an uncomfortable warmth through his mouth. It was time to take over.

"Granddaddy, I'm gonna call around town and find somebody to help out around here and get this place cleaned up. It may be best if I checked you in somewhere."

"I don't need no—"

"You need to let people help you!" There was an exchange in the silence that followed Kyle's proclamation, a passing of authority in a single instant of life. The building of Kyle's tenure as a man was made complete by his denial and demand of authority. "Now, I'm gonna call around and get you some help in here tomorrow morning and I want you to do whatever they say do. If they do somethin' you don't like, tell me and I'll handle it. But right now, I'm going down to the View and kick everybody out."

Andrew looked up with concerned eyes. This person standing here was foreign, but he liked him. A dingy smile gleamed across his face as he clapped his frail hands one time.

"That's my man right there. Hand me that phone before you leave."

Kyle conceded the request and watched as Andrew's shaking hands found their way to the oversized pushbuttons on the phone.

Seven punches later, Andrew awaited the end of ringing. He cleared his throat, not wanting to be interrupted by the bothersome cough.

A quick unpleasant voice on the other end answered, "Albany View."

Andrew spoke with stern diction, "Hello, this is Andrew Scales, yo' boss. My grandson is here and he's on his way down there to kick some tail. If I was you, I'd run outta there like roaches on a radiator."

യ80

Kyle walked into the office of the View and skipped salutations, "You're fired, you're fired, and you're fired! Get out! Don't touch another key on the computer. Don't flip through another stack of papers. Don't speak another word into a phone and don't even breathe another sip of air in this office. I want all of y'all out. Goodbye! If you see me on the street, run the other way 'cause if I see you, I'm gon' curse ya. Then I'm gon' smack you so hard it'll make your great-great-granddaddy's next door neighbor's cousin spit fire. Good riddance!"

Twenty-One

Finding Out

ᘓᘗ

THE FIRST BILLBOARDS OF THE VIEW WERE LOCATED IN the parking lot of a liquor store. On the corner of Jackson and Highland, Kyle gazed up at the back-to-back signs, one advertising malt liquor and the other heralding a public service announcement for drug abuse.

Old and young converged at the parking lot to carry out checker challenges. Sitting on empty peach boxes and milk crates, people watched conquerors defeat prey. Spectators outnumbering the checker pieces, were often joined by the men sitting at the gray line waiting for work.

The gray line was where the anxious unemployed awaited daily jobs. Men with willing bodies and empty pockets sat at Roosevelt and Washington awaiting employers needing labor. Each truck with empty beds stopping in front of the crowd was bombarded by eager men. The will of the group outweighed their experience, which translated into cheap labor. After more hours than trucks had passed by, the men made their way over to the liquor store parking lot to watch the checker Olympics for the remainder of the day and well into the night.

For years beyond Kyle's existence, the billboards had

remained in its birthplace. Scattered throughout the south side of town were painted billboards on the side of buildings. These paintings were the genesis of Andrew's small town fortune. Kyle had thoughts of owning the buildings now. His ambitions for the View were delusional yet, at the same time, attainable.

By finding clients other than malt liquor, he could gain credibility. With credibility he would generate more revenue. And of course with more revenue, he would gain more billboards. Kyle wanted the herculean billboards floating over East Olgethorpe Boulevard.

His daydreams were interrupted by sharp jabs in his side.

"You wanna buy a newspaper?"

"No ma'am," Kyle replied to a frail old lady barely able to stand. Her cane was merely an accessory. It didn't aid her walking—nothing could.

"Say what?"

"No, thank you," he replied a bit louder.

"You want a newspaper?"

"No, thank you! I don't want a newspaper!" Kyle yelled with as much respect as screaming lungs could garner.

"What's yo' name boy. I ain't seent chu around here much."

"I'm Kyle. Andrew Scales' grandson."

"Say what?"

"I'm Kyle! Andrew Scales' grandson!"

"Oh, you is? Sho nuff? I know Mr. Scales. We go way back. He used to be good friends wit' my husband. His name was Mack. We used to own a funeral home on South Madison. You ever heard of it?"

"No ma'am, I don't—"

"Say what?"

"No ma'am, I don't think so!"

"You ain't never heard of Mack's funeral home on South Madison Street?"

"No ma'am!" Kyle continued yelling.

"We coulda been the biggest funeral parlor in southwest Georgia if them police didn't kill my husband. Yo' grand-daddy tried to help us out, God bless his soul. I said 'Andrew we shol could use yo' help.' Me and Marcus both went to see him. Marcus is my brother-in-law. Andrew said, 'Times is tough, Emma. All I got is twelve thousand dollars.' I said, 'Andrew, I shol' appreciate it, but that ain't gon' be enough. We need at least ninety thousand. We can pay you back with interest.' Andrew said, 'I can see 'bout somebody up in Atlanta helpin' you out with some type of investin'.' I said, 'Andrew, whatever you can do to help, we appreciate it.' Nobody ever did help us out. So we had to turn it over to the bank and somebody else bought it, but they ain't never had much luck wit' it. Some peoples think that old building cursed now.

"I know you done seent Meadow funeral home on South Madison."

"Yes ma'am, I know about Meadows!"

"We coulda been five times as big as Meadows. Anyhow, you sho' you don't need a newspaper?"

"How much is it?" Kyle asked with lowered volume, hoping she wouldn't hear.

"It's fifty cents. I got change if you need it. How many you want?" Emma heard him very well this time. Kyle missed the woman's bait and switch. Digging through his pockets for the silver exchange, he paused for a moment. Kyle was running through the calendar of his life.

"Ma'am, when did you say all of this happened?"

"Say what?" Emma was back to her routine.

"When did you say all of this happened!"

"Oh, this happened in seventy-seven."

Coins lay in Kyle's hand midway down his pocket. Movements froze and his mind was a blaze with confusion. Either Emma had the year wrong, or she was simply babbling about events that never occurred. For it could never be that Andrew had an abundance of money to lend and not have helped his friend. That was a grandfather he did not have, Kyle thought.

"I don't know if—"

"Say what?"

"I don't know if it was seventy seven 'cause that couldn't have happened that year!"

"Sho' it was. I remember clear as day. I remember it 'cause that's when you spent yo' first summer down here."

Kyle was immovable. She'd just confirmed her story with his personal time stamp. Not only had she called the date, but she'd placed a reference for Kyle's life as well. If she was accurate about a trivial detail such as his first summer in the town, then the more important dollar figures must have been accurate.

"Here's your money."

"And here's your paper," Emma announced without Kyle having to repeat himself.

Off she hobbled to the sidewalk beginning her laborious task of crossing the street. Placing her cane onto the stretch of road, she disregarded the presence of cars. Once in the street, the slow shuffle of feet exchanging strides interrupted by the cane's stability, seemed to go on for days.

The episode would eventfully last ten-minutes. A line of seven cars waited impatiently as Emma's show ended on the opposite side of the street.

Kyle had been watching as her multicolored, polyester dress rocked with the rhythm of her sauntering. Her wardrobe was older than he was. It reminded him of curtains he'd seen in someone's home and a housecoat worn by Virginia. It was a hybrid of decorated windows and early morning garments. The crown she wore was a feathered church hat. Portions of white wings swirled about the accessory, hiding the mangled mess of hair which hadn't been combed since the hat had been found years ago.

Staring up at the billboards, Kyle was disturbed by the

discovery. Of course the validation would come with a line of questioning for his grandfather. Kyle was finding Albany quite different now. Despite its hidden beauty and its natural treasures, his childhood memories were growing darker.

C380

Andrew was placed in the safe and clean confines of a retirement community. It would allow Kyle time to restore some sanitation to the house and get the business in order. The evening hours called for soothing conversation and Kyle needed relief from the exposure of time's reality. After he finished disinfecting the room in which he would sleep, Kyle summoned the sweetness of his girl from Bainbridge.

"Hello, Camilla?"

"Hey, Kyle."

"What's goin' on?"

"Thinkin' about my man."

"Is that all?"

"That's enough for me. How's everythang up in Albany?" Camilla asked, her voice twirling in the thick drawl.

Kyle sighed with frustration as he thought about the early discoveries. "It's not what I had expected at all. My grandfather is in pretty bad shape. He's run off his help and the house is just nasty."

"What?"

"I mean it's terrible. When I walked into the house, I almost threw up."

"Are you serious?"

"Very. He's probably been sleeping in his own urine for days."

"Oh, my God! There's no one there to help him?"

"They tried, but he ran them off."

"What about your family? Don't you have an aunt?"

"Yeah, but she travels quite a bit."

"That's terrible, Kyle. I had no idea."

"Neither did I. If it weren't for you, I don't think I could stay down here for good."

"That's sweet, baby. If you need me to come up there and help, I will. I've got a little time."

"No, Camilla. I couldn't have you stay here. Besides, you need to work on your job search, don't you?"

"Absolutely not." You forget that you're talkin' to the queen of connections. I start in two weeks at Vigoro Industries. It's a plant here and I'll be working in accounts payable. I figure a few years as a grunt and then I'll be on my way to comptroller. If not, I'll just move up there and try to get on at Miller or Proctor & Gamble."

"You didn't waste any time, did you?"

"Baby, I don't know how to waste time. What about you? What's going on with your plans for your grandfather's business?"

"Well, I fired the whole staff and—"

"What?"

"Oh yeah, they're all gone," Kyle answered. He spoke with the conviction of an experienced executive.

"Why did you do that?"

"They were stealing money from the business."

"That was fast. I didn't know you had already performed an audit."

"Camilla, I didn't need to audit anything to fire those fools."

"But where's your proof?"

"In my grandfather's word, that's where."

"Kyle—"

"What? He knows how much money is in the bank and how much should be going out. He obviously felt like it didn't match up. And I rectified the problem."

"I hope you're right because you've just contributed to the unemployment population of southwest Georgia."

"Please, Camilla. Three crooks are hardly gonna hurt the economy. And why are we talking about this? Let's talk about when we're gonna see each other again."

"I just want you to be careful. This isn't D.C. where people can find another job just like that. It's a bit more complicated here, so just be cautious. Besides, what are you gonna do for help?"

"I've already sent the word over to Albany State for some co-ops or interns. Everything'll be fine. Now, like I said, when are we gonna see each other again? I've got somethin' for you."

"Really? Like what?"

"Like I'll show you when I see you and then you'll see for the rest of your life."

There was a pause. Camilla wondered if an assumption was appropriate. If so, she knew exactly what to assume. "What did you say?"

"I said then you'll—" Kyle was interrupted by the call-waiting signal disturbing. "Hold on a second, baby. Hello?"

"So you grown, moved down to Albany to run your granddaddy's business and now you can't even call your mother and tell her you made it okay?"

"Hey, mama! What y'all doin'?"

"We trying to work our way into your busy schedule and come down to Albany on the fourth of July."

"Hold on, mama. One second." Kyle pressed his finger into the flash button and clicked over to Camilla.

"Camilla, this is my mom on the other end. Why don't you come up for Fourth of July weekend? I think my parents are coming down from Atlanta. You all can see each other again and we could celebrate the announcement."

Camilla was aroused once again by Kyle's teaser.

"What announcement and why can't you make this *announcement* earlier?"

"It's only a week away. Do you think you can come up?" Kyle asked, rushing her.

"I'll try. That's my first week of work so I may have to work late, but I'll try."

"Good. Call me later when you know for sure. I gotta run, baby. My mom's on the other end waiting."

"I love you, Kyle."

"Not as much as I love you," Kyle declared to his soon-to-be, bride to be.

"Hello, mama?"

"Must have been a big business deal, huh?" Ingrid said sarcastically.

"Nope, that was my honey."

"Lord have mercy. Boy, you are too grown for me."

"So when y'all comin' down?"

"We'll probably leave Friday or Saturday. A friend of ya daddy's is runnin' in the Peachtree Roadrace and he's gonna try to go watch him. If it rains, we'll just head on down there Friday."

"Okay, that's sounds good. Camilla's gonna try to come up, too."

"Oh good! It'll be really great to see her again. That is such a nice girl. When ya'll gon get married?"

"Come down here and find out."

"What chu say?" Kyle was throwing hints like Mardi Gras beads.

"I said just come on down here. But y'all might want to stay at a hotel or over at somebody else's house. It's really bad at granddaddy's."

"What do you mean?"

"Mama, when was the last time you were down here?"

"I don't know. It was probably when you were here for Spring Break that last time. But we call down there all the time."

"The house is nasty. You couldn't fall asleep here if you were dead, it smells so bad."

"He had some help stopping by there, though."

"That's what I thought, but he ran 'em off."

"Oh, daddy. What is he doin?" Ingrid paused in her fear and frustration. "How bad is it?"

"He was layin' in his own mess when I got here."

"What!"

"It smelled like he had been that way for days."

"That's ridiculous. Nobody couldn't even call us? I bet they kept gettin' paid even though he kicked them out. What are they doin' down there? You know what, I'm gonna come down there tomorrow. This doesn't make any sense." Ingrid's anger fueled her rambling.

"Mama, don't worry about it. I'm getting' him some better care already. Just come down when you planned and it'll be all right."

"No. Uh huh, somebody needs to be held accountable for the way that house is being kept. I mean not even a phone call or a note or nothing."

"You know just as well as I do when granddaddy gets somethin' in his head, nobody can do anything to stop it. He might have told the help not to call anybody. Really, mama, let's just make it better from this point on."

Ingrid sighed and struggled to form her thoughts. "It's just that… you're never ready for something like this, Kyle. I wasn't ready when my mama died and I guess I'm not ready to see my daddy wither away." The hurting daughter dwelled in her pain followed by tears. "He used to be so strong and so big. When I was little he would throw me high in the air and catch me every time. I never ever thought that he would drop me or miss me on the way down, you know?

"He could whip you so fast you wouldn't know what you had done and in the same minute give you a speech to make you think that you were the most special person in the world. He took such good care of us. And now I feel like nothing because I'm not taking care of him. I should have been there living with him after mama died. Kyle, I should have been right there holding his hand and cleaning his mess. That's what he did for me. He did for all of us. Now it feels like we abandoned him."

Ingrid's words yielded to her tears and seconds of silence. "Would you do that to me or your father? Would you leave us alone to rot away?"

"Mama, you can't blame yourself for this. Besides, no one knew. If you talk to granddaddy and he tells you what you want to hear, you assume everything is fine. If you wanna help, just come down when you planned and bring him a smile full of sunshine. It's gonna be okay, really."

Kyle's words provided no relief for his mother. Ingrid sniffed and wiped her wet release as the phone became useless. No words were being exchanged.

"Mama...mama."

"What is it, baby?"

"I'll take care of everything. It'll be fine."

"I know you will. That's why I'm so scared. If you didn't love him so much, there's no tellin' what could have happened to him. He might have already—" The speculation hurt and speaking was too painful now. It had to cease.

"Mama."

"I gotta go, Kyle. I can't—"

Kyle heard the phone fumble its way to the hook as his mother rushed away from the detriment she would have to face in a few days.

The premature patriarch hung up the phone and began taking deep breaths as he rethought his decision to move here again. A few more breaths, deeper with each repetition, he smelled a reminder of work left undone. The entire house had to be organized, disinfected and fumigated. He thought of starting at the source of it all, his grandfather's bedroom. If Kyle could conquer it first, then his tasks thereafter would be minimal.

Walking to the back porch where the cleaning supplies were stored, he saw a string hanging from the ceiling. It struck him as odd because it hadn't been there during his youth. The wound fiber was the only addition to the house and seemed peculiar in that it hung so low. Tied to the handle of the attic door, the string was five feet from the ground. It could have easily been reached by a frail old man, but Andrew was in no condition to climb the stairs.

Kyle feared the mere thought of what creatures inhabited the attic. He kept walking and retrieved the supplies from the back porch. Nearing the bedroom again, he dropped a bottle of bleach and stooped to pick it up. As he stood erect again, he felt a sliver of something easing its way down the back of his neck and fighting its way down his shirt.

Kyle jumped and jerked, swatting what he couldn't see. The supplies littered about him, he looked around as the jitters infected his body. There was no living being on him or below him. He looked up and there it was. The string, oscillating. He'd grazed the string when he picked up the bottle.

It kept swaying in front of him as if to say, 'don't ignore me.' Kyle reached for the string while a heated sensation whirled through his veins. He pulled the enticing fiber and the attic door creaked as it opened. When Kyle could reach the handle, the compacted stairs began to unfold.

Hanging from the rafters in the attic was another string. Same woven fiber as the one tied to the attic door handle. Dust and cobwebs decorated this string. Kyle reached for it and pulled. A rough tension fought back as Kyle yanked harder. Suddenly a light popped on in the attic. The string was tied to the chain of a light bulb.

Had he not been committed before, the curious man was now attached to the endeavor. Kyle loaded the first step and the wood began to crack so he quickly jumped to the next, which proved stronger than its predecessor. Fearfully, he climbed the structure and poked his head above the opening and into the attic.

Just as he climbed one more step a creature scurried in

front of him. He slipped down a step, but caught his balance while losing a steady heartbeat. The warm tingling transformed into bubbling heat on his skin. Fear was fighting curiosity and indecision compelled the movement. Kyle ran up the stairs and looked in the direction of the creature's sound. A rat was trying to camouflage itself into the darkness of a corner. Chewing and scratching, the rodent escaped into a hole that had been too small for its growing body. The garden treats and fallen morsels in the kitchen had doubled its size.

Scanning the attic, Kyle found himself the only being here. The attic was strangely empty save for piles of hatboxes.

Each box was stacked atop another. Every container had a range of years written on a white piece of paper. Some of the dates spanned two years, others five years or more. Columns of boxes in rows of three were gathered in a cluster. Kyle quickly counted four stacks of three boxes of different sizes and shapes. No uniformity existed amongst them, not even the brand name or color. The only likeness was the duct tape suffocating the cardboard figures. Tape wrapped the boxes horizontal, vertical, and diagonal. Whoever had sealed the contents did not want them easily opened.

Realizing this, Kyle climbed back down the steps into the kitchen, retrieved a knife, scurried back up the stairs, and began cutting away the tape from the first box. He began with a dated box which read 1972-1979.

Minutes later the top was removed and Kyle loathed what he had just discovered. Anger swept power into his hands as he cut away the tape from the other boxes and uncovered each top, exposing the duplicated contents.

Twenty-Two

Albany Uncovered

⋆⟋⟍⋆

QUAIL PLANTATIONS WERE OBLIVIOUS TO KYLE. DURING his summer visits, the city consisted of the Flint, downtown, Mercer Avenue, and local restaurants such as Carter's and Jimmy's Hotdogs. Simplicity had surrounded his young innocence.

After Kyle had made the attic discovery, when Joshua called later that night, a break from old Albany seemed refreshing.

He and another friend were playing golf at the private golf course he'd talked about. Kyle, excited about the networking opportunities, accepted the invitation with enthusiasm. It was a chance to get close to some old money as well as escape some he hadn't known about.

The Pinefield Plantation was twenty miles below Albany. Its owners were a white real estate developer and a black bank executive, both from Atlanta. The two were hardly at the hidden oasis and almost never appeared simultaneously. A meeting of the two during eighteen holes at the prestigious Radium Springs Golf Club formed the matrimonial merger. Both men were in search of umbrellas for Uncle Sam's downpour. The developer had real estate and the president had cash. Pinefield Plantation was the revenue-generating solution.

Sam Williams managed the facility. A University of Georgia graduate, the horticulturist and MBA held the position for only a short time. He was handpicked by an associate of the developer. Sam and Joshua were good friends and the friendship was infectious to those they knew, hence the invitation for Kyle. Sam's duties entailed reservations, arranging quail hunts, overseeing the lodging staff, and in charge of upkeep—upkeep of the private golf course tucked backed behind the fifteen hundred acre plantation.

Kyle and Joshua had arrived together that morning. Sam met the duo in front of the plantation lodge. The bulky manager appeared in front of them dressed in sturdy work clothes. He was clean-shaven, a contrast from many of the clients who sported full beards infested with crumbs from the morning breakfast. Sam presented himself as professional as a hunter could be, removing his hat to greet his golf guests. Reddish brown hair was trimmed high and tight with a part down the left side. Patches of pink colored his cheeks, a side effect of the cold conditioned air inside the lodge.

"What's goin' on, J?" Sam asked.

"I'll let you know in about nine holes," Joshua replied.

"Sam, this is my buddy I told you about, Kyle. Kyle, Sam."

"Nice to meet ya," Kyle offered, gripping the man's hand with vice power. He grinned the face of salesmen walking through a forest of money. Kyle was thinking of quail slogans, avoiding the reality that drivers near the liquor store had no use for quail hunts.

"Same here," said Sam, stripping his pants. Revealed were the popular khaki Bermuda shorts and ankle socks. Universal summer golf apparel. "J tells me you learned to play golf up in D.C.?" Removing his work shirt, he covered his chiseled torso with a collared golf shirt.

"I play a bit. It was practically advised in my MBA curriculum."

"You're an MBA?"

"Yeah, that surprise you?"

"No not at all. I got my MBA from UGA. We had a golf group of MBA's up there."

"I would imagine so since the campus has its own golf course," replied Kyle.

"Ah ha, you've done your homework."

"Always learning, friend."

"I like him already, J."

The three smiled with delight at golfing among pals. Sam capped off his transformation from hunter to golfer by lacing up his black and white saddle-oxford spikes. Placing a winter white cap atop his autumn colored strands, he jumped in the driver's seat of a strange contraption.

"This what y'all use for golf carts around here?" asked Kyle.

Joshua and Sam's laughs filled the morning air. The visitor's remark was original and hilarious to those in the know.

"You've never been on a quail plantation, have you?" asked Sam.

"When was the last time you saw black folks on a plantation?" Kyle replied.

Sam roared with laughter as Joshua gave an obligatory snicker having already heard the comment.

"And we ain't in a hurry to get on any more," he added.

"Man, where did you find this guy? He's outrageous."

"I found him runnin' a red light?"

"Well, don't worry about that out here." Sam's laughter subsided and he explained the contraption's purpose.

"This is a huntin' jeep."

Sam got out and walked around the front of the massive machine. A large iron rack six feet wide and three feet deep was attached to the front of the jeep. Attached to the back was another rack that was twice as deep and erected almost seven feet high. There was a shallow grate used for storing the quail carcasses collected during a hunt. Silver cages were pulled by a wagon attached to the already fully loaded jeep. It was a dragon with an engine.

"We can take four hunters plus a driver out on one of these things. We've got room for the dogs and all the gamebirds our clients score. You can shoot from the jeep up there on the perch or you can roam the field if you like."

"And all you do is hunt quail here?"

"Oh, no, sir. You can hunt turkey, deer, and dove, but not all year 'round. South Georgia is the quail huntin' capital of the world. J, we need to take our friend here on a quick tour before we—"

"So you mean to tell me that quail fly down here just to get shot?"

The laughter roared again.

"No, they breed 'em here," Joshua said, flexing his quail knowledge.

"We can breed an entire population of quail right on this land. One hen'll lay at least twelve eggs in the wild, sometimes double that in captivity."

"You learn all that with a Georgia MBA?" asked Kyle.

"Shoot naw. I learned all that from puttin' in eighteen hours a day. Get in. Let's tee 'em up."

As Kyle placed his foot into the jeep a gunshot disturbed the tranquility. Its boom and recoil lingered in the air. Echoes rode the sound waves, mixing with the wind. Kyle, the only foreigner to the environment leaped to the ground and lay face down to avoid indiscriminate bullets.

As the gunshot's echoes died with time, Kyle heard gasping from Joshua and Sam. Lying on the hood of the jeep, their hands banging the metal, the two held their stomachs from the pain of laughter.

Sam's pink cheeks had become rivers of red. His lungs

seemed to be confused by the strong heaving that laughter brought. Joshua pulled his hat off and threw it to the ground. Air restored the sound to his diaphragm and he burst into laughter again with an even deeper bellowing laugh.

Kyle pushed himself from the ground feeling a bit angered at not knowing the source of the laughter. A prank, perhaps, or an initiation for the visiting black guy. "What the hell is so funny!" Kyle demanded.

"You really are scared to be back on a plantation, aren't you?" Sam managed between gasps.

"Oh, oh, oh, man," Joshua's laughs ended before Sam's. "Somebody's shootin' clays, Kyle. Oh man, we've gotta get you out here more. Oh man, I'm dyin'. It's not even huntin' season, for God's sake."

"Okay, so where's the golf course?" Kyle demanded.

"Let's go." Sam's beet like face was soaked in tears and exploded with incremental bursts of more laughter.

The men loaded their golf bags and headed further into the plantation aboard the customized dragon.

⋘⋙

Roads on the plantation were made by frequent trips of the modified jeeps. The way asphalt was constructed on the city streets, nature's strands had been pressed down, leading the way to desired destinations.

Kyle held onto bars of the jeep while they rocked and bumped past by the shooting course. Clays were taking flight, spinning and elevating like miniature UFO's. During the abbreviated flight, the shot rang out again. The UFO exploded, bursting into aborted pieces then a puff of colored smoke. It was a collision of things that knew no corners but produced sharp edges. A flat round clay structure met the spherical buckshot and finally produced the shattered results.

Clay shooting was a rhythmic flash; the shooter yelling 'pull', mechanical contractions originating by a launching device at the tower, a spinning whiz of the object as it divided air, the powerful tympani strike of a shotgun, and a quick crack, ending the measure.

Passing the target range, the visitor looked out at the piney woods. Trees escaped the ground in clusters, much too short to meet the clouds. The trunks here lacked the structure of the perfectly lined pecan tree groves. They seemed to simply stand tall, challenging nature to make them sway one direction or the other. Its fragile, layered bark was almost human in that it resembled the magnification of skin cells.

They drove on and Kyle noticed wiregrass meadows filled the vast opening where trees segregated themselves from other features. Sagebrush covered the floor, giving camouflage for creatures too small to fight and too smart to run. A pond halted the intrusion of trees and plants at its watery edge. Here the growth could do nothing but gaze at its natural kaleidoscope reflecting off the rippling mirror.

Sam drove the jeep away from the worn road and maneuvered to an area familiar only to him. He quenched the fiery engine of the dragon by killing the ignition.

Kyle was nervous. There was no golf course in sight and he was alone in the woods with two white guys that hunted—often.

Stories occasionally resurfaced about people reliving the old hanging days. Over the years one or two blacks had been reported missing. It was usually concluded they were in the woods somewhere. Kyle quickly realized his mistakes. Not telling anyone where he was going. No one knew where to start looking. He hadn't even driven to the location, so there would be no trace of his car.

Sam leapt from the jeep. Kyle eyed him the entire time. Joshua remained in the front seat, his demeanor calm as though he had witnessed this procedure before. Sam retrieved a large stick from the back of the jeep. Gleaming a sinister smile, he approached Kyle.

"Now this is something you'll never forget," Sam announced.

Having embarrassed himself before at the sound of a shotgun, he would wait until the last minute to fight back. As soon as the stick was raised, Kyle would thrust his foot into Sam's chest and the rest would be improvised.

"Listen for a second," Sam continued, still watching Kyle's eyes.

Kyle returned the look and obliged. There were no sounds, only that of blood-pumping thrusts through busy veins. His heart was pulverizing his chest cavity, holding it captive. Sensations of heat crawled down his back, and sweat purged though his skin.

Just as Kyle could feel his urine ready to force its arrival propelled by fear, there was a sound.

Two high-pitched notes and then a pause followed by three more high-pitched notes.

Bob-White. Ah- Bob-White.

"That's South Georgia's fastest and hardest flying Bob White quail right there, son," Sam said, boasting as though the birds were his own brood.

Kyle relaxed, but still kept his guard asking, "Where are they?"

"Over there in a covey," Joshua answered.

"What's a covey, a quail tree or something?"

More laughter ensued, albeit controlled.

"No, city slicker. You know, as manager of this fine facility, it's my duty to educate you Washington, DC MBA's on southern culture. The covey is how the quail protect themselves. It's not a tree. It's a group or a gathering of quail. They all get together and face outward in different directions. When danger approaches, they fly out every which way. Birds of a feather flock together don't just sound good, it's the way they survive."

"Those survival skills obviously don't help too much since they're too stupid to fly off the plantation so they won't get killed," said Kyle.

"Until they grow bigger brains and bigger balls, they'll always be hunted and we'll always get 'em," Sam replied.

"How many are over there?"

Sam tossed the stick into the air, catching the opposite end. "I thought you'd never ask." He began walking carefully towards the concert of two and three notes. Once within his reach, Sam flung the stick forward. It traded end for end in the air, rising quickly and then plummeting towards the earth. The stick crashed against a brown floor layered with underbrush. Like a handless magic wand, the stick produced a feathered flutter. The sounds of a thousand fans wafting into the summer air penetrated the sky. Paddles of wings flowed downstream as though the river had been elevated while the birds floated.

Certainly beauty such as this was kept hidden for a reason, Kyle thought. Perhaps it was as sacred as the command of the imaginary water wizard. A show this stunning belonged to the public and not tucked away along makeshift roads.

The potbellied birds disappeared by the frequency of their flaps. Visions of brown specks gave way to the blue sky. Kyle was amazed at the delicate balance of freedom and captivity, breeding and banishment.

"So what do ya think?" Sam asked. "Breathtakin', ain't it?"

"I never knew anything like this was here. This is somethin' I might expect to see in a zoo or down at Chehaw park. What's really funny is that those birds are perfectly happy waitin' on their execution. I guess some things don't know how to go free."

"Sam, Kyle, can we get to the course? You two forest freaks are killin' me tryin' to become one with nature."

"Well, look who's talking. Reverend Josh himself."

"Oh, cut it out, Sam."

"It's true. Just wait and see."

"Josh, you a preacher and a cop?" Kyle asked.

"No-o-o." Don't listen to that moron. I'm a deacon over at Saint Paul's. Sam came to one freakin' Sunday School class that I taught, and now he swears I'm gonna be in the pulpit one day."

"He is. You should have seen him, Kyle." Sam stood on the front of the jeep as though it were a pulpit. "The word of God this and the word of God that. Brethren, I swear unto you if thine this thou shall not that thine Bible babble."

"Okay, when the lightin' strikes, we'll know who it's here for," Joshua said.

"Joshua, what about that whole church and state thing?" asked Kyle.

"What about it?"

"I thought there was supposed to be a separation."

"Kyle, the earth is the Lord's and all its inhabitants."

"Alrighty, enough with the bible lesson," Sam said, walking across the hood over the windshield and into the driver's seat. He fired the dragon once more and the men were off.

Joshua tried expounding on his text, but Sam tossed his passengers about the jeep, swerving around trees and making three hundred sixty degree turns. Holding on was difficult enough. The sermon would have to wait.

The jeep finally charted a straight road, which lead to a steep hill. Joshua and Sam took the opportunity to fasten their seatbelts.

Once the metal and fabric secured them both, the ride was nearing its end. Reaching the hill's crest, Sam slowed the jeep by releasing his foot from the gas, allowing momentum to take over. The vehicle pulled itself over the hilltop and then coasted down the other side, beginning its descent into an emerald colored miniature metropolis.

The hill's crest was a division of contrast. On one side lay the brown landscape of a hunting backdrop and on the other was the earth's green carpet. Riding down the hill, Kyle took an encompassing look at the private beauty. Here was yet another world he never knew.

Oak trees were lined in a row at the entrance to the course. Their old extended branches seemed to welcome visitors like open arms at family gatherings. The road then wrapped itself around a small glistening pond with a fountain at its center. Water recycled itself through the fountain's sprout, each drop anxious to be showcased in the oasis.

By now, the southern sun was baking its contents. The insulation of morning dew had long diminished and the battle of heat had begun. Sam stopped the jeep behind one already parked. They exited the vehicle and walked toward a small shack which ivy had been allowed to swallow. The worrisome growth was trimmed with precision. Freshly snipped leaves were lying on the ground. Someone had obviously been trimming in the early morning.

Flowers of bright golds and brilliant reds outlined the walkway to the shack. Birds serenaded the day's occasion aided by a few of the plantation's gamebirds. Older quail had survived and used the sanctuary for fowl retirement.

Sam and Joshua walked inside the shack to load up on golf balls, beverages, and sunscreen. Kyle remained outside, still gazing at this place that resembled the beauty of Oz rather than southern backroads.

"Beautiful, ain't it?" Joshua said. He was the first to exit the shack, his face and arms saturated with protective lotion.

"This is unreal. You mean to tell me that one man owns this place and it's not open to the public?"

Sam emerged from the shack. "Actually two people own it. It's their own little playground. You're public and you're here. We like to think of it as 'by invitation only', if you know what I mean.

Kyle was sure to pitch a billboard sale now. He didn't care what they advertised, but anyone with this kind of money could throw a little of it his way.

"Well, boys, what about a little two-man best ball? Kyle, me and you will take on Josh and the old man. Us MBA's gotta stick together so we'll just—"

"Hold on there, Sammy," a commanding voice hailed from inside the shack. An accompanying body came forth with a slow stride. It was the old man Sam had referenced, the Chief. Arriving long before the three, he was prepped for the golf outing.

The Chief looked at the young men and announced, "Why don't you and your bosom buddy team up and I'll take Kyle." Walking up to the visitor, the Chief draped his arm over Kyle's shoulder, smiling. "I want to catch up with him, see what's been goin' on in his life." As the Chief's smile vanished he said, "Besides, we need to have a long talk about his grandfather."

Twenty-Three

Regretful Golf

⸙⸙⸙

THE FOURSOME STOOD ON THE FIRST TEEBOX WAITING for no one. They had run of the entire course. Four hundred and twenty yards down the fairway, small figures ran onto the putting surface and quickly disappeared.

"Who's that?" Kyle asked.

"That's the grounds crew. They're puttin' the flags in," replied Sam. Everyone except Kyle looked in different directions. His focus was on the three regulars and their demeanor. They all seemed to patiently wait on something that had not yet arrived.

"What are we waitin' on?" Kyle asked.

"Waitin' on Quinton," Sam replied.

"Oh, you guys got another buddy comin'?"

"Nope. Quinton is the official starter for every round of golf here. If Quinton doesn't come out, we don't go out. As long as I've been workin' here, Quinton runs the show."

"Foolish if you ask me. Just plain foolish," the Chief remarked.

"Well, where is he? Why didn't we just give him a ride from the lodge?"

"He gets around just fine on his own. In fact, I think I see him comin' right about now."

"Kyle, you ain't gon' believe this," Joshua said whispering in his ear.

"Here he comes," Sam said pointing towards the pond.

An overly plump quail made its way towards the tee box. Worn with age and years of flight, the bird waddled and paused, strolling as though the world would wait for its decision.

With an arrogant bobble, Quinton's head was a combination of complimenting hues. His crown was brown, meshing with a black separation of a white throat and eyeline. The black areas invaded his eye and resembled a masked hero of some sort. Super-starter, perhaps. The distinct colors mottled at his lower breast. A contrasting pattern was the only similarity of its head and body.

Quinton looked like a crossbreed of penguin and pigeon. An experiment yielding surpassingly beautiful results. Alas, his plumptitude had taken its toll. The short wings, having aided Quinton in escaping many hunts, were used sparingly now. His claws were the preferred mode of transportation in this stage of his life. Flying was labor for the plantation icon.

Finally reaching his prestigious position, Quinton stood in the middle of the tee box, looked at the golfers, strolled up to Joshua and pointed at him with a lazy beak. He turned to look down the fairway and walked back towards the pond.

"Okay, now we can start! Josh, you're first," Sam yelled with ebullience.

"You gotta be kiddin' me. You mean to tell me that bird walks out here before people play golf and picks out who tees off first?"

"Every time. I said you wouldn't believe it."

"And I told you it was foolish."

"Shouldn't that thing be shot by now?" Kyle asked.

"Not Quinton. We figure he's been around for quite a few years now. Survived every hunter. We brought him out here and he learned to stay. Guess he's the one that had the brains and the balls," said Sam.

"There's always at least one to prosper despite the death of others," said Joshua. "Jews have holocaust survivors, Blacks have slave descendants, Christians, immigrants—"

"Grandsons," the Chief interjected, staring at Kyle.

Kyle chuckled with absence of knowledge. "Joshua, you rich because of somebody's dying?"

"No, but you are," the Chief replied.

"What? What are you talkin' about?"

"Hey, guys, come on. Quinton's gone. Let's tee off before we get cooked out here," Joshua insisted. "It's gonna be a long day."

"Sure is," the Chief added as the round of golf began.

The private golf course was deceptive in its appearance. Though it was constructed with nine putting surfaces, the entire course was played as eighteen holes. Each tee box could be used to play two separate fairways. Yardage markers for every hole were painted quail statues: blue for 200 yards, white for 150 yards, and red for 100 yards. The course used only four golf carts and the paths for the carts had been made by several trips over the course by its visitors. Grass was precisely cut in a cross-hatched pattern and over-seeded during the winter months. This ensured the green playground would remain that way all year long.

Trees on the course stood in the center of circular pine straw trimmings. Each circle was five feet in diameter. From the tee box, they looked like small ornaments.

Joshua and Sam teed off followed by Kyle and the Chief. Four perfect tee shots and four perfect approaches landed them all in the center of the green on the first hole. The men took turns putting and the teams were at even par on the first hole. While walking to the carts, Kyle began the shop talk.

"Sam, you guys ever thought of any advertising for this place?"

"Can't. It's not open to the public, er uh, I mean, it's by invitation only.

"Not the golf course, but the hunting area."

"We've got a few things going like the phone book and we're listed with the Chamber of Commerce."

"What about a billboard?"

"Hey, you two gonna chatter all day or play golf," asked Joshua.

Everyone loaded up into their carts and headed toward the next tee box. This time three balls lay in the fairway and one in a water hazard. The Chief had pulled his tee shot left and blared profanity.

Sam and Joshua placed their approach shots five feet below the hole. A birdie was inevitable. Kyle's approach shot landed just off the fringe. The match was building now.

Once at their ball, Kyle and the Chief studied the contour of the grain and faced the decision of whether to putt or chip. Kyle suggested a putt while the Chief was adamant about a chip shot. Some arguing ensued until Kyle's patience gave way to persistence. The Chief would chip. He lined up behind the ball, taking aim then stance. Placing himself ahead of the dimpled object, the Chief took the practice swings before executing the shot. There was a crisp impact with the eight-iron and the ball darted off towards the flag. Its speed was much faster than expected and was sure to run by the hole some ten feet. However, the flagstick seemed to have a magnetic feel for the ball as it remained directly on course for the hole. When the ball seemed destined to go on forever, it crashed into the flagstick and disappeared into the hole.

Everyone gave a boisterous shout at the feat. The Chief darted off towards the hole, intentionally leaving Kyle to celebrate by himself. The other two made their putt for birdie and Sam addressed the sales pitch.

"I don't think the owners want to advertise hunting on a bill board. Animal rights and all that. So I guess the answer is no."

Kyle lost his stride as his business meeting had just been destroyed. He was ready to head back and pitch some other potential customer. But here he was, in the middle of nowhere on a beautiful private golf course with no client.

"But one of the owners left a message that he wanted to speak with you about cooperative advertising near some billboard over at liquor store or something?" Sam said.

"What!"

"The bank president. He wants to talk you. Most likely he'll want to advertise the bank on your billboard."

"But how did he know I was coming?"

"Oh, we have to have every golf course visitor approved before they can play. He heard that you were coming to help out with your grandfather's business and, well, you know how capitalists are."

"Man, why didn't you tell me this back at the lodge?"

"'Cause you never would have made it out to the course," Sam replied with a smile. Kyle hopped into his cart with an even bigger one.

The men headed to the next tee box 200 yards away.

"You gonna be like you grandfather, young man?" the Chief asked.

"I hope so. He's a great man and I respect him a lot."

"Hmm. Respect, that's a tough word to use these days. There's respect for your elders, respect for one another, respect for the dead."

"Yes, sir," Kyle replied, confused about the Chief's rhetoric.

"People here have a lot of respect for my career. That's why I'm running for state rep."

"I'm sure you'll do well, Chief."

"There's only one blemish on my record. Do you know what that is, son?"

"No, I'm sorry I don't."

"When you were a little boy, one of my officers was killed. No one was ever arrested for that murder. Do you remember that?"

"Vaguely. What happened? Were there no witnesses?"

They arrived at the tee box. "Oh, there was a witness all right. But she's dead now. You know someone that knew the witness very well."

"Who?" Kyle asked before the Chief exited the cart.

Grabbing his club from the bag and removing the head cover, the Chief walked around to Kyle and replied, "Your grandfather."

Kyle sat erect in the cart, his body functions seizing up and then losing control. A scattered pulse, erratic heart, itching scalp, loose bowels, excited bladder. Death was next, he thought. He was snapped from the siege by voices.

"Hey! You hittin' from back there or you gonna get out of the cart?" Sam asked.

Joshua looked at the Chief and then towards the ground.

"What did you say to him, grandpa?"

"The truth hurts," he replied.

Kyle emerged from the cart with a three wood. Without making eye contact, he walked past the men, placed his tee in the ground and then the ball atop the tee. He addressed the ball without performing a pre-shot routine. His swing was awkward and uncomfortable. After impact he lost his balance and the ball sailed off to the right, resulting in a boomerang slice. Kyle watched the ball ride away on the curved loss and then stepped aside without saying a word.

"What got into you?" Sam asked.

There was no response, not even a glance in their direction.

Joshua could determine the context of the conversation without asking.

He'd known about the allegation towards Andrew. Although the Chief never informed him directly, there was always talk around the station about the Chief's imperfect record. He'd tried to convince his grandfather not to play golf with them that day. When the Chief heard Kyle would be playing the course, he'd rearranged his entire schedule to play in the group. Campaign appearances and strategy meetings were all set aside in hopes that he could inject Andrew's virus into his own bloodline.

After the other tee shots had been scattered to different areas of the fairway, the men once again jumped in the cart. Kyle sat there waiting to press the gas pedal. He wanted the cart to telepathically appear at their destination or an instant transformation of some sort in which they could be transported without conversation. Now he feared any sound that would pass over the Chief's lips.

The day had been so beautiful, an exhibition of things unknown and places unimaginable to foreign occupants. He wanted to become a quail, fleeing the covenant of its covey. A feather within its wings, a speck upon its decorated breast, any minute object that would allow him to avoid what was next.

"You gonna drive that cart, or we gonna *will* the next shot?"

Kyle thrust his foot into the pedal causing a jerked acceleration of the cart. The Chief quickly grabbed the side rail to steady himself. He looked at Kyle, smiling, realizing his words had served their purpose.

Waiting on the tainted scroll certain to be revealed, Kyle prepared for the worse.

"Don't even think about doing anything about it," the Chief began.

Agitated by the man's mere existence, Kyle replied, "What did you say?"

"Your tee shot. There's no way you'll find that ball. Don't even think about doing anything about it."

"Oh," Kyle replied.

RPMs of the golf cart's engine were the only movements until they reached the Chief's ball. He was stewing Kyle in a pot of discomfort. While he simmered with suspense, the Chief played a perfect approach shot within six feet of the hole and subsequently sinking the putt for another birdie. As they drove to the next hole, Kyle expected silence, but it was not to be.

"Your grandfather knows about the shooting. He knows about the witness, and I dare say he knows who did it. You should check your granddaddy's jewelry and see if he's missing anything. Spilled blood is around your family, son, and unless you clean it up, it's gonna keep runnin'."

"What the hell are you talkin' about? If you got somethin' to say, then just say it! Stop playin' these games and say it!"

The golf cart stopped and the gasoline engine fell to a purr. Sam and Joshua heard the shouting and stopped their cart short of the tee box. Joshua knew all too well the sound of his grandfather's rolling thunder. Had he not leaped from his own golf cart to protect his visitor, the Chief's vengeance would have destroyed him.

"Grandpa, why don't you ride up here with Sam and I'll ride with Kyle. Somethin' tells me we need to keep an eye on each other's score cards."

"Never you mind, son. I think I threw my back out on that last putt," the Chief lied. "I'm gonna catch a ride with the greenskeeper and head on back to the shack. You boys go on without me," he said, pulling himself out of the golf cart. The Chief burned Kyle with a look of death resurrected. "Besides, my work here is done. Sammy, good seein' you again," he yelled. "Joshua, hit em' good and tell your father to get those people at the plant to vote. Kyle," he began with volume only the two of them could hear. The Chief extended his hand with a gentleman's gesture. Kyle reached to return the offering and the Chief quickly retracted the offer.

"Wash your hands, so I won't have to."

CﬔℬꙄ

The abbreviated round found the three men back at the lodge where Kyle was able to speak directly with the bank president. He'd given Kyle the name and contact information for the company's marketing vice-president.

Considerable tax breaks were being offered to companies demonstrating involvement in empowering rural and urban areas. The president had learned that advertising was an acceptable offering of corporate presence.

Kyle was to call the vice-president and settle the terms for a thirty-six month campaign using the double-sided billboard. When Kyle threw around figures near twelve thousand per month, the bank president never paused when he replied, "Brad's got a check with your name on it. Send him an invoice and we'll nail down the particulars after the Fourth of July holiday. We'd do it today, but I'm runnin' in the Peachtree Road Race, ya know."

His first major score for the View simply created itself by happenstance. A celebration, however, was shrouded by the accusation and threats from the Chief. The images inside the box were flickering in his mind like a strobe light penetrating his brainstem. The discoveries were beginning to hurt and there was but one medicine that would soothe the pain. His grandfather's truth serum.

Twenty-Four

Digging

ↂ℧

Tʜᴇ ᴄᴏᴜɴᴛʀʏ'ꜱ ʙɪʀᴛʜᴅᴀʏ ʜᴀᴅ ᴘᴀꜱꜱᴇᴅ ᴛᴡᴏ ᴅᴀʏꜱ ᴘʀɪᴏʀ and the retirement home staff was removing decorations from their annual Fourth of July festivities. The home was always festive. Any reason to decorate brought about balloons of hues not matching the holiday's color scheme. St. Patrick's days were often red, white, and blue. Some years Halloween was orange, black—and purple. Columbus day settled for transparent balloons.

Colors were of no importance. The act of decorating, celebrating, and breaking the mundane activities of pill consumption and board games was the true occasion. Streamers were recycled from holidays, aiding to the already clashing catastrophe on the walls. There was little concern for decorations. Much of the emphasis was placed on care for the residents.

The facility boasted the best reputation for elderly care in the Albany. Staff workers often made personal sacrifices to ensure expert care. Overtime was common among the workers, however, compensation for extra hours was not. It was a family affair that inspired selfless magic created within the walls. Residents were known to leave property and money to their favorite staff worker.

The new building was the result of a deceased resident's willing her entire estate to the facility. It was that type of unprecedented care which inspired Kyle to place his grandfather here.

Andrew had been on bed rest since his admittance. Though his atrophy was retreating at the hands of nutrition, the old man's spirit had declared defeat.

Kyle entered his room and Andrew's face unzipped a lost smile. Cleaner than their first reunion, he spoke with joy and sharpened faculties.

"Hey, that's my favorite grandson right there."

"What's goin' on, granddaddy? You feelin' all right?"

"Aw, boy, I ain't no good. They got me up in here like a baby in a hospital. I can't get no work done from here. I need to be back home."

"Naw, you on't need to be at home. You need to be right here where people can take care of you."

"But you gon' need help down at the View."

"I got that all taken' care of. In fact, I came to tell you that I just got a new client."

"Sho nuff?"

"Yeah, got him signed on for almost three years."

"Say what?"

"Sure did."

"Must be Miller or somebody. You know I been after them for I don't know how long."

"No, actually it's a bank. They want both sides of the billboard, too."

"You kiddin' me?"

"Nope. I figure I can get some smaller businesses to advertise the building spots. After the three years are up, I bet we can get a spot over on Oglethorpe."

"Lord hab mercy. I can't believe this. You ain't been down here a good month and you done already turned the business around. If I didn't—" Andrew's diction trailed off to a weeping staccato.

Kyle dressed his shoulder with a comforting hand. Words weren't necessary for gratitude.

"It's okay, Granddaddy. I understand."

Andrew gathered his emotions and shuffled them, losing sorrow and trading it for joy.

"If I didn't have you, I wouldn't be here now."

"That's not true. You still got mama and 'nem. They'll be down here later. I bet they can't wait to see you."

"You don't understand. I loved Virginia more than my own life. And when she left, my love for you was all I had to keep goin'. Grandson, I love ya. I trusted you with my life a long time ago and you ain't never let me down."

Kyle felt a resurgence of discomfort he'd felt with Emma, the boxes, and the Chief. The feeling was surfacing with frequency now and it was gaining strength.

"Granddaddy," Kyle said. He wanted to talk about the riddle he'd just delivered. He wanted to talk about the discoveries. He wanted to know what had happened to this euphoric place that was now saturated with deceit. "What do you mean you trusted me with your life?"

"Aw, don't pay no attention to me. I go in and out sometimes," Andrew replied. His attempt was unconvincing and fueled Kyle's inquisition.

"You should get some rest." Kyle was coy. He was baiting his grandfather and, for the first time ever, was unsure about the man's honesty. "By the way, I ran into one of your old friends today."

"I got plenty of people that think they old friends."

"This lady seemed to know you pretty good. Her name was Emma?"

Andrew's motions ceased. The fidgeting he'd begun came to rest like a deflated balloon losing all hope of ever rising again. Kyle picked up on the reaction and continued.

"She said y'all go way back. Her husband died and they

used to own a funeral home or something. You know who I'm talkin' about?"

"Yeah, I know her. Knew her husband, too. Good friend of mine."

"That's what she said. It's a shame what happened to their business."

"White folks used to be so cruel down here. Came in there and took that loan from them for no reason," Andrew replied, shifting the point of inquiry.

"It was good that you tried to help them get back on their feet though."

"Didn't have enough money. Gave 'em what I had though."

"That's what she said, too. Said you gave them almost nine thousand dollars but they needed way more than that. That was around 1977, wasn't it?"

"Mm-hmm. If I had it back then, I would'a gave it to 'em."

The hot sensation jolted from Kyle's head diverted through the neural highways in his body. Blood pulsated with an insane force as his heart followed the chaotic concert beneath his skin. Hair on the back of his neck straightened, protruding through their own follicles attempting to flee his body. Everything pure about their bond tried to flee him. Memories of affection and love, images of special summer time, sounds of laughter between them—it had all just become tainted by Andrew's words. For the contents of the hatboxes served as infallible proof that Andrew was lying.

Kyle wanted to leave. He needed to leave before Andrew unknowingly shattered the picture, the picture of a flawless image of his grandfather. He'd spent a lifetime painting it in his mind. Andrew had begun to destroy it in one instantaneous moment, but leaving would not satisfy the hunger Kyle had developed.

Evil epiphanies were evolving everywhere he turned.

The source of each awakening seemed to be lying here bed-ridden. Weak from life's choke, his deceit had become an all-consuming pot of poison. Pushing through the pain, Kyle continued his questioning.

"How much money did people make back then, Granddaddy ? I mean how much money did you and grandma have?"

"Maybe a couple thousand dollars?"

"But didn't y'all have rental properties and some farm land you sold?" Kyle fought the lie. He challenged the dis-honesty to grow. If lies would be told today, he wanted each one to reveal itself.

"Yeah. It wasn't worth much," Andrew replied, think-ing he could slip answers in the way he did on the back porch during Kyle's youth.

"What about money in the bank and maybe stashed away somewhere?"

"You shol' is concerned about money, boy. Where you get that from?" Andrew gave a cunning smile. He saw his own prideful hoarding in Kyle.

"Are you tryin' to tell me that when I was little, all you had was a couple thousand dollars and you couldn't help your friend with a bigger loan?"

"I didn't have it to give."

Kyle locked his eyes onto his grandfather's. He was searching for the good in the ancestor. It was then he knew it. Perhaps his words had been blended with confusion and medication. Maybe he wasn't understanding the questions. Kyle searched for the excuse which would restore the belief in his hero.

Though the hurt was now sickening, Kyle pressed even further after a long silence. His voice oscillated.

"Granddaddy...what happened to that policeman that got killed when I was little?"

Andrew fidgeted again. His hands began to quiver with uncontrollable vibration. Kyle appeared, not as his grandson, but as a ghost revealing secrets of death. Andrew's dry throat struggled to produce the liquid which would lubricate the lies he selected.

"What you talkin' about?"

"The policeman that was killed. Did you know him? Was it that same time when that man came to the house and you took me all over town with you? I remember that mornin'," Kyle said, rewinding the show his mind. It was one of life's snippets which copy images into memory. Did you have anything to do with that p oliceman?"

"Naw, boy. That was a long time passed. We was talkin' about somethin' else. We was talkin' about—"

Andrew stopped. The lies had run dry. He stopped talking because he knew the buried confession would pry its way through. His head rolled over the pillow and his stare fixed against a picture he could not decipher. Andrew looked but saw nothing. Knowing that if he saw the face of his grandson, he couldn't lie again.

"Granddaddy, I know about the boxes. I found them in the attic."

Andrew shivered.

"I saw the dates on the boxes. The one for 1972-1979 had more than three hundred thousand dollars in it. You had the money to help your friend, but you didn't. Why did you lie to me about the money? It's over five million dollars up in that attic, granddaddy. All you had to do was tell me the—"

Kyle's words were drowned in his weeping. He cried for the lies, for the shame, for the lifetime of secrets he had yet to find. He cried for his grandmother. Sitting in his facial fluids, Kyle smothered his face into his own hands.

Andrew wiped his own tears and released the reign over his life's deception. The sins and burdens of his life had left him ill and alone. He'd shared the evil with the two people he'd loved the most and it had killed one of them. In an effort to salvage what was left of his soul, he attempted to save Kyle's life.

"I did it for you."

Kyle stopped his movement. Wondering about the reference of his grandfather's comment.

"It was all for you. Not for my sons or daughters. They didn't know nothin' 'bout no legacy. Didn't understand what it meant to have one. I knew as soon as you sat on my lap that first Christmas. The way you put your hands around my neck for no reason at all. I knew you was my legacy. The one who would carry on the name and all the work I done. It was for you, son. That money is yours. It's for yo' children and yo' children's kids. I don't want yo' bloodline to work as hard as I did. I want them to live the life of a king.

"Wasn't nobody touchin' yo' treasure. I don't give a damn what they needed or who they was. Every family got to make they own legacy and I made mine. Made yours. I ain't proud of some of the things I done. But you got to know that I did 'em for you. I lied so you won't have to. I stole so you won't have to. I ki—. I did things so you wouldn't have to.

"In yo' life, it's gon be times when you wonder why things happenin' to you. You gon' wonder why you got things other people ain't got, good things. And that's because of sacrifices I made for you. Don't you forget that, you hear me? What I did for you is between us. People got a funny way of redeemin' the past on things they see in the present. I worked too hard for people to destroy this empire I built for you. If they found out things they don't like, they'll destroy my name and yo' future.

"Remember how we used to sit in the garden for hours and make the ground ready for the seeds. Didn't care what we was plantin'. I just needed time to talk to you about us and about life. I wasn't plantin' seeds for the vegetables. I was plantin' seeds in you wit' time and patience. Look what you become, Kyle. All that nurturin' and look at you.

You more of a man that I could ever think of bein'. And if I got rocks in my dirt just so you could reap the best harvest this family ever seen, then so be it. I don't care 'bout me no more. I did it for you. All of it ain't been good and I'd give my soul if it could just rain and wash away my dirt. Just wash it all away."

Kyle was momentarily restored by his grandfather's admission. The man possessed a love for him Kyle never knew. An unconditional, transcending, yet dangerous love.

"Granddaddy, rain is sweet for thirsty crops, but that water washes up stuff you didn't want people to see."

Kyle left his grandfather's room and walked through the hall of the retirement home. Smiles and salutations passed right through him. He acknowledged no one, afraid that even they might reveal secrets about the man occupying the room he'd just left. Kyle needed to get home and examine his grandfather's small shiny gift that was now as heavy as his grandmother's headstone.

Now standing outside, Kyle was tapped on the shoulder by small wet fingers falling from the sky, as if the soul-snatching spirit of doom had been waiting in prey for this day. Deceptive rain began to seep through the earth's ceiling over South Georgia.

Twenty-Five

Alberto's Birth

ᏣᏂᎤᏋᏫ

Thousands of miles away from Albany, Alberto had *been the year's first inbred offspring of air and sea. Depending on its strength, Alberto would either become a tropical depression, tropical storm, or worse, a hurricane. The conception of the meteorological misfit had been much further east of Georgia—Dakar, Senegal, a city that was Africa's westernmost offering to the Atlantic Ocean.*

Here a long, yet narrow, small Senegalese boat called a piroque and three fishing rods could yield an exotic catch. The Atlantic's salty swishes ebbed into the Saloum Delta brought with it fifty pound barracuda and two hundred pound stingray. At times the waters produced ten barracuda catches without rowing one single stroke. The long flightless amphibian was an easy catch—unlike the Captain fish. Masking its talent with family members ranging from six to eighty pounds, the Captain fish was feisty and arduous to retrieve. Those without the proper gear could find it yanked into the ocean.

It was that same fighting spirit from which the coast of Africa produced the tropical wave in search of a destiny.

An assignment rationed out by forces known, yet unseen, the wave of Dakar would find its way to a place it had never before visited.

The technical concept of tropical waves had its genesis some forty years prior to Kyle's existence. Scientists had discovered that the African easterly waves originated from Northern Africa, which was Dakar's geographical relativity.

While Kyle had been reveling in the notion of returning to Albany, searing temperatures of the Sahara Desert had begun the seasonal contrast with the balming, cool temperatures on Africa's coast. Separated by miles of water, Albany would soon become the recipient of Africa's residual climate.

Tradewinds did just what they were; traded breezes across the tropospheric flow through the agitated Atlantic. Seventeen days prior to Kyle's discovery of his family's burden, the African easterly waves unleashed one of the sixty annual seedlings and it began to flow.

Sunrises and sunsets wafted the creature west. Casually riding and residing in the Atlantic, a brewing wave measuring fifteen hundred miles in length made its presence known. Adorned in a cluster of seductive clouds, it showered the Lower Antilles, the arc of islands bowing off the Caribbean Sea's border.

Turning north, the thing bellowed thunderstorms, this time barely missing the Virgin Islands and Puerto Rico. It had sniffed U.S. soil, although a purchased decoy for the mainland. Still active it subsided a bit, holding its burst for what it searched for.

More days passed and the watery path reached further north, a direct path for the central Bahamas and then it would head for the Eastern Shoreboard. When its way had been found, a trough moving west sheared it apart and the course of this indecisive storm was altered. The trough that pushed it further west had been another of the annual sixty *waves from the east. It was as though a force had seen the original wave's premature ascent north and unleashed another to direct its final approach—further west towards the Florida panhandle.*

The National Hurricane Center had witnessed a meeting of two more small separate tropical waves, one moving east and another to the west. Using its water vapor imagery and sounding data, the NHC observed as Alberto flowed directly into what appeared to be a landing area formed by the two opposing troughs. Not only did the creature have an assignment; it had tutorial help. As a result of the welcoming committee, Alberto moved across Cuba and was given yet another vertical wind shear.

Eleven days had passed while Alberto searched for its entry to the United States. The storm system crossed Cuba's Isle of Youth and poised near the country's western tip. Data reported by the National Oceanic and Atmospheric Administration revealed that the tropical wave had begun to circulate. Alberto was slowing its westward thrust and calibrating an attack. Circulating more than four thousand miles from the African origin, its winds ripped at twenty-five knots and Alberto had an official classification—a tropical depression. If the winds increased to thirty-five knots, Alberto would become a tropical storm and those in its path might be in grave danger. There it sat, slowing its temperament for the west, and building a swirl.

Hesitating inside Mexico's gulf, Alberto was aided by yet another trough. The depression was experiencing precise adjustments by accompanying forces.

On July's first day, a navy vessel in Mexico's gulf, the Robert E. Lee, reported that the Tropical Depression was thrusting winds at 44 knots. The westward wave from Dakar, Senegal had, in fact, grown to become Tropical Storm Alberto.

Now realizing its plight and potential, Alberto heaved itself directly north in line to collide with Destin,

Florida, eastern Alabama and western Georgia. But the storm's journey had been too tiring even for itself. The miles and the forceful waves had weakened its might. Just off the coast of Florida, the fight ended and the Tropical storm was no more. Though the fight was over, the mission was not yet complete. Alberto gave what it had to its cause, which would be more than sufficient. It would be devastating. Retreating into the gulf, Alberto left its remnants in the form of torrential rains. Almost cosmically destined for each other, a force, a place, and a person would be forged together. The meeting's attendees meshed by prophetic alliteration, Alberto, Albany, and Andrew.

Rain reinforcements came later during the day Kyle's parents arrived. They'd stopped at Lisa's house—Ingrid's sister—and settled there for the night. It was vacation time and her sister had placed a key under the mat before they'd left for California.

Once back on Mercer Avenue, Kyle continued the sanitation of his grandfather's house. He'd had intentions of a small family cookout, but the day had escaped and was later washed away. Housekeeping was disturbed by the blaring sound of the rotary dial phone.

"Hello."

"Hey, baby."

"Hey, mama. Y'all still in Atlanta?"

"Naw, we're over at Lisa's house."

"I thought they were out of town."

"They are, but we decided to watch their house for 'em since we were coming down."

"Smart move. You sure don't want to stay here. Actually it's not as bad as it was. I've been cleaning for a while now."

"You are so precious. Sometimes I can't believe you're mine. Now you just get ready to relax. We'll be over to help you get the house together."

"When, tonite?"

"Shoot naw. It's rainin' like a fool out there."

"I know. And it came down all of a sudden. It's better to stay where you are. I was gonna try to have a cookout tomorrow. Maybe it'll be dry enough by then."

"Well, we wanted to go and spend most of the day with Daddy. Why don't you meet us over there?"

"I was over there today. I don't need to go back."

"What's wrong? Is everything okay?"

Kyle stopped cleaning and stared out the kitchen window, watching the liquid night consume the glass.

"Kyle?"

"Mama."

"What is it, baby?" Ingrid asked, her maternal radar sensing discomfort.

"Do you remember when I was little and Granddaddy and 'nem came home late. The next mornin' you were askin' a lot of questions and he wouldn't talk about it?"

"Vaguely. Why do you ask?"

"Do you remember a policeman being killed down here a long time ago?"

"Oh, yeah. It almost tore the city up. But it was later found out that one of Daddy's friends did it and the police shot 'em or somethin' like that."

"What was his name?"

"The policeman?"

"No, the man they shot."

"Oh. Mack something. He used to own a funeral home but after they found out he shot the policeman, his business dried up. What made you interested in that?"

"Just askin'. You know how it is down here. It only takes a thought for somebody to give you a history lesson."

"Don't I know it and then they won't stop talkin'. Listen, I gotta run. Ya daddy's over here getting frisky."

"Ugh, mama. Y'all nasty."

"Don't be mad at me us 'cause we're still in love. We'll meet you in Daddy's room tomorrow, okay?"

"I'm not goin' back down there. I, uh, got some work to do down at the View," Kyle replied.

"Okay, then. We'll stop by the house after we leave there. You want somethin' from Carter's? Hold on, Kyle. Ya Daddy says hey and he loves you."

"Tell him hey and I love y'all back. Bring me some peach cobbler if y'all stop by Carter's."

"Okay, we'll talk to ya."

"Bye mama."

Twenty-Six

Swept Away

⸏ ☙

Kᴋᴇ's ᴏɴʟʏ ᴀᴜɴᴛ, Lɪsᴀ, ᴡᴏᴜʟᴅ ᴏᴄᴄᴀsɪᴏɴᴀʟʟʏ sᴛᴜғғ his favor with hot dog's from Jimmy's or entertain him at the zoo during his summer visits. Ingrid's only sibling, ten years her junior, had just adopted a six-year-old girl. California was to be their first vacation together. Unlike most cross-country expeditions, this one would not be by plane. Lisa wanted to show her daughter, Tammy, the America she had never known. Therefore, the two would drive to San Francisco to visit Lisa's high school sweetheart. Lisa and Tammy had departed that morning and made a stop in a city thirty miles north of Albany called Americus.

While devising the trip with her mother, Tammy'd said, *"If we drive across America, we have to stop in Americus."* The new mother agreed and planned a route through Americus, then to Columbus heading over into Tuskegee.

Coincidentally, Lisa's co-worker was scheduled to perform at a concert in Americus. Tammy and Lisa planned to attend the event, spend the night with the co-worker's family and depart Thursday, the following morning, before sunrise.

Wednesday, the night of the performance, a scarcely occupied building was given the news of the show's cancellation. Rain had continued to submerse the region, prohibiting several orchestra members from arriving.

A woman dressed in a long, flowing evening gown addressed the mumbling crowd fifteen minutes after the concert was to begin. Clearing her throat, the stylish woman made a very unusual announcement.

"Ladies and gentlemen," she said, fighting her southern drawl. "It seems we have a slight problem on our hands. I'm afraid the concert for this evening must be postponed."

The crowd's mumble evolved into shifting and movements.

"As you can see, we haven't a full orchestra. I'm quite sure it is a direct result of my next announcement. We have just learned that Americus in now under a flood warning. Therefore, those of you that brought umbrellas must now use them for boat oars."

Releasing amusing comments and laughs, the audience stood to their feet and headed for departure.

"I'm very sorry for the inconvenience. Please retain your ticket stubs for a refund or admittance to the next concert."

Unconcerned, the people formed lines at the coat check for raincoats and umbrellas. Lisa escorted Tammy to the stage where she grabbed her co-worker's attention.

"We'll meet you back at the house," Lisa informed her.

"Do you remember how to get there?"

"Yeah, we'll figure it out. Besides, Tammy has to get a Happy Meal," she replied with a frustration sweeping over her face. They didn't check their umbrellas or raincoats, so the mother and daughter bypassed the growing line and witnessed a raging disaster outside.

The sky's offering saturated the town unaware of its purpose. Alberto's rain had missed its intended city. Perhaps mistaking Americus for Albany. Waters were swelling from within the city as its residents remarked at the heavy rain. No one had realized the potential until the flood warning was issued. A rainy Wednesday had just become a detrimental doomsday.

Streets were taken over by currents fighting to destroy previously immovable objects. Hidden by the summer night's darkness, the flood rapidly engrossed Americus, Georgia.

Prior to the concert, the plummeting rains were torrentially teasing the Mayo Street Bridge. Exactly two hours later, waters had risen two inches and the smashing current began pounding absurd amounts of water against the structure each second. The rain was pouring its power onto the people at a rate of one inch per hour and would continue to do so all night.

Lisa and Tammy began searching for familiar streets. Windshield wipers were futile fans against the rain-coated glass. Lisa jammed the wipers to the maximum speed and each swipe danced from left to right, arcing up and down with useless frequency. The panicked driver was operating blindly.

"Mommy, I can't see," Tammy yelled from the back seat.

"I can't either, sweetie. It'll be alright."

"Look for the yellow M-mommy."

"Okay, Tammy." I just want to see the road. Lisa said to herself, as if to conceal her fear.

"I'm scared, mommy."

Armies of liquid fists slammed against the car. A cadence of no particular rhythm accompanied the wiper's song of sorrow. The interlude was deafening. With no vision and the duet of danger slamming her eardrums, Lisa attempted to drive the car across the Mayo Street Bridge. Rocked by Alberto's fury and water from Town creek, now flowing across the structure, Lisa could feel the vibration.

She accelerated, attempting to escape. A flow of water

up ahead on the bridge caught the speeding car and elevated its tires, fighting gravity. Lisa had no control. The car returned to the surface swerving over the center line and then spinning, crashing into a guard rail near the bridge's end. Vibration of the bridge grew to a rumble and seconds later to cracking. Lisa yanked at the wheel and tried to drive the few feet which would have put her on the other side. Her steering wheel was stuck as was the car. Cracks in the structure continued and Lisa looked out at the night illuminated by her headlights and watched as the Mayo Street Bridge collapsed.

The car was hanging onto the last piece of what had not succumbed to the current. Lisa unstrapped her crying daughter and pulled her out of the back seat. The door was opened and the two stood atop the car.

Drivers who had arrived at the bridge just before the collapse jumped from their cars. A couple yelled across the raging waters, "Hold on, we're calling for help!" a man yelled, pulling out his cell phone.

"Help us!" Lisa screamed above her crying daughter.

"We should swim across and get 'em," an onlooker suggested.

"We'll never make it. Those waves are higher than the ocean. We'd get swept away as soon as we got out there," the caller replied. "If help doesn't get here right away, they're dead."

"Help us!"

The current banged against their feet now, slowly submerging the car.

"Mommy! My feet are getting wet, mommyyy!" Tammy screamed.

Lisa added her tears to the wet night. She could see that the pace of the water was faster than that of any rescue team's ability.

"Hold on, baby. Just hold on."

Minutes later the water was already at Lisa's hips and

Tammy's shoulders. The little girl simply cried. She had never known these feelings and sensations at the same time—wet, cold, fear. Standing against the rushing waters stole the mother's energy. With every fiber of muscle she could find, Lisa picked Tammy up and held her above the current.

The people across the creek were still. They couldn't move. Lisa realized they could not help. She offered a final plea for her life then for her sanity.

"Helllp us! God, don't let this happen!"

Screaming and holding her daughter, Lisa felt the force push against her waist. The current was being fed by more rain and it began to toss Lisa.

Observers covered their eyes, not wanting the picture snapped in their minds developing there forever.

Men who watched the water swallow more of the mother and daughter each second, began to cry. The weeping grew heavier as the water pushed and surrounded the two until there was nothing left but their memory.

∞

Kyle awoke Thursday morning and tuned into the news. He was searching for clear skies through the magic of a local meteorologist. What he saw instead was shocking. The news anchor delivered the message.

Flash Flooding swept through parts of Southwest Georgia late last night. The remains of Tropical Storm Alberto have stalled over the region and begun to claim lives. Jessica Moran has the details from Americus.

The camera switched to a reporter as she completed the story.

Authorities say moments after a car drove onto the Mayo Street Bridge, the swift current forced the bridge to collapse. Witnesses say that's when the horror unfolded before their eyes.

The observers from the night before retold the story with great dramatics and eyes still overtaken with tears. They conveyed the helplessness they felt watching it all and regret for the young girl's life. Kyle was drawn closer to the set with each word until he learned the rest of the story.

Authorities have already notified the family members of Lisa Scales and her six-year-old daughter, Tammy. Both were residents of Albany. The rest of Southwest Georgia braces for flooding. From Americus, Georgia, I'm Jessica Moran, Channel Seven Action News.

Kyle ran away from the set. He stumbled over furniture in an attempt to put distance between himself and the shock transmitted from the tube. Sitting on the floor, his chest rose then collapsed with repetition. Breathing returned to normal after the disbelief subsided. If they'd contacted the family, his parents must have known. Kyle dashed towards the phone and ripped at the dial until the seven digits had been rotated back to the silver hook.

Mama, did you hear? he would say. *That was Aunt Lisa and her little girl that died last night,* he would confirm. The phone mocked him as it returned ring after ring. He needed to hear the voice of his family, but there was no answer. Kyle pressed the white bumps protruding through the phone, released them and began ripping at the rotary again. His parents must have gone to the retirement home early. A woman's voice answered the phone in Andrew's room.

"Hello."

"Mama. Did you see the news?"

"Kyle, this is Nurse Jones. Yes we've heard about your aunt. Oh, honey, I am so very sorry. Your grandfather is taking the news hard."

Kyle's insides churned at the announcement of his grandfather's pain.

"Will you put my mother on the phone?" Kyle managed while fighting the hurt.

"Your parents are not here, Kyle."

"What!"

"We've been trying to call them all morning. They left a message yesterday evening saying to expect them for a visit today. But we haven't seen them yet. It's still early."

Something was wrong and the concern for his parent's whereabouts disturbed him deeply. He began thinking of places where they might be and stops they could have made before visiting Andrew. Suddenly his thoughts were intruded upon by a booming knock at the door. Relieved, he ran to it smiling a bit, realizing his parents had obviously stopped by to pick him up. Kyle gripped the door and flung it open, holding his arms out only to find a police officer.

"Sir, you need to evacuate the area immediately. Flooding is expected to wash away this entire area."

Kyle was lost in a paranormal daze. The officer couldn't be standing before him demanding that he leave. His aunt couldn't have been killed last night. His parents couldn't be missing. Then it became clear. After hearing the news of flooding, his parents must have fled the house. *But where had they gone and why didn't they call*, he thought.

"Sir, did you hear me? You need to evacuate the area. We're goin' door to door. If you can help your neighbors, please do so."

"But there's no water over here," Kyle replied.

"I would advise you to leave the area. Just because you don't see it now, doesn't mean it ain't comin'. You do realize you're less than five miles from the river, don't you?"

Kyle waved to the officer as he shut the door, retreating back in to the house. He would reflect over the loss of his aunt and wonder where his parents were.

Twenty-Seven

Departures and Arrivals

ALBERTO WAS DONE. THE ORDAINED FORCE HAD reached its destination and delivered a watery explosion. What remained was the unyielding aftershock. Rain had vanished and the sun made a futile cameo. Despite the downpour's retreat, the invasion of Albany continued.

Americus had been a mere bystander of the Flint River. The city evaded the winding waters some fifteen miles to the east of the riverbanks. It was damaged mostly by flash flooding of the lakes and numerous creeks. Albany, however, was not as fortunate in its locale. The Flint wrapped around parts of the city, slithered within its main vein and almost bisected the town segregating east from west. The Flint could easily strangle the city. Four bridges allowed occupants to cross over the river on normal days. The bridges had now become links of death.

Albany was the recipient of wayward water channels in search of allies. The Flint, Albany's main marriage of land and water, was fed by Lake Chehaw, which was fed by Kinchafoonee Creek and Muckalee Creek. There was even a power reservoir lying at the city limits held back by a single dam at the entrance of Albany, a bottleneck waiting to burst.

Cities north of Albany such as Macon and Montezuma poured drained waters into the downstream tributaries. Water that the Flint offered to smaller channels was reciprocated, but with brutal force. Every creek and every lake joined in the detrimental drainage, growing in power and size at every turn. It was this merging of water and gravity that would serve as Alberto's legacy, its sole purpose for the journey.

Just below Americus, the Flint poured into the vast eighty-seven hundred-acre Lake Blackshear. Another dam at the end of the lake served as a controlled funnel, supplying water and restricting flow as needed. With the surging of the Flint River Valley and its south stretching branches, the fifty-seven square mile city of Albany stood in the path of more than two hundred fifty miles of water rushing towards it at a rate of over one million gallons per second.

Kyle disregarded the evacuation order and continued to clean the house. He was confident that his parents would call before the day's end. In between sweeping and sanitizing, he walked to the front door and looked up the street. No cars and no water. There was no massive flood as the policeman had mentioned, not on Mercer Avenue, not yet. He retreated into the house and returned to scrubbing.

The television, he thought. He might learn more from the news, however disturbing it might be. Cameras rolled as he witnessed more destruction, this time much closer than Americus.

The television seemed to spill over with water ramming and running past the Broad Avenue Bridge.

"That's right around the corner!" Kyle yelled. He darted to the door, expecting a tidal wave to roll down the street at any moment. Instead he saw melancholy clouds closing the curtains on the sun, but no water. Again he ran inside to check the accuracy of the reports. It was indeed Broad Avenue, less than three miles from the house. At this rate, the dwelling could be deluged in a matter of minutes. Astutely, he focused on the television.

Rust-colored currents composed of red clay residue and rain rocked the bridge's foundation. The peaks and valleys of the waves were sure to rise and wash out the bridge, if not reduce it to crumbled stones first. Kyle looked closely, searching for his parents' car. Only authorities occupied the bridge announcing that it would close along with the other three bridges. East and West Albany had just been separated. Alberto's remains were dividing and conquering.

Kyle jerked the television's dial and rotated the circular clicker to another station. A helicopter carried the news crew over the raging catastrophe and captured the drama of Lake Blackshear.

Water was boiling at the dam. Hydrologists had derived an approximate amount and the reporter broadcast the astronomical figure.

Thank you, Jon. We've just learned, experts have calculated that more than twenty-three billion gallons of water are within the confines of Lake Blackshear at this very moment. Of course confines is a relative term. This water is searching for somewhere to run and the dam cannot hold it all. You are watching live as the effects of Tropical Storm Alberto swell over Lake Blackshear.

David, do experts have a plan for diverting the water? Can anything be done at this point?

Jon, we spoke with the chief operator here at Plant Crisp and he said that he hopes they won't have...Oh my God! The flood has breached the dam here at Lake Blackshear! You're watching live coverage as the floodgates are opening and the water seems to have taken on a life of its own! We can see where the current was once building. It is now rushing south at an enormous pace! Jon, I was just about to say that the chief operator hoped they would not

have to open up more floodgates. Prior to this blast of wa-
ter, the dam was operating with three gates open. It now
appears that all fourteen gates have been opened and Lake
Blackshear, which encompasses over eight thousand acres,
that water is now on the loose, Jon. As you can imagine,
this means even more water has been unleashed to flow
south and looks to be headed straight for Albany. I've
never seen, in all my years of broadcasting, a force of this
magnitude!

Kyle ran outside again. It was his routine now, checking for the inevitable waters that would swallow his street.
Still, Mercer was being spared. Panicked, the young man
found himself wandering about the house aimlessly. This
was indeed a place he knew, searching for comfort and security by the presence of his parents or grandparents. The
newscast was too much to bear. He banged the power button yet the tube remained illuminated. He bashed the button
harder and the high pitch whistle of the tube ceased.

Remaining in the house was of no use. Kyle felt the
urge to go out into the waters and find his parents. At the
very least he would go wait for them at his grandfather's
room. The hurt of his dishonesty might erase the fear of
raging waters.

Dashing for the door grabbing only his car keys, Kyle
was benumbed by the grinding bell in the telephone. Anxiety choked his senses and blood jetted through veins. Chills
protruded through his skin, covering his arms with bumps.
The phone had not completed a full ring before Kyle
grabbed the receiver.

"Mama!"

"Hey, baby," a woman's voice replied.

"Mama?"

"No, it's Camilla. Kyle, is everything all right?"

Kyle collapsed into a chair from disappointment. He
wanted to scream because no one was who they should
have been.

"Kyle, are you okay?"

He replied barely audible with dissipating strength, "I can't find my parents."

"What'd you say? I can't hear you. Speak up, baby."

"My parents. I don't know where they are."

"Are you serious? Did they make it from Atlanta okay?"

"Yeah, they got here a while ago, but they were supposed to go see my granddaddy. They're not over there and no one's answering the phone where they're staying."

"Do you think they were out in the city when the waters first came in?"

"I don't know. I don't think so because we talked the night before and they said they were gonna be with my grandfather the next day."

"Are you okay? When are you leaving?"

"I'm not going anywhere. There's no water on this street."

"What! I was watching the news, Kyle and they've got shots of the bridges closing. Aren't you close to a bridge?"

"Less then five miles and I'm tellin' you our street isn't flooded. How are you? How bad is it in Bainbridge?"

"I don't think we're getting half as much water as you all, but we're expecting it. The main concern is the plant where I work. They're afraid the chemicals could get in the water. Kyle, we live right down the road from the plant."

"What!"

"I'm really scared."

"You've got someplace to go right?"

"Not really. You know my mother can't be moved from the bed. Even if she could, there's nowhere we could go. The shelters are still within reach of the flood area. We can't go north 'cause it's worse up there and we don't know anybody in Florida."

Kyle massaged his temples within the vice of his thumb and middle finger. If he squeezed hard enough, he thought he might pass out and the nightmare would have concluded upon regaining consciousness.

"God. Why is this happening!" Kyle shouted.

"Baby, it's gonna be all right. I'm sure they'll turn up. Maybe the phones are out where they are."

"Well, I'm not gonna sit around here until they bring tin cans and wire. I'm gonna go look for 'em."

"Oh, no you're not!"

"Watch me."

"Kyle, don't be stupid. I mean—. I'm sorry. But please think about it. You can't go anywhere. The bridges are closed and most of the roads might be washed out. I know you're upset, but you goin' out and gettin' lost or killed isn't gonna help anybody."

Camilla sat in concerned silence listening to her boyfriend's heavy breathing. His lungs filled and emptied with profusion.

"Kyle, I love you and I don't want anything to happen to you. Promise me you won't go out looking for them. They'll turn up, I'm sure."

The silence lingered until Kyle broke through.

"I love you, too, Camilla. But if I make that promise, I don't know if I can keep it."

The frightened man hung up the phone and copied his footsteps to and fro. His pacing was partnered with stressful feelings of fright. If the flood was ever going to submerge Mercer, it would be soon. Thoughts flickered to the vision of his parents driving down the street just before the waters would rush. But it was not to be. Ingrid and her husband were still inside Lisa's house.

ভজ্ঞৎ

Kyle denied his sweetheart's plea and entered the tumultuous tide eating the city. Protected by rubber shoes and weatherproof golf clothes he sat in the car contemplating.

Which route would he take? The bridges had been closed. His parents were staying over on Desota Street in East Albany near the college. Insanity ruled his rationale thinking. Someplace between desperation and hope, Kyle thought he could devise a route to cross the city's oceanic voyage. Maybe there was an area south of the city's limits where cameras hadn't been and the police had forgotten.

Visions of the newscast pulsated in his mind. He remembered the dam at Lake Blackshear opening and releasing the billions of gallons of water. He visualized his car being tossed downstream like a spec of inconvenient dust from God's fingernail. Looking through the windshield, Kyle imagined the clear glass transforming into the asinine aqueous brown blur seen by submersed pupils. The shield that protected from the wind would be useless if the car would somehow became washed away. Seconds would pass before the vehicle's interior lost its delicate balance of hydrogen and oxygen. In less than a minute, H's outnumbering O's could fill the car retracting air for water, trading breathing for suffocation.

The images were so vivid Kyle began coughing from his own imagination. The purging of his throat made him realize the car hadn't moved nor had it even been ignited. Each frame of terror was deleted by thoughts of his parents. He knew they would have scaled the trenches of doom to find him, had he been lost. With his initial insanity masked by his restored bravery, Kyle drove out into the flood in search of his parents.

Desota Street was northeast of Mercer Avenue. Kyle would be forced to drive into the direction of flowing waters and cross the closed bridge. If things were impossible, this was one of them. A route south would have taken him two hours out of the way. Going north through the city of Cordele would amount to the same. He might miss his parent's arrival, if there was ever to be one. His thoughts were the point of impact for two jousting enemies—logic and stupidity.

Kyle drove north up Madison Street heading for the waters. Onto Broad Street he turned and saw the flashing lights near the bridge. He thought that showing desperation in the face of authorities would somehow garner their help in his task. Sloshing through the brown blob, Kyle finally arrived at the Broad Avenue Bridge. The obnoxious river seemed to toy with man-made strength. Cars which had undergone strenuous crash testing and mechanical wear analysis were washed along the banks like wayward branches dismembered from aged tree trunks. Concrete, scientifically formulated to combine natural elements creating rigid stability, crumbled as though it were crackers in the hands of a child.

It all overwhelmed him and he put the car in reverse. Dazed, Kyle accelerated backwards looking only at the images in front of him growing smaller with each revolution of the tires.

The car gained momentum from the street's ramp and he felt the car slipping from his control. Quickly glancing in the rear view mirror, another car was in sight. Kyle whipped his head around to check the reflection's accuracy. Just as he had feared, the car was much closer than it appeared. The brakes were smashed in a useless attempt to ease the impact. It was too late and the car slammed into the front of an approaching car.

Steam rose from the hood of the car like ghosts wafting away from haunted depths. Kyle was thrown across the passenger's seat unguarded from his seatbelt. Darting from the car to check on the safety of the victims, he was frightened by the sight.

Inside the car a man lay across his wife, holding and consoling her. Though both conscious, the woman was in terrible pain. Kyle yelled into the car, "Is everybody okay?"

The man, vigilant in the comforting of his wife, sat in the car unresponsive. Events outside the car did not concern them. Grabbing herself, the woman released a deafening scream. Her husband, still lying across her gently, held her hand and tried healing the pain with words. But the woman's hurt knew no sounds. It only knew time and the time had come.

Kyle tried again a bit louder, "Is there anything I can do?"

This time the husband glanced up at Kyle. Fear painted his face and the reaming picture was revealed as he moved away from his wife.

"Please help us!" he begged.

Exposed now was the woman's shape. Her delicate body, though thin among her limbs, was round and firm at her womb. She was deep into the labor of their first child.

They'd been en route to the hospital before the collision. Only in minor pain prior to the impact, physical surges intensified compounded by cadences from her heart and rushing bloodstream. Stress flowed through her body as the water flowed through the city.

"Aggggh!" the woman shrilled.

Kyle was terrified. The presence of life and death was surrounding him. Images of his aunt transposed onto the woman's face. He stood locked in shock as he envisioned his parents living this predicament and he himself swimming in the womb.

"It's coming!" the woman screamed. The infant's arrival knew nothing of the danger which would take place. Just as the woman fixed herself in delivery position, waters from Lake Blackshear began rushing through the town. The current was gradually making its way to the car and rising with each movement of the unborn fetus.

"Hold on, honey. It'll be okay, just do your breathing," the panicked husband attempted. "Please, can you help us? Looks like we're gonna have to do this ourselves. If you could come around to the driver's side and hold her head. I'll, uh, I'll come on that side and work the delivery."

"We need a doctor!" the woman yelled out.

"We don't have time, honey. We've gotta get ready."

"Noo-ho ho!" she cried. It was to be her first child and the worst of her fears were manifesting.

"Okay, what's your name?"

Kyle responded with only a hypnotized glare.

"Hey! What's your name?"

"Huh? Kyle."

"Okay, Kyle. I'm gonna need your help, guy. Come around to the driver's side and hold her head, okay?"

Kyle pulled back from the window and sloshed through the water building near the back of the car. He reached the driver's side and was stricken with fear of watching disaster appear before his eyes. Realizing he could not stand by and watch the exit of life or the arrival of death, Kyle took one last look at the couple and ran away.

"Hey, wait! Kyle, wait. I need your help! Jesus Christ!"

"Where is he?" the laboring lady inquired.

In disbelief the man replied, "He ran away. Can you believe that?"

"I knew this was gonna happen. I just knew it!"

The woman dropped her head back on to the seat. She'd all but given up and waited for a tragic end to her nine-month fairy tale. Her release of hope drained her energy as an unconscious state tried to possess her body. The transformation from panic to hopelessness calmed her, and the threatening blood pressure slowed to slightly above normal. Her body was trying to shut itself down. The fetus slowed its entry, but still inched forward with time and gravity.

"It's okay, honey, we can still do this. I just need you to prop yourself up on your elbows, okay?"

"No, it's no use," she cried. "We weren't supposed to have this baby. My mother warned me." Sorrowful, the woman had given up.

"What? No, really it won't be that bad. Just prop yourself—" Threatened by the sight below him, the husband shouted, "Oh God!"

"Is it already dead? Is it stillborn? This is how my mother said it would be. I didn't listen."

"Stop talking like that! It's just—. I need to get you out of the car and onto the hood."

The woman looked at her husband, paused for a moment, then laughed with lunacy.

"Just stop. I told you my mother said—I"

"Will you stop it! I've got to get you out of here! The water is coming into the car!"

"What! Agggggh!" The notion of drowning was very real and it restored her senses as well as the pain. "Honey, help me, please. I don't want to die. I don't want our baby to die!"

"It's okay. Just breathe. Just breathe. I've got to try and lift you out of here, okay?"

The husband placed one hand under the fold in her legs and the other beneath her back. He made a slight tug that strained his own muscles and riveted pain in the woman's body.

"Aggggh! Wait, wait! This won't work."

"I can't move you by myself."

"We can do it, honey. We can deliver it by ourselves." Her hope was returning. But now it was too late.

"I know we can, but the water is starting to fill up the car. There's no way I can get you out after the baby comes. We'll have to—"

"Try dammit! You gotta try! Aggggh!"

It had all resurfaced, the hysteria, the stress, the desperation, and the baby's entry.

As the man derived ways to get the child and his wife out of the car, a wave of current surged from behind the car. Water rippled into the compartment faster than before.

Now the husband was thinking of a painless end to the inevitable. Delivering the child and choosing which life to save would be unbearable for the survivors. Drowning would end the nightmare simultaneously and yield no suffering survivors. Once again the waters rushed from behind and invaded the car as high as the gearshift.

There was only one task left, convincing his wife to lay back and accept his decision. She would fight, but the struggle would be in vain. The strongest surge yet, came only seconds after the last and the sobbing husband waited as his wife screamed.

"Aggggh! Honey do something, pleeeease!"

"It's okay, just relax." Tears washed his cheeks as he stared a look of solace into his wife's eyes. He caressed her head as he had done many nights. Her husband had always been her soothing relief. He continued to stroke her, easing pains for the last time.

More surges came, but rhythmic this time and with more repetition. They came as pulses with the frequency of footsteps.

"That's them right there!" a voice called out.

"Is everybody all right?" another voice shouted.

The husband looked out of the rear window and saw the source of rushing waters. Men were wading toward them. They'd just exited a roaring Humvee, all-terrain vehicle with the words National Guard blazing on the doors and hood. The monstrous truck had been driving closer to the car causing the waters to flow further upstream and into the car. Tow trucks were further back to retrieve the cars from the waters.

Uniformed men trailed a few steps behind one man in civilian clothes. Out-wading them all was Kyle. The young man, who was brought into the water by irrational thinking, had gained his composure and retrieved help for the couple. Two men surrounded the car and pulled the woman from the vehicle while a third drove the Humvee closer. Once the Humvee was loaded with the team and couple, the woman's pain intensified. She screamed without cease as the vehicle pushed through thigh-high water for three miles. The group arrived at the hospital on Third and Jefferson where a medical team rushed to the vehicle with a wheelchair and gurney. They were too late.

Staring into the vehicle the medical staff saw a sobbing husband and crying wife. Looking with amazement, they witnessed the sight of Albany's newest resident. A six pound fifteen ounce baby girl crying out to the world that she had arrived.

Twenty-Eight

Submerged

⌘⌘⌘⌘

By Friday morning, July Eighth, water was as high as first floor ceiling fans in some areas of the town. There was no more rain, only images that looked like the Big Dipper had poured itself on the city.

The rising current had marched into Albany Thursday night. Some of those who chose not to evacuate were awakened by a tapping on their windows, the upstairs bedroom windows. A resident on Desota Street had spent the night and morning maneuvering through the neighborhood by boat. Knocking on the windows of his neighbors, they were surprised to find him in a boat outside their house, at the second floor no less.

An elderly man came to the window and upon seeing the boater drew the curtains closed. He jumped back into bed assuming the floating gesture was a nightmare.

The friendly ferry operated for hours until most of the neighbors had been accounted for. Other boats with motors propelled their way from other neighborhoods to help. Everyone had seen the early broadcast of Lisa and her daughter's tragic death. A ribbon was placed on the rooftop of the two-story home, for they thought it was vacant now that the residents were deceased. The rescuers had no idea that Kyle's parents were trapped inside.

When others were being extracted from windows at night, Ingrid and Angus slumbered. Awakened by what Angus thought was a childhood habit returned, the sheets were wet. The two had jumped from the bed only to land in a pool that had completely flooded the second floor bedroom. Outside the window was more water blocking their escape. Had the neighbor known of their presence, he would have captured them both.

The attic was their only option, and there they had remained hostage by the water, shivering and hungry for thirty-six hours.

Yelling had proved useless. Voices were masked by the boats' motors and waving waters. Silence surrounded the house, which meant no one was close enough to hear the shouting.

"What are we gonna do?" Ingrid asked, weakened by the wait.

"I'm sure someone will come by soon. It's been almost two days now. Kyle knows where we are and he's probably getting some help for us." Angus was calm. He'd been trying to help his wife get through the situation.

"But why is it taking so long?"

"They've got a whole town to rescue, baby. I'm sure there are people much worse than we are."

"What if they don't come?"

"Then the waters will drain and we'll just walk out."

"How long will that take?"

"It depends on how much water is out there. I swear I've never seen anything like this."

"Angus! How long will it take?"

"I don't know two, maybe three days."

"Three days!"

"Maybe."

"We can't stay up here for three days. We'll starve to

death."

"Ingrid, ain't nobody gon' starve to death in three days," he said, smirking.

"This ain't funny. I'm going to be sick if I don't get some food and water in my system."

"Baby, just don't think about it. Put your mind on something else. Think about Kyle." The mother instantly forgot about her own needs at the mere mention of her son. Thoughts eventually drifted to a place where she would not see him. His survival and her starvation painted the picture. If she didn't eat, the mother thought she'd never get to see her precious son again.

Ingrid walked towards the folding ladder attached to the attic door. She reached down to open it when Angus grabbed her.

"What are you doing?"

"I told you I'm not gonna sit up here rotting and starving to death. I gotta get some food and water."

"Ingird, come one now. Don't be silly, let's just wait a while and see who comes by."

"Wait! What do you think we've been doin' for almost two days? What if they come by and we're dead because we didn't eat or got dehydrated? This waiting would have been useless. I'm going to get something. Let me go!"

Angus did as his wife requested and gave in to her reasoning.

"Baby, wait. I mean hold on. I'll go get something for us. You know you're not the best swimmer."

"Not gon' be much swimming. Just drop in and walk under water to the kitchen."

"Okay, but still," Angus said, shaking his head and pulling her away from the door. "I'll get it and come right back. I'm getting' water, canned food, that's it," he added, hanging on to what little authority he had.

"Get some salt and pepper, too."

"Ingrid."

"Just kidding. Please be careful."

Angus opened the door and the ladder sank down into the brown murk consuming the house. More water had filled the dwelling since their climb and debris was floating through it.

A baby doll that would never feel another hug or a pull of her artificial hair floated by. CD cases with music heard for the last time bobbed up and down with the movement of other belongings. Inanimate objects would no longer serve a purpose except to be inanimate.

"Look at all that water!" Ingrid exclaimed. "It wasn't that high when we first got up here."

"I know. Good thing we woke up when we did."

"Do you think it's gonna get any higher?"

"I hope not."

"But what if it does?"

"I don't know, Ingrid. We'll just have to get a plan together." Let me get the stuff first and we'll think of something."

"Angus, are you sure you want to go?"

He looked at his wife with frustration. It was her demand that put him here ready to lunge down into their own private creek.

"Okay, okay. I know I asked you to go. Just be careful and hurry back. We need to get out of here 'cause the water might get higher."

Angus shook his head again and slowly began moving down the steps on the ladder. The murky waters inflated his pants creating a cold bubble around his leg. Chilling liquid unnerved him as he traded steps with each foot. Halfway down the ladder, water wavered over Angus' chest. When the two had escaped to the attic, water was barely as high as the third step. He paused and the nervousness showed through his shaking.

"What's wrong?" Ingrid asked.

Not wanting his wife to sense his fear, he lied. "Nothing. The water is cold. I don't think—. Nothing."

"What is it?"

"Uh, I don't think I remember where the kitchen is."

"Don't be silly. It's right down the hall."

Angus gave a false laugh, more for himself than Ingrid.

"I, uh, I'll be back in a minute." Mentally he had already swam the short length. He rehearsed shutting off oxygen for about one minute and then bursting upwards when in the kitchen. When the refrigerator was located, he could hang on to it while he breathed. Retrieving items from the pantry would be a feat so he though of two trips, one for water and the next for food. The second trip would be easier. Finally he was ready.

Two more steps off the ladder and the swimming, or paddling, would commence. The first of the last two bowed on contact and he shook with fright before grabbing the ladder's sides.

"Whoa! Be careful, Angus. What happened?"

"Jesus! This step is weak. It feels like it almost broke. The sudden movement caused mini-currents. More debris was unleashed underwater. Papers awakened from the bottom rocked to and fro with disturbed patterns of waves before losing their buoyant flight and resting back again on the bottom. A picture of Lisa and her daughter, facing upwards, floated for a moment and then landed, this time face-down. Trapped under other items was a small purple ball. Released from the clutter its air began pushing it toward the surface.

Angus found the courage to continue and unintentionally placed his foot on the rising ball. The meeting of flat and round, even under water, was a fatal contradiction. Angus lost his footing and fell away from the ladder. Ingrid screamed at him, then for him. Reaching for the wooden security again, only his fingernail scrapped the structure. The falling man panicked upon submersion into the waters and paddled without cause. He rolled over and over in the fashion of a fighting crocodile drowning its victim. Angus was his own victim now. He was drowning himself.

With orientation lost and no vision in the brown water he stretched hands and feet hoping to touch or land on something.

"Anguuus!" Ingrid screamed, trying to guide her husband towards the ladder. Vocal sound waves bounced off the splashes and the frantic paddling under water. Suddenly a hand emerged from the water and Ingrid grabbed at it. She would pull her husband from the water. Instead her protrusion through the small attic opening and unleveraged body-weight pulled the would-be heroine into the water as well.

The outstretched hand meant that Angus had found his orientation and footing. However, he was pushed further to the bottom by the addition of Ingrid and he was fighting again. Now he had to match his feet with the bottom, paddle his way to a float, and help his wife to the ladder, all while using the one breath that he never took.

Rolling ensued again. Ingrid, unaware of her own position, paddled downward while Angus attempted to move from beneath her. He was captured by her movements of madness. Bubbles were forced from his sealed lips and his lungs heaved one last time before his efforts ceased.

Ingrid's energy was stolen by the futile paddling and the stress signals her brain received telling her life was about to end. The struggling widow had no thoughts of finding orientation, reaching for the ladder, her husband's body, or refraining from panic. She only knew to paddle until there was no paddling left in her, or breath, or life.

Twenty-Nine

Wild-Kingdom

———————— ೮୫୫೦ ————————

Po-Shank, THE FREE FREELANCE WRITER AND FORMER maintenance man, sat atop his roof waiting for a boat to row by. At the hands of the merciless tides, Albany had gone wild—wildlife. Waddling on the far side of the roof was a family of ducks. Even these endothermic habitants of water, air and land were seeking refuge from the flood.

"Now that's bad," Po-Shank said to his younger brother, Keith. The ducks are runnin' from the water. Keith, you hear me?"

"Ouch!" a voice yelled from the other side of the roof.

"What is it? What happened?"

"It got me. Doggone, I thought I could get him."

"Keith, what you talkin' about?"

"This rattlesnake bit me."

"What!"

"Yeah, it's the third one I done seen today. Guess the flood just bringing everything downstream and out of the woods."

"You better sit down! Man, you gon' die!"

"Hell, ain't nobody gon' die. A boat'll be by here

'rectly. If you just calm down and don't let ya blood rush and git all crazy, people be all right. Faster ya blood run, faster the poison spread."

"Now what make you a expert on snake bites?"

"I'm a' expert on the count o' this make my fifth snake bite," the cool victim answered.

Keith's prophecy soon came to pass as the two men heard the circular swishing of a small motorboat. A driver sitting in the back, steering the vessel called out to Joshua who was riding in the front. Joshua had been helping with rescues in this neighborhood.

"Hey, y'all right, Mr. Shank?" Joshua yelled as the boat sent ripples towards their roof.

"Got a snake bite. Other than that we're all right," Keith replied. Po-Shank was in shock simply from being near a snake bite.

"Get on in. We'll get you close to a ride so you can get to the hospital," said Josh.

All four men were safely inside the boat and headed off down the street. A red object barely standing above the water projected white letters commanding cars to stop. Boats had no brakes, nor any use for stop signs when the only traffic lay sunken beneath it.

"How's everything goin', Josh?" Po-Shank asked.

Josh turned to face him, then looked back out at the rooftops. He recognized the question was just small talk. By simply observing, anyone could see how things were going, "Not too good. Another four thousand people evacuated today. Except for the library, all the buildings at Albany State are partially submerged. We got reports from Chehaw Park that some of their animals have escaped. The sewage is going right by the treatment plant so the river's got sewage pouring into it. We found the bodies of two young boys and I still haven't located Kyle's parents. That's just the things I know about."

"Kyle? Kyle, Mr. Scales' grandson?" asked Po-Shank.

"Yeah."

"Don't they live in Atlanta?"

"They came down for the fourth, I guess."

"What about Mr. Scales? He all right?"

"I think so. Kyle said all the people in the retirement home are okay."

"Thank Jesus and his daddy," Po Shank offered.

"When I drop you off, I'm gonna meet up with a recovery team. There's a man and wife that has these two trained bloodhounds. Seems they can track the living and find the dead. I just hope it'll be tracking instead of finding."

"Yeah, I heard about them dogs. Say they can find anything."

"You okay?" Joshua asked, facing Keith. The bitten man was slightly sedated.

"Just fine. Tryin' to stay alive and survive," Keith rhymed.

Josh maneuvered to look at the boat driver. "Let's go down that street and see if anybody needs help. The water gets shallower down there anyway. It's a good thing we came by when we did you havin' that—"

Josh was interrupted by a jagged scraping underneath the boat.

"What was that?" Po-Shank asked. "Is that shallow water already?"

"No," the driver replied. We've got another hundred yards to go before we get to—. Whoa, what in the world?"

The force was stronger this time. Each man steadied himself as the boat began rocking.

Keith's civility was becoming edgy with the commotion.

"Look right there!" the driver pointed.

Skimming the surface was the pointed skin of an alligator. The snout extended from the tail some fifteen feet. Its body was three feet wide.

A quiet fear filled the boat. Josh signaled for the motor

to be cut. As the rocking lessened, Josh reached for the boat's oar. He placed it gently into the water and gave smooth slow strokes. The boat gained momentum and distance from the alligator. After the jagged threat was many head starts behind them, the driver started the motor and darted off to safety.

"Good Lawd!" Po-Shank exclaimed. "Was that one of the Chehaw Park animals?"

"I don't think so," replied the driver. That's probably just a gator from the river. The flood brings everything out. Cars, houses, gators—h"

"Rattlesnakes," the calm Keith added, reminding the men he needed first aid.

For a brief wade in the water, there was laughter amongst the men.

Joshua smiled and said, "The water's probably four feet deep here, but if you'll look over there a bit, you can see it's back up to the roof of that house. That's why everything didn't get water, just the low lands. If you cut right through there, we can dock and there's an emergency truck just beyond that stop sign. Tell officer—"

Another disturbance frightened them once again. They heard rampant splashing behind them. Before each man turned back to look, they thought the alligator was charging towards the boat.

The sounds drew closer as the men turned about to watch their own doom. Brown flashes of water consolidated with a lighter brown prancing through the shallow area. Petrified in their terror, no one moved. The stampede of water marched closer to the boat and almost magically began parting, moving around the floating foursome. And the occupants saw the wet wonderment. Two elk were galloping past them, pounding the water below their hooves. The sprouting antlers bobbed up and down like massive claws turned upwards scratching the air.

Feeling attacked, the men lay down in the boat, covering their heads for protection. The elk darted by, changing direction as quickly as leaves blown wayward without purpose. And the men were indeed attacked—with water. As the stampeding duo became only a distant sound, they giggled once again.

"Now *those* are the animals from Chehaw Park," the driver jested. Giggles became full-blown laughter, bringing relief during the trying times.

"I'm glad this is funny," Keith said, still simmering in the snakebite. "But if you don't mind—if we don't plan on gettin' to the hospital—could you please tell me which of these wild animals is gon' be the death of me?"

Thirty

Ashes to Ashes Dust to Water

෯෯

LATE FRIDAY NIGHT, THE FAMOUS TRACKING BLOOD-hounds accomplished another morbid task. The dogs had indeed found the dead. Floating amongst debris in the house, barking heightened as the canine team found Kyle's parents.

Joshua had worked his twenty-fifth consecutive hour. The days knew no end now. He couldn't even imagine the strength to go on, nor could he find the courage to inform his friend of his parents' demise.

Saturday, after he'd had a brief affair with sleep, Josh would set aside a few hours to comfort and minister to the person this flood had made an orphan.

෯෯

Kyle sat in the house still soaked from the adventurous baby delivery. He hadn't removed his clothes. He hadn't bathed. The house which decayed his grandfather was having the same affect on him. Waters had yet to find a path to Mercer Avenue.

A knock on the door reeled him from his depressed state to one of optimism. Perhaps this knock, perhaps this disturbance, he thought, would be the salvation he'd been longing for.

Kyle wanted to throw open the door and fall into his mother's arms, grab his father's hand and simply cry, releasing the hurt he'd been drowning in since the flood began. He didn't run to the door anymore. Instead he dragged his feet. Each time the phone rang or a car drove by, he lazily approached it. A stagnant robe of despair weighed him down.

Slowly he answered the door and saw Joshua. A glow shone from behind him. There was a beam of hope entering the house. After all, Josh was the person who'd said he would find him. Those were the last words he'd given Kyle: *We'll find them.*

Josh was pulled inside quickly while Kyle squeezed the sides of his arms. He tried to squeeze the good news out of him as though he were a tube filled with paste to clean stains.

"Did you find them? Did you find my parents?" he finally asked.

Josh waited a few breaths, then took a deeper one.

"Yeah, we found them Kyle. We found them."

"Well, where are they? Are they at the hospital? Is everything okay? Where are they?"

Josh lowered his head, hiding his eyes. It could have easily been reversed, he the recipient and Kyle the messenger. The old friend raised his head and continued.

"They, uh. They didn't make it, Kyle. We found them in your aunt's house. They drowned. I'm sorry."

Kyle was immovable. His thoughts were abstract. Feelings were instruments inflicting internal pain; comfort was an offering that would be in vain.

The grit and ash on his face was disturbed only by a single stream of wetness replenishing itself until his eyes blinked.

"Kyle, Kyle sit down," Josh offered, trying to guide him to the couch, but he was a rock and Joshua could not move him.

Kyle did not want motion. He simply wanted to stand in this spot, in this time until it all went away. The reality that it would not go away and the fact that his family was disappearing with each day began to rumble.

Melancholy siphoned out of his gut and into his lungs, causing him to breathe hurt. The hurt spread into his chest and surrounded his heart with sorrow. His heart pumped the sorrow into his throat and filled his mouth with anger. His lips parted and projected the toiling emotions.

"NOOOO-HO-HOOOOOO!!! WHYYYYYYYYYYY!!!"

Veins bulged from his neck. Tears flowed heavier. His body quivered. His hands and fingers were rigid hooks. His knees buckled and the burdened man collapsed onto the floor. There he remained, crying, screaming, wondering, waiting for pain to vanish and answers to be revealed.

Joshua sat in the floor with his hands placed on Kyle's back. He wanted to draw all of the tribulation out of his friend's body. There were no words, which could accomplish the feat. It was a place Josh had never known. He'd never been this close to a personal tragedy and even this distance was uncomfortable.

The hand rested on Kyle's back for well over an hour. It felt the heaving of his lungs purging air created by the departed parents. It felt the vibrating bass in his voice crying out the words 'mama, daddy.' It felt the recoiling coughs of rejected saliva failing to soothe the strained throat. It felt the rattling of his torso while vibration emanating from his snoring. After emotions had their way with him, his body shut down and slumbered.

CℨℬↃ

Awakened by the discomfort of an awkward sleeping position and the hard floor, Kyle found Joshua still at his side. The boy who'd rescued him from danger in the woods was the man comforting him in absence of family.

Kyle cleared the string of sleep pouring from his mouth and rubbed his swollen eyes. The sight of the room and Joshua near him was a reminder of what had happened. It seemed as though the announcement had been a horror movie and sleeping was a commercial break. It was time to face the reality.

"You okay?" Joshua asked, rising and sitting on the couch.

Kyle stared at the patterns of the floor. Wondering if the wood felt pain when separated from its own tree trunk. He thought about a piece of string's torture of being pulled away from its spool. Kyle finally shook his head.

"Anything I can do for you? Have you had anything to eat?"

Kyle lifted his head and looked at Joshua and asked, "Did I do something wrong?"

"What do you mean?"

"Did I hurt somebody? Have I been evil? Why is this happening to me?"

Josh sighed and searched for solutions unknown. The best he could offer was, "Everything happens for a reason, man. It's happenin' to the whole town."

"The whole town ain't losin' two family members a day! I got a two death per day quota in my family!" Kyle boisterously laughed insanely. It was the only emotion he had yet to experience. "Am I cursed?" he asked, as the laughing transformed into queries. "Is my family cursed?"

Josh clasped his fingers together and said, "We're all cursed, Kyle. Each and everyone of us."

Kyle's dementia was broken by the unexpected response.

"What?"

"We all have these curses, Kyle. I'm not trying to say this is all your fault. You have to be the one to answer that question."

"What the hell are you talkin' about?"

"It's like this. People always ask me when am I gonna get married. I know this doesn't have anything with your loss, but it's the only way I can explain it. There's no way I can get married until I get my curse off of me."

"What curse?" Kyle was enticed by the statement and temporarily forgot about the tragedy upon him.

"Womanizing and abuse. I mean, I was never abused, but my daddy used to hit my mother. He doesn't do it anymore. Probably because he's too old," he said, thankful for the passing of time that had been his mother's only defense. "My aunt told me about it a few years ago after I was out of college. He had more than his share of women on the side, too. You know I may have a few brothers and sisters somewhere up in North Georgia.

"I hated my Daddy when I found out about it. Then I found out that my grandfather did the same thing to Nanna. And I understood why my father did what he did to my mom. Then I understood why I could never keep a girlfriend and why I had arguments with girls when they wouldn't give me what I wanted. That wasn't me. It was the ghosts and the sins of my father and my father's father. We all got 'em, Kyle. They just come in different packages.

"You know how when you got somethin' in the fridge and it spoils and rots? What happens when it stays there? It starts to stink and then it starts spreadin'. Suddenly, you got that smell on everything in the fridge. It's in the water, it's on the eggs, and it's in the meat. So then what happens, you got this bacteria all over your food that you're gonna put in your body and feed to your family. From this one small, rotten, bad piece of food, people are gonna get sick and maybe even die when all we had to do was find out what on the inside was bad, deal with it by cleanin' out the insides of the refrigerator, and throwin' out the garbage. Then we go back and check the insides often, makin' sure that nothin' else is goin' bad. If it is, throw it out right away. We should do that once a week, preferably every Sunday. I have to do it every day 'cause the rot was two generations old in me."

Kyle struggled, going in and out of the conversation. He'd heard most of it and followed the message. Yet he failed to make the personal connection.

"So what does that have to do with me?"

Josh walked through the verbal door Kyle opened. He knew Kyle's curse, knew the source, and it was time for him to abolish it.

"Kyle, there may be something in your family that you might not know about. Something that happened which has nothing to do with you. It might even be a habit or a problem someone in your family has. Maybe even a secret."

Kyle examined the intimate patterns again, reflecting over those still living.

"My grandfather," he began.

"What about him?" Joshua asked, sitting near the edge of the couch now.

"I just recently found out that he—" Kyle couldn't do it. He couldn't defame his hero.

"It's only gonna spread, Kyle. If you don't deal with it, somebody is gonna have to pay for it. It might not be you. It might be your children or grandchildren."

Kyle immediately thought of his love for Camilla at the mention of children. Earlier news reports had told of the small town being the next victim of the floods. If parts of Albany were being plummeted by the waters, Bainbridge would be completely destroyed. It was time.

"My grandfather is...he's selfish and a hoarder of money. I found out he could've helped one of his friends keep his business. He lied about having the money. He had plenty of money to help. I always thought he was very giving to his friends and family. This guy lost his business and I think he died or maybe he was killed. You think that may be one of the reasons I'm anxious to make his business succeed?"

"It's possible. That's a good start."

"But what's that got to do with all these people dyin'? This doesn't make any sense."

"The friend. It wasn't Mack, was it?"

"Yeah, how'd you know?"

"I'm a cop, remember?"

"See, there's another death. I mean he wasn't my family but he was a friend of the family. Do you know how he died?" Kyle had escaped the tragedy in his mind. Joshua's conversation was transporting him elsewhere. Somewhere Kyle never thought he'd go.

"Kyle, I need to be honest with you. Now I want you to know that this is for you and not because I'm a cop. It's too late for me to do anything about anyway. But if you really want to deal with your stuff, you've got to face it. All of it."

Having dwelled in a pit of devastation for the last few days, Kyle thought he was prepared for anything. There couldn't possibly be any more surprises.

"Go ahead," said Kyle.

"The guy who died? Mack? He was killed by a policeman."

"What?"

"My granddad was there the night it happened. He and some other officers showed up at a meeting they were having. Your grandfather was there, too."

"My grandfather saw him get shot?"

"Yeah, my granddad and his men were there to investigate the murder of another officer who'd been killed a few weeks earlier."

"Okay, I remember that."

"Kyle, it's widely believed that—"

"What?"

Josh was hesitant now. He felt perhaps he'd gone too far. The journey was interrupted by discomfort and intrusion.

"Maybe I should just leave it alone."

"No, you better not. If it's got something to do with me, you better say it," Kyle was baited and slightly angered now.

"Kyle, this is for you now. There's nothing I can do about it."

"What the hell are you talkin' about?"

"It's believed by several people that your grandfather killed that officer, but Mack was shot and blamed for the murder."

"What!"

"The meeting was being held by some group of black businessmen in the city, the Black Business Association or something. The only convincing evidence was buried in Mack's grave. Seems that the men of the group threw all the evidence in Mack's coffin during the funeral. Kind of a protest, I suppose."

"What evidence?"

"My granddad said everybody in the group was supposed to bring the proof that they didn't kill the officer. And the only thing that could clear each of them was what they threw in the coffin."

"What was it?" Kyle's life began rewinding in his mind. Rescuing babies-newscasts-plantations-college-high school-junior high-summers-spring breaks. That moment. The moment the rewind was searching for. The moment that had been hiding from him all his life as if an act of innocence. The moment Andrew gave him the gift. He could hear the words as though Andrew were standing behind him—*After this day, never show it and never talk about it.*

"It was a pair of cuff links. There was one found at the scene of the crime belonging to somebody from that group.

Whoever didn't have both cufflinks was the culprit. After Mack's funeral, he was blamed for it and supposedly the real evidence was buried with him."

"So what makes you think my grandfather did it?" Kyle covered himself with denial and became defensive.

"I'm not saying that I know. I'm just saying what other people say. You were looking for answers and I thought—"

"You think that because somebody tried to make my grandfather the scapegoat people are dying. You think my grandfather brought this flood!"

"Whoa, calm down, Kyle. I told you, this wasn't for me. This was for you."

"Well, thank you very much, Deacon! Thanks for the sermon! It's just what I needed. My family is drowning to death everyday and you come in here and tell me my grandfather is a murderer! A cop-killer at that. You want me to confess some made-up crime that people say my grandfather committed. And the only piece of supposed evidence is six feet underground in a dead man's coffin!"

Kyle lifted himself from the floor and began frantically walking around the room. He was running from the truth, although he was boxed in by its presence. The truth would not leave this house now. Deceit would be forced to vacate this time. It was all too much: death, lies, and reckoning. Joshua sat watching the struggle before him. He'd done all he could to help his friend. The rest was on Kyle's list of generational to do's.

Let it fester and peel itself off, Kyle thought to himself. It was not his murder, though now he knew what the precious gift meant. The secret had survived for years, dormant, undisturbed. Even if he wanted to confess his grandfather's transgression, what good would it serve besides slandering the family's name and very likely the destruction of the empire to which Kyle was the heir? There could be no validation of the murderous claim, only cahoots of hearsay. Without the coffin, the cuff link meant nothing.

As Kyle pondered over the discoveries, the thought of his parents resurfaced along with the anguish. He began reflecting over the last conversation with his grandfather, how he'd called for the cleansing of dirt through rain. The first drops that he encountered outside the retirement home refreshed his thinking. Had his grandfather brought the flood? Kyle's head throbbed with agony and indecision. He entered the kitchen in search of the headache medicine he'd recently come to depend on.

Joshua called out from the couch, "Kyle, I need to use your phone. I just got paged 911."

Kyle waved his hand, fending off the need for conversation while giving permission.

"Hey, this is Josh." Kyle could hear him in the kitchen. "What! How?" A long pause followed. "This is unbelievable. When is this gonna end? We're gonna need some federal help down here. We ain't got the manpower for this! Good, he needs to come and everybody else up in the White House needs to come too. Tell 'em all to bring rubber boots. So what are we gonna do about these? All right. I'm right around the corner on Mercer. I'll be there in five." Joshua ended the conversation, looked up at the ceiling and shook his head.

"Somebody else dead?" Kyle asked cynically. "Who is it? My grandmother's great aunt twice removed on my father side?" Sarcasm was showcased now.

"You're not gonna believe this," Joshua began. "Some of the water in this area is twelve feet deep. The deeper the water, naturally the more water you have. Lots of water. And lots of deep water increases your water pressure."

"Just tell me who's dead so I can shoot myself."

"Well, that's just it. All of this pressure is bringing up anything underwater that has air in it."

"What do you mean?"

"Kinda like a football or basketball that you hold under water. As soon as you let it go, it shoots up through the water like a missile."

"You tryin' to tell me balls are shootin' up through the water?"

"No, think about it," Joshua said heading for the door. Kyle had been reeled in and was following. "What around here has air in it and covered by the ground like a hand pushin' it down."

"I don't know. Rocks?"

"No, Kyle…coffins. The coffins are comin' out of the ground at Oakview cemetery." Joshua opened the door to leave, "And they're floatin' down the river."

Thirty-One

Finding Pharaoh

⊱⊰

Josh ARRIVED AT THE FLOATING CEMETERY AS CITY workers chased after the dead in boats. A large gentleman struggled with a rope while a co-worker steered. The two were herding coffins as though it were a floating rodeo. With rope and oars, the two had been capturing the run-away coffins. Vessels themselves, the decorated boxes filled with air sailed with speed in the current. Josh was about to jump into a boat when he was joined by Kyle.

"What are you doin' here?" Joshua asked.

"I wanna make sure my grandmother doesn't float off. I've already lost my living parents. I can't lose my dead grandparent," Kyle replied, lying to his friend. He wanted to be the first one to spot Mack's coffin and push it further down the river. If he could push it off to a secret area, Kyle thought of returning later and removing its contents. Despite the obvious lies, he still had loyalty to Andrew.

Kyle knew nothing of funerals and coffins. The post-mortem ignorance propelled his questions.

"Where are the names," Kyle asked one of the city

workers in the boat.

"What names?"

"The names on the coffins so you can tell who's in 'em."

"You jokin', boy? Who in the world builds coffins so you can pull 'em outta the ground, much less pull 'em out of the ground away from the headstones?"

"You mean—"

"Ain't know way to tell wit' out the burial papers and most of the office is underwater. Them papers floatin', too. We gon' have to catch those, dry 'em out, sort and then try to match the coffin brand name with the departed."

"What about the ones you can't match up?"

"It's gonna be a painful thang for the families, but it's gotta be done. We gon' open 'em up."

"What!"

"You got people in here?"

"My grandmother. Virginia Scales."

"You Andrew Scales' grandson?"

"Yessir."

"Nice to meet you. Fine man, yo' granddaddy."

"Think so?" Kyle asked, looking at Joshua. He was searching for goodness in the old man rotting away in his bed.

"Know so. Mr. Scales got me this here job when I was just a wino tryin' to find work on the gray line."

"And how did he manage that?"

"Well, his family was...hold on a minute. Y'all steady yaselves. We got some bubblin' right over there."

"Is that when it usually happens, Billy?" Joshua asked.

"The real big ones happened just like that. Y'all just hold on. We seen some big ones today, but that one is really bubblin' hard. Suppose the water over here is the deepest so the water pressure is big as a house right 'round here."

Air and water separated on the surface as the gurgling

water produced large bubbles. The melodic bursting continued and the water grew turbulent in a small contained diameter. Having witnessed the flood's sideshows, Joshua and Kyle thought they were prepared. But nothing would ever resemble the sight yet unseen.

At the peak of the underwater disturbance, bubbling ceased and made way for the gargantuan protrusion. A large silver object was emerging from the waters with great velocity. It was pointed vertically and took on the form of a long rectangular torpedo. The coffin blasted out of the water by the strength of the deep-water pressure. This object, normally carried by six mourning men, projected six feet above the surface until splashing back down, sending boat-rocking waves all around it.

"Do you see that!" Kyle shouted.

"Is that how it always happens?" asked Joshua.

"Yeah, but I ain't seen one go that high all day. Somebody in that coffin got something to say," the experienced coffin catcher replied.

Kyle and Josh turned to each other, their thoughts identical. It must have been Mack's coffin.

"That makes number two hundred right there. Last year up in Hardin, Missouri, more than a thousand coffins came up. It ain't right when the dead rise. Somethin' goin' on when the dead come back like this."

"Did they get all of the coffins back in Missouri?" asked Kyle. He wanted to know what the chances were of Mack's coffin never being found.

"Oh, I don't know, but we'll find all of these."

"How can you be sure?"

"Because we got a little friend in the sky."

"Hallelujah, Billy," the spirited Joshua replied.

"Not that friend, Josh. I mean some—listen. Here they come now."

Billy looked upward as the sound of a hundred fingers thumping the air headed towards them. The thumping grew louder and became thunderous chops against the sky. Though high above them, the helicopters cut through air with pounding power.

The choppers used for searching out drugs were on humanitarian missions today. National guardsmen, assisted by other law enforcers, circled the area spotting the coffins.

"I thought the helicopters weren't coming until tomorrow," Joshua said.

"I didn't know they was coming at all until I saw 'em at Central Square downtown. Good thang they here though. They spotted a coffin downstream about ten miles."

Kyle was dismayed by the discovery. If a displaced coffin had been recovered ten miles away, he'd have to carry Mack's coffin back home to keep it hidden. Even deception itself was being evasive.

The boat eventually calmed with the passing of ripples and waves. Billy uncoiled a rope to retrieve the body-carrying missile. Maneuvering around tree trunks and brushing the dangling Spanish Moss, the men saw a gathering of limbs—human limbs.

"Oh God, look at that," Kyle said, covering his nose.

"That ain't the first of it. We caught a few more of those this mornin'. Everybody can't afford airtight coffins. And some 'em just open up and dump the body out. Foreman said we gotta get shots for tetanus and diphtheria."

Joshua paddled the boat away from the exposed bodies and the men continued the day's heroics of catching coffins.

C3&O

Sunday morning the sun observed a spillage it could not possibly evaporate. Josh had worked another non-stop shift. Kyle had an all-night bout with sleep. Insomnia won. Thoughts of his parents could not be dissolved. The moments he did sleep, dreams of Ingrid tapping his shoulder awakened him. Another time, he walked through the house swearing he'd heard his father's voice. Finally, the first glimpse of light through the window caught him slumbering until the knock on the door came.

"We all goin' to church this mornin'," a neighbor yelled before darting off for the next house. Assuming she meant Mt. Zion, Kyle returned to bed and fought the intrusive rays penetrating the house. The light reminded him it was daytime and the pillow covering his face reminded him he was trying to forget it was daytime. There was no sleep to be had and Kyle decided perhaps there could be something found in a service. Maybe divinity would help cure the wounds and answer the questions.

After showering and dressing in his Sunday best, he walked outside and stumbled over the papers on the front porch. Tucked in a plastic bag and rolled together with rubber bands were two newspapers. A red sheet of paper surrounded both editions. Printed on the paper was a message:

WORKING TOGETHER DURING HARD TIMES
The Albany Herald & The Albany Southwest Georgian

Kyle removed the rubber band and found both newspapers wrapped within each other. The Herald, with its large circulation, had joined with the Southwest Georgian, the widely read paper amongst Albany's blacks.

By joining forces, the news was sure to reach all of Albany's remaining residents. Each paper screamed the stories of twenty thousand evacuees and deaths in the flood. Kyle quickly flipped through the pages, trying to avoid spotting the names of his parents.

Another section foretold of the good news. Muckaleee and Kinchafoonee Creeks were continually receding. Pictures of high waters and homeless residents covered a centerfold of one section. An article detailing a planned visit by the President caught Kyle's attention. The President's visit continued into the politics section next to an article about voting in the upcoming primaries.

The Southwest Georgian ran an interview of the black State Representative who was concerned about low voter turnout. Normal voting areas were engulfed by the waters and residents were either disassociated from election interest or displaced from their homes. The State Representative's district was sixty-five percent black, but five of his precincts had been relocated. He was facing two Republicans who now had the upper hand in his own district, one of whom had a familiar face.

In a small corner of the paper was a listing of church services and their locations. The Mt. Zion church service was to be held at a Jewish temple. Kyle wanted to attend just to see the Baptist soul fill the sanctity of a synagogue.

Just before he began folding the paper, he noticed a full page ad covering the back of both papers. Standing in the center of children from different ethnicities, shapes, and sizes was the Chief. Below was a caption that read:

> "We are Albany and Albany is us.
> Elect me as your
> State Representative."

The Chief's credentials were listed. He'd done everything from dog catching to drug busts. Kyle rerolled the papers and headed off to church.

The flood was changing everything in the city. Shifting winds and rolling tides were transforming Albany. In time, the water would retreat, leaving what had been washed up, exposed.

ೞ

The synagogue reserved for Mt. Zion Baptist Church services rang with gospel harmonies and hailed of hallelujahs. The congregation could have filled the massive building three times. Brown faces contrasted the structure's white walls and ceilings, yet complemented the brass fixtures. Hebrew writings scrolled upon the hanging fabrics would not be read nor interpreted during this service, but simply kept company.

Kyle strolled in and took a seat in the back pew just after the choir took their seats. An animated and worn pastor conducted the order of worship. His opening prayer asked for the healing of pain, the salvage of lives, restoration of hope, and finally rest. It was not to be the normal service by any means. The building was strange. The saints hadn't strength to go marching in. And weeping was enduring for much longer than a night.

Someone pulled at the door from outside, trying to enter before the prayer was finished. The usher, a thin woman with a thick mustache, quickly pulled it shut. Her action produced a disturbing crash as the wooden door collided with the steel frame. The pastor looked up and some of the congregation turned to witness the calamity. Disturbed by the boom, the pastor ended the prayer and proceeded with the order of worship.

A deacon took position at the microphone as he prepared to welcome the visitors. The thin usher opened the sealed door and held a brief conversation with someone outside. Her duties entailed simply being a doorkeeper in God's house. She took it a bit far. Instead she was God's bouncer. Calamity ensued at the rear of the church while the deacon spoke.

"This temple does not belong to us. It belongs to God. We are in God's house."

Cosigning *Amens* and *Alrights* followed each phrase.

"We are visitors in this here temple. But we are permanent residents in God's house."

The pastor smiled with approval of the speech.

"And since we are residents."

"*Well*"

"We need to welcome those who are visitors amongst us.

The organist offered a friendly chord to complement the verbal dish.

"So please welcome yo' neighbor with a friendly hand-shake, hug, or a kiss."

Members mumbled happy remarks about the context of the deacon's request. Smiles refreshed the faces until the usher's antics shocked everyone.

"I said y'all at the wrong church! Go away!" the aggressive woman yelled out of the door.

"Katie Sue, is there a problem?" the pastor asked, making his way out of the pulpit and down the center aisle. Deacons in tow, a parade of aids, strolled behind the Pastor.

"It's all right, Pas'or. Some people outside can't read the newspaper and don't know where they supposed to be at for services," she replied.

At the rear of the church, men readied themselves for a forceful retaliation. They had no idea what lurked beyond the door. Evil had ridden into town on a ferocious wave and their defenses had remained vigilant.

"Step aside, Katie Sue."

"Pas'or, I can handle—"

She submitted to the man's powerful glare and humbly moved aside. A white man dressed in a versatile blue suit appeared. He looked as though he could hold a service or maitre d' a fine restaurant. With a bible in hand, the man stood in the door of the temple and gave the previous gate-keeper a scornful look once inside.

"God bless you, Reverend. There must have been some confusion about our service today. We were sched-uled to meet over at the recreation center, but no one was there to unlock the door and…. I'm sorry. Forgive me, I'm

Reverend Hutchinson from Friendship Missionary and this is Reverend Dole from Pleasant Grove.

"Nice to meet cha," they all exchanged. The congregation moved about and talked amongst themselves as they tried to ascertain the disturbance.

"Y'all simmer down. Pas'or is handlin' this here sichuation," Katie Sue yelled out. Fearing her skinny wrath, the people obliged.

"Revered Dole was supposed to meet over at Civic Center, but that's under water. And now people are simply trying to meet in each other's house. There's just no room. Do you think you could find it in your heart to allow our flocks to worship here with you?"

"Of course. Are they on the way?"

"They're right outside, Reverend."

The pastor and deacons walked through the doors and beheld a sight the town could never have created with a thousand brushes.

People were lined up outside and around the block. Different shapes and sizes and creeds and colors stood in the morning sun shining like a kaleidoscope of saints.

A lady swaying as her housecoat barely survived on her shoulders, stood in front of a young black boy wearing an Albany State T-shirt. Emma leaned against a large man whose overalls caged a bulging belly and exposed red skin below his chin. A well-dressed man with arms around his family stretched a bit further to rest his hand on a little Hispanic girl while her father parked the car.

No one saw colors and no one noticed classes. If there was healing and hope beyond the doors, they wanted to taste its flavor if only for a moment.

The pastor witnessed the amazing sight and quickly ran back into the church.

"Settle down everybody," he commanded. "Stella, you and the missionaries go on back to the fellowship hall and get ready." He turned back to the door and waved the other clergymen in. "Looks like we gon' have a few more mouths to feed after service. Now, let's try this again. Moses may have parted the Red Sea, but Alberto has brought Albany together. Welcome all visitors!"

Albany poured into the temple and fellowshipped with each other as they had never done before. Members picked up purses and made room for others. The solemn building was alive with the hope and miraculous powers of faith.

ൟ

After the congregation had settled and the order of service had progressed, the pastor referenced the text for his sermon. He spoke of Pharaoh and the death of his son as a result of imprisoned Israelites. Placing a long glare upon his extended congregation, he announced the title of his sermon, "The Sins of our Fathers are being Washed Away."

Kyle felt the queasy knots forming in his stomach again.

Chimes of *all rights* rose from the pews to the ceiling. Members shuffled to retrieve pen and paper in preparation of copious notes.

"Help us, Father!" someone shouted.

The pastor settled them with, "We've heard it several times before, that old familiar phrase, Go down Moses. Way down in Egypt land. Tell old Pharaoh. Let my people go. Had Moses known the difficulty of this task, perhaps he would have thought otherwise."

Well, well. The cosigners revved as they did throughout entire service.

"Had he known the stubborn disposition of this evil selfish, idol worshipin' man they called Pharaoh, perhaps he would have taken another route. If he had kno-o-o-own that the task would only be accomplished by threats and demonstrations of death, perhaps he would have rethought his plan and walked right into Pharaoh's house, never bothering to find the man, but instead searching for his son and upon finding the young ruler to be, telling him to his young face. It is because of your faaaather that you will die very soon. It is because of your faaather that you won't see too many more sunrises, but your last sunset is coming rather soon.

Well, well.

"Young man, I'm not here to frighten you. I am here to let you know that the sins of your father will be washed away, but unfortunately for you, young man, they will be washed away in your blood.

Come on in here Reverend.

"Perhaps Moses could have saved himself the pain and anguish of wasting his ti-i-ime with a stern conviction of the Pharaoh. He coulda saved himself some energy.

"Besides he had other things to do. He had to get ready to part the Red Sea. Now I ain't never parted a sea before but I suspect it's a lot of work. I have a hard enough time partin' my little girl's hair when my wife's away so I can only imagine what it was like to part the Red Sea," the Pastor remarked and turned to face the other ministers joining him in the pulpit. All of the people laughed for the first time and the building itself seemed to exhale.

"So you see, by talking to the son of Pharaoh, his purpose would have been better served. Oooh, but Pharoah! This Pharoah. This man whose evil ways had produced the smell of death for thousands of people. This man who had the souls of demons emanating from his own breath. This man who could *swallow* the hearts of children and wash it down with the blood of his own mother! This man who was the poster child for damnation. This man whom the devil himself viewed as competition. This man----was blind."

Oh, help us preacha!

"I'm not speaking of blind in the practical sense, but he was blind from insight, from foresight. He, like many of us, could not see into the future. Did you hear me?"

Yes, yes, yes!

"He, like many of us, could not see into the future. I'm not talkin' about space ships and space stations. I'm not talking about livin' on Mars or cures for cancer. I'm talkin' about the future twenty minutes from now, an hour from now, a week from now, five years from now. I'm talkin' about lookin' into the *ey-y-y-yes* of our children, our grandchildren, and realizin' that WE ARE THEIR PHARAOHS!!!!"

Preach on, preacha!

"Just like in Egypt, there was a father who would not banish his own sins and the price was the death of his son. The next generation!"

Well, Well teach us preacha!

"We are our next generation's Pharaohs. Because we have not released our own sins, we have not repented our own sins. And when we die, those sins will go unpaid. What happens when big mama dies and big mama still got debt on her house? Huh? You know. We got to pay it! Who's gonna pay for our sins? Yo' eldest boy, yo' youngest child, yo' grandchildren? They're gonna pay just like Pharaoh's son paid. Maybe not with their lives, but with deep sufferin', so deep they won't know what's goin' on in their lives. So deep they won't even know anything is wrong until they wake up one morning cryin, screamin' and yellin, MY MAMA WAS LIKE THIS! MY DADDY HAD THIS PROBLEM! THIS IS THE SAME THING MY GRANDDADDY DID!

"And that's when they'll know. That's when they'll realize that we, their ancestors, didn't wash away our sins.

"Our sins of drug abuse, our sins of alcoholism, our sins of domestic abuse, sins of child molestation, our sins of adultery, our sins of murder, our sins of hating other races. Our sins that we have because *our* ancestors didn't wash their own sins away! And now here we are swimming in their sins in the streets of Albany, Georgia, today!

That is why God sent Moses to Pharaoh first! He was giving Pharaoh a chance to wash away his sins. God tried to save the life of Pharaoh's son. That's why Moses went to tell him 'Let my people go!' To save the next generation!"

Well, well. Come on in here Pastor!

He paused in his fury, allowing the people to digest the difficult message.

"Some of you may be asking yourselves, why in the world is he preachin' about sins and death when we sufferin' out here every day 'cause of this flood? If I was a visitor in a Jewish Synagogue listenin' to a black Baptist preacher, I'd be askin' questions, too."

The people giggled as the Pastor's misleading smile transformed into tightly pressed lips, ready to spit the truth.

"I'd be askin' why is this happenin' to us? Why is this flood here? I might even take on the mind of Jesus and ask My, God, My God, why has thou forsaken us?"

An old man sitting in the middle of the building cried out, *"Why, Father, why!!"* He stood up and continued, *"Why, Father, why!!"* Any remaining strength he'd reserved from flood fighting was consumed by his outburst and he collapsed back into his seat. Ushers came to his aid, but the people were captivated by what they hoped would be an answer.

"When I ask myself why is this flood here, I look before me and see this rainbow of people staring at me. I'm reminded of God's covenant that he would not destroy the world with water again. When I ask myself why is this flood here I look into eyes which I have never seen and tell myself.

Look what had to happen before we came together!

Moses is here, but his name is Alberto. He has come to give us the chance to release some of us from our generational sins. We, like Pharaoh, are being given a chance to save the lives of our sons and daughters. Not loving each other is our sin. Not loving our enemies is our sin. Not loving black, white, yellow, red, that's the sin of our fathers and the flood is washing it away.

"There may be someone here today living in the sins of their ancestors. This can be the day to look back upon history and tell yourself. That's the day it ended. That's the day I grabbed Satan by the throat and cast him out of my bloodline.

"Reverends, will you help me? We're going to pray with every soul in this building that wants to realize the generational sin and release it from any further hurt, harm, or danger. We can do this together and transform this city, this state, and this world. Will you come today?"

Just like the water that had run into the town, the people flooded the alter, their feet running, their eyes dripping and their hearts heavy with pain of the past.

Kyle, moved by the message, jumped from his seat, ran into the aisle and out of the church. He spoke to no one and thought of nothing as he sped for the last time to his grandfather's bedside.

Thirty-Two

A Hero Dismantled
─────────── ⳕ⳨ ───────────

"DID YOU DO IT?"

"Well, hello Kyle. How's that sweetie pie of yours?" said the nurse.

"Excuse us please," Kyle snapped, never giving her a glance.

"Did you do it?"

"Do what? What's wrong wit' you, boy?"

"Granddaddy, you been lyin' and hidin' long enough. I want to know if you was the one that killed that police officer when I was little."

"Who you think you talkin' to? Boy, if I wasn't in this bed, I'd raise up and—"

"Smack me? Then throw me to the ground. In your anger, would you kick me? Would you kick me in my skull until I died? Is that how it happened?"

"Don't you talk to me like—"

"I got to know, Granddaddy. Do you understand that I have to know? I have to know the lie that you gave me to live with.

Andrew fixed his eyes upon the calendar in his line of

sight. The dates had no meaning. The days served no purpose. His mannerisms humbled and his voice softened.

"It was different times then, Kyle. People was different. Things wasn't the way they is now."

"Things are exactly the way they are now 'cause of what happened back then," Kyle replied. "This stuff that we see now, this death and destruction. It's all a cost of what happened."

"You tryin' to tell me that——"

"I'm tellin' you that I need to know. 'Cause I want to get it off of me. I want it off my children and their children. Don't you see, as much as I love you, this is yo' burden, not mine. I don't know what happened or I don't know why you did it, but it didn't have nothin' to do with me or mama and daddy or...or Aunt Lisa and her daughter until you started hidin' it. Can't you see that I'm next? There's nobody in town from our family but me? Granddaddy , help me. I got to get rid of this thing." Kyle paused. "Did you do it? I'm gonna have to tell some—"

"Tell who! What the hell for! What's done is done and whoever dead is dead! I ain't lost no sleep over that dead fool! He woulda killed me if I didn't kill him first!"

Andrew flung open the doors from his darkest vault and finally spoke the truth. It had evaded the last moments of his wife, the salvation of his children, and nearly the love of his grandson. Kyle stood in the midst of the epiphany that his grandfather was not perfect or even innocent. At the same time he sank in the reality that they were all the other one had. He was shocked beyond movement. Kyle knew it were true before he'd stepped inside the room, but the resounding confession shattered whatever minutia of disbelieving hope he'd ever had.

And suddenly the calendar dates were active. They now symbolized distance between what had been discovered and what would be revealed. Kyle wanted to run through the streets of Albany screaming to the world, his grandfather had killed a man thinking it would cleanse him. An instant passed and a part of Kyle began thinking of ways to conceal his grandfather's legacy, hoping it might preserve his name. He was torn between the lessons simmering in his conscience and the selfishness he'd inherited in his heart.

Kyle turned his back on Andrew and walked away from him. There was a picture on the windowsill of Andrew, Virginia, Kyle, and his parents. It was taken one Christmas and Kyle gleamed upon his bicycle next to the sofa.

He looked beyond the image and realized that the sofa was broken and his bicycle had long been dismantled. Kyle picked up the picture and held it toward the light. Rays and reflections changed the picture with each angle. One direction made his grandmother vanish and the opposite direction made his parents disappear. Always showing, no matter the turns the picture frame took, were Kyle and his grandfather.

"You gon' run outta here and change the world wit' that little piece of knowledge you got? It ain't gon' make nobody happy. Ain't gon' do nothin' but kick up dust that have people chokin' and gaggin'."

Kyle set the picture down gently, watching all the images reappear. "Sometimes you gotta cough a little bit to get all the mess out of your system."

The nurse interrupted the tension with a hectic knock.

"Kyle, is Camilla still down in Bainbrigde?"

"Yeah."

"You talked to her lately?"

"No, I tried a few days ago. I think some of the phones aren't working down there. Why? What's wrong?"

"I heard that Bainbridge just got its first taste of the flood and they expect it to be real bad down there. You know they got that chemical plant. Say if the stuff gets in the water, won't be no survivors."

"What!"

"Sorry to interrupt, just thought you'd be interested."

"My God, I can't take another one, not another death," he mumbled. Emotions and memories of lost family were fresh and drained his ability to cry out. "That's it," he said. "I'm gonna see if I can get in touch with her. See if she's all right," he remarked to no one in particular. This has gotta stop right now."

"Where you goin', Kyle? What you gon' do, son?" Andrew asked, with a final plea for discretion.

Still not willing to exchange a glance with Andrew, he replied, "I'm going to check on Camilla right after I make a stop downtown."

"Kyle. Kyle!"

Thirty-Three

Running

———— ☙ ————

It was Tuesday which marked the last week of campaigning for Republican and Democratic primary elections. Mail services had been disabled and the Chief knew he was missing hundreds of voters without direct mailings.

To combat the problem, he decided to hold an impromptu rally. His location of choice was the area where many Albanians were gathering, the Federal Emergency Management Association office. FEMA had rushed into Albany, setting up disaster relief headquarters. The city's destitute bombarded the makeshift office of draped vinyl tents crowded with chairs, folding tables, and homeless citizens.

The flood-ravaged people sought funds for the restoration of their businesses and others simply wanted shelter. Mobile homes would soon be imported to Albany for those completely washed out. Streets and avenues that resembled America's slice of life, with children playing and lawnmowers rumbling, would become improvised trailer parks.

When the FEMA relief opened the doors, more than

one thousand residents were waiting in line for the low interest rate miracles. It was here that the Chief thought he could raise interest in the election's importance.

Equipped with a portable PA system, directions to the polls, and the schedule times of his own personal shuttle bus, the Chief launched a campaign of desperation.

"Citizens of Albany. Your presence here today is a testimony of your bravery and courage. It shows your love and appreciation for this city, our city. Other folks from other cities would have left and never thought about coming back home. Home. Home is all we have left, fellow citizens. Yes, some of them are ruined, some of them are underwater, but we can rebuild! We can rebuild together!

"I know you're tired. I know you are hungry. I know you are discouraged. However, it's of the utmost importance that we start thinking about tomorrow, today! As you may or may not know, the elections are one week from today. We all have other things to be concerned about right now. What will the FEMA team tell us? What will the President say when he arrives tomorrow? Where will we sleep tonight? These are all very important questions. Here's another good question. Who will lead us into the rebuilding of our city? Fellow citizens, I want to lead you. I want to be your state representative and the first step begins with the primary elections next week. I want to lead this city into its rebirth and I need your vote. Together we can—"

"Shut up!" A voice burst from the crowd outside the offices.

Murmurs followed. Some in agreement and others in disbelief. The Chief carefully devised his next words. He couldn't possibly lash back. Instead he diplomatically pushed on with political rhetoric.

"Together we can overcome obstacles and—"

"Shut up, I said!" The voice was louder this time. It was attached to a feisty old man. "We can't do nothin' with

y'all," he said. His bones wrapped tightly with wrinkled
mocha colored skin. "It's yo' fault we in this here situation
now." The line turned to face the Chief, waiting for more
accusations and then answers. "What you got to say to
that?"

"Sir," the Chief smiled, fighting back his building
scorn. "I'm not sure I know what you mean."

"You know good n' well what I mean, white man!"

Murmurs became audible phrases amongst the crowd.

"Sir—"

"Y'all sent that flood straight to the black folks!"

The Chief abandoned the microphone and exchanged
dialogue with the man.

"Sir, are you saying that someone controlled the flood
waters and directed them to certain areas?"

"I already said it! Now, what you gon' do about that,
politician!"

"Sir, may I ask your name?"

"Mad as hell wit' no place to sleep. That's my name.
What's yo' name? Happy all day wit' a place to stay? Is
that yo' name?"

The crowd laughed a bit and listened for more.

"Sir, there is no way that anyone could have controlled
all of—"

"Then how come all these peoples in line looks like me
and the people that looks like you is at home eatin' breakfast?"

People gave shouts of inquisition now.

He right. Look like only black folks in this line.

Yeah, why is that?

"I'll tell you why it is," the instigator continued.
"'Cause they controlled the flood."

"People, people!" the Chief shouted. "Let's not get excited. Believe me when I tell you it is impossible to control
billions of gallons of water. How can—"

"Didn't y'all open the floodgates at Lake Blackshear?"

"Yes, but—"

"Didn't the flood get to the po' folks' neighborhood first?"

"You can say that poor-—"

"Ain't this line full of black folks?"

"Yes, but—"

"Well then, how you gon' stand there and tell us y'all didn't flood the black neighborhood. You might wanna get the microphone and get back in yo' car befo' we jump out this line."

There were shouts from the crowd now. The people wanted so desperately to pour out their filthy frustrations, and the Chief seemed like the perfect sewage drain.

"Are you threatin' me, sir?" asked the Cheif.

"Aw naw, I ain't threatin' you yet! When I tell you that I'm gon' jump out this line and beat yo' brains out, that'll be a threat!"

Red pigment flushed over the Chief's face. The growing rage in him subsided only by common sense. If the man had jumped out of line, there would surely be others. Not only would it bring him a lost election, but bodily harm as well.

Retreating to the microphone, the Chief found ingenuity for the situation.

"People, people! I hear you and I understand your concerns. I must tell you, it is highly unlikely that the floodwaters were controlled—"

Shouts interrupted the speech as the Chief turned his hands towards to the crowd asking for control.

"People, listen! I will take this task upon myself. I'll meet with the city manager."

"We want Jesse and the coalition!"

"That's fine. If he wants to come down, so be it, but we can handle this ourselves. I'll talk to the dam officials, some engineers, I'll even swim the river if I have to. If—"

"Won't bother me if you forget how to swim while you

in there."

With a heavy sigh, the Chief continued, "As most of you know, I was Chief of Police for many years and I pride myself in the ability to serve the people and to complete thorough investigations. That same pride will accompany me to the State House of Rep—"

"Yeah, we all know how good you investigated yo' officer that got killed way back when. Had to blame it on a dead man. Somebody gon' have to die befo' you find out they sent the water to the black neighborhoods.

Nothing came from the crowd but silence. The spiteful man had touched the taboo. Even he lowered his head after releasing the statement. His comments up until now had been laced with malice, but this was issued to hurt the Chief.

The Chief waited until patience was traded for tolerance and tolerance gave way to scorn. His scorn subsided and was taken over by forgiveness.

"It's funny you should say that, friend," he said as his lips brushed against the microphone. The Chief wanted these words to be heard by all within earshot. "My career as a law enforcement officer has been blemished by one imperfect case. This obstacle has haunted me personally because I am an advocate of justice. The same way I searched for answers to that one case you have so eloquently described," he said pointing to the man, "is the same way I will search for answers to your accusation today. If it takes my entire life, I will find the answer just as I am about to find the answer to my one imperfect case."

"What you talkin' about? You already blamed it on Mack and he long gone."

A satisfying smirk spread over the Chief's face before he said, "Let's just say that someone has returned from the dead to reveal the truth. You will all soon learn the truth, about everything and everybody."

Thirty-Four

Resolutions

———— ෬෧ ————

Family and friends were forced to revisit the interment of their dearly departed among rows of retrieved coffins from the river. The finely polished vessels had become scratched and stained from the current and its intercepting tree branches. Some coffins were cross-referenced with the brand name from the purchaser's paperwork. Others were forced to undergo the painful identification process.

Counselors offered their services to anyone seeking comfort through words and therapy. It was an event always regretted but almost never repeated, the burial of loved ones. A few rare cases assumed the gruesome task of viewing partially decomposed bodies. Families with no papers or those who could not identify the coffin were forced to bear the unsightly scene.

A family in the identification center prepared themselves for the unveiling. Precautions were taken for the spreading of disease. As the center's personnel began opening the coffin, each member clasped their hands with the others, interlocking fingers and restricting the blood flow. Oblivious to the physical pain yet overtaken by the pain of knowing, they watched. The top was raised, as was their breathing. Air rushed into lungs and flushed from nostrils while the coffin opened as the body came into view.

It was indeed their family member. She was wearing the dress from the picture, the one with a purple pattern and lavender lace. The favorite dress she'd sent to the cleaners twice every month. It was the dress she'd worn while gliding across the floor in the arms of her husband to the sound of soulful tunes. It was the dress a grandchild spit up on during their first meeting. She'd dressed up special for the grandchild's visit. After cleaning off the infant's accident, they all assembled on the front porch and posed for camera clicks. It was the picture of her in the favorite dress she swore to take to her grave. So they knew it was her. A man fell to the floor when the rushing and flushing of air was not enough to sustain consciousness. The identification was made.

In a secluded corner, men gathering over another coffin noticed the commotion, but paid little attention. A greater task loomed before them. It was the coffin of controversy.

"We really should get the family's permission," a personnel member said.

"Just do what I told you. Let me worry about the family."

The other men stood silent, one with a camera and the other, a note pad.

"Look, if I lose my job, I'm gonna—"

"If you don't do what I said, you won't have a job to come back to, understand? Now you look for 'em and tell me how many you find.

After the command, protected hands began fishing in the coffin. He disturbed the body as little as possible and uncovered the items. The entire length of the coffins was searched. Even the crevices of the satin-lined walls were searched until the man was satisfied.

"Here, that's all there is. Looks like ten. Five pair."

"That can't be right. Count 'em again."

"Two, four—" the searcher began. "It's ten, that's it."

"That doesn't make sense! There were six men. One was dead and one should have only had one. It should only be nine in there. Dammit!"

"Sorry, what can I tell ya. It's ten and they all have the initial BBA on 'em. Wait a minute. These two don't have anything on 'em. In fact, these are completely different from the rest of them."

"What! Let me see those." He snatched the trinkets and examined them closely. "Son of a—"

The man replayed events long gone in an instant. "He threw in a pair of ordinary ones when everybody else threw in the real ones. Ha! I got 'em! Boys, you make sure you meet me down at the FEMA tents tomorrow. Get every reporter you can find. Let them know that Albany's oldest crime has been uncovered. Joshua, make sure you're there to witness your grandpappy's defining moment, hear me? Oh, and make sure you bring that scientific person we met. Tell them to bring all information about how water flows and the city's topography and that gibber jabber. You know all the stuff that proves Mother Nature is a mean old heifer when she wants to be. Last thing I need is a broken promise. Here, take a picture of the evidence. This'll get me elected by a landslide for sure."

As the camera flashed and the blank notepad became headlines, the Chief smiled, holding in his hands the BBA cufflinks and Andrew's secret.

CdEO

Lines stretched beyond sight the following day at the disaster relief offices. All of the weary had not been served the previous day and had returned for more waiting and wishing. Among the recycled was the old agitator.

The Chief noticed him while setting up. He smiled with satisfaction knowing there a special recipe of crow for the old man. More people were waiting today. Word spread of the expedience at which the loans would come. The relief line was now the town lottery.

Rumbling began as the people noticed the Chief's return and his entourage of equipment-wielding news people. They watched as he tested his microphone and cleared his throat.

"Fellow citizens of—"

"We done heard that part. Just tell us what we already know." The spokesman gave no room for salutations. Noticing the tension, reporters perked up, sensing a real story. A smile was offered by the Chief, then a shake of the head.

"Sir, I have exactly what you need to hear. May I present to you Brenda Hodgins. Mrs. Hodgins is a hydrologist. She studies water and things associated with water. Mrs. Hodgins can tell you the temperature, contaminates, and origin of water almost by lookin' at it. Now, why someone would want to study water is beyond me," he jested. "But Mrs. Hodgins has volunteered her time to give you a brief explanation of the flood pattern you've been askin' about."

A short woman stepped to the microphone and adjusted the height to her fitting. She blurted a few words and the instrument squealed through the speakers. The Chief aided her by moving it a few inches outward. This time her speech was clear and concise.

She spoke of Alberto's path and the massive rains which had swelled branches of the Flint. People were amazed as she conveyed complicated numbers with practical examples. She then explained the structure of Albany's land and the way south Albany was simply a low-lying area. It was where the flood chose to go, she told them. Water obeys gravity and it could not travel uphill without being pumped there. Then she spoke of the floodgates at Lake Blackshear and how the waters would have flowed over the top eventually and the floodgates would have never even mattered. Finally the woman spoke softly about how she had never in her life seen anything like this great flood and hoped there would never be another. Her emotions and speech were returned with a quiet sympathy from those who'd given their attention. Except for one.

"So white folks knew back in 1836 that the south side might flood one day. They made that land cheap and that was all black folks could afford. Ain't that right?" Pondering produced the familiar murmur as they struggled to analyze the old man's theory.

Hodgins replied, "I'm no historian, sir, but I suppose there may be some accuracy to your thinking, be it accidental or intentional. Let me say this. If that is the case, it is a price laid upon our heads by our forefathers and foremothers and it is our obligation to relieve ourselves of that taxation through forgiveness."

She exited the stage to a small token applause, gripping handshakes, and back pats from those standing in line.

"Thank you, Mrs. Hodgins," the Chief said, capitalizing on the good feelings. A reporter followed her with more questions. "As I said yesterday, Albany needs someone to help heal the wounds and move forward. I want to help you. I will get answers, I will find you solutions as I have today with the gracious help of Mrs. Hodgins.

"I will also be persistent for you. Persistent until the end if need be. What I'm about to say hurts, but I think of you as family so it's okay." The Chief lowered and raised his head. Everyone focused intently on the forthcoming speech.

"Several years ago, one of my best officers was killed in the line of duty. Life is precious and even more precious is the life of one that protects this country's citizens. That case was closed, but never solved. It has haunted me to this day that the murderer of a policeman might be living in Albany having let another take the blame for the crime. Dougherty county officials, along with my own private investigation, have recently uncovered the true perpetrator of this crime."

Movement rushed through the people as they consulted with each other as to who it might be.

"I do not rest until my job is done and I will do the job of state representative for you thoroughly as I have finally closed the last chapter on my law enforcement career. Dear citizens, it will surprise you to learn that this murderer is still living and breathing today."

Again the crowd reacted. Reporters scribbled feverishly and focused cameras carefully.

"This killer is still in our city. The man never came forward. This person knew he was guilty. This man is—"

"My grandfather!"

A voice boomed opposite the stage boosted by a police bullhorn—Joshua's bullhorn. A hand reached up to the device pulling it from Kyle's mouth and placing it near his own. All of the BBA members had come to stand together with Kyle's decision. It was the first time since the funeral.

"This person is my friend!" shouted Gus. The bullhorn was passed again.

"This person is my classmate!" yelled Tyrone, who then gave the instrument to Ulysses.

"He's my fishin' buddy!" Ulysses passed it on to D.J.

"He's my colleague!" D.J. said, then lowered the device, but continued holding it. He held it steady for Emma. Standing frail, yet proud, she spoke, "Andrew Scales is a good friend of my late husband and he's my church member."

D.J. retrieved the bullhorn and continued.

"Andrew Scales is my church member, too. The same church that you and your men stormed into years ago without warrants. And you made this woman a widow with the haste of yo' actions.

"What Andrew did was not right, although we think he did it in self defense! His grandson…come on up here, Kyle. His grandson has come to each and every one us individually, confessed and asked forgiveness for what Andrew did. We forgive him. We love him. We respect him for his honor. We pray for Andrew and God will take care of the rest! Now as for you, Chief!" The line shuffled as people moved towards the stage.

"It's time for you to repent on behalf of yo' men. Yo' grandson Joshua wants to rid himself of yo' burden, too. These two young men are the future leaders of this city and they can't do it with the tainted spirits of you and Andrew. You know good 'n' well you don't need to be runnin' fo' no office tryin' to run the State House when you ain't got yo' own house in order!"

"Get yo' old self off that stage!" the old agitator shouted.

"People, I—" he began.

The crowd's movements and chants rendered the microphone useless. Disgruntled and defeated, the Chief exited.

Emma hobbled toward Kyle and Josh, holding each of their hands in her own.

"I told you, the truth'll set you free."

"Thank you," they both replied.

"Huh?"

"Thank you!"

"Aw, you welcome."

Emma slowly turtled her way through the crowd. The people parted as clean-shaven strangers with earpieces escorted a friendly gentleman wearing jeans and a striped short-sleeved shirt. His hands were soft but he had come for labor. He introduced himself to all even though everyone knew him. The guest touched the shoulders and shook the hands of everyone near. Kyle and Joshua were stricken with jaw-dropped awe as he greeted them both, "Hi, Bill Clinton. Pleasure to meet you. I'm here to help."

While others were shaking the presidential hand and basking in a moment of rescued happiness, Emma made her way to the front of the emptied line and sat down in the first available seat.

"Hello," she said to the FEMA representative. "My name is Emma and I need ninety-thousand dollars."

"Ma'am, you'll need to fill out these forms."

"Huh?"

"You'll need to fill out these forms!" the person yelled.

"Okay."

"Here's a pen if you need one."

"Huh?

"Here's a pen if you need one!"

"Aw, okay. You wanna buy a newspaper?" she asked, placing the small bag of papers on the table.

The person saw the desperation in her eyes and asked just above a whisper, "How much are they?"

"Fifty cent. I got change if you need it."

Thirty-Five

While on the Way *Back* Home...

⟡

IN THE FOLLOWING DAYS, THE WATER HAD MIRACU-
lously receded from the town of Bainbridge. Kyle was able
to reunite with his sweetheart and claim her as his fiancée,
as family. Embracing his love, Kyle began the painful and
lengthy mourning process. Had he not been occupied with
the pursuit of truth and the salvation of lives, his sorrow
would have surely killed him as well.

The grieving continued long after the quintuple funeral,
which took place for his parents, his aunt, her daughter, and
finally Andrew. His burden, though revealed, claimed him
with a heart attack even more massive than Virginia's
stroke. Andrew was buried next to his loving wife. Her coffin was never disturbed during the flood. Virginia didn't
have to rise from the dead to right her husband's wrongs,
although she'd spent a good portion of her life trying.

The other portion was spent pouring her righteous ways
into Kyle with pinches of her presence. A pat on his head, a
squeeze of his cheeks, a kiss while he slept, a hug for his
soul.

Virginia knew she could never be as close to him as
Andrew. Instead she planted her own seeds in him, having

faith that they would one day flourish.

Numbers told of the needed relief and devastating realization in southwest Georgia. The President's visit prompted nineteen millions dollars in flood relief for the state. Four million dollars was approved to help the unemployed. The thirtieth fatality was found in the town of Dawson. Crops were submerged, amounting to more than three hundred thousand acres of ruined vegetation. Emergency food stamps were issued, totaling almost two million dollars. Homes were lost or inhabitable for nearly twenty thousand Albanians. Flint's flood stage capped off at twenty feet. Water in the town had reached forty-two feet—more than twice that which could be controlled. An anonymous donation of over three million dollars was shipped to the FEMA office—in old dusty hatboxes. Alberto and Albany had come to blows, leaving casualties strewn about like pebbles washed ashore.

Rather than facing the mockery of a landslide defeat, the Chief withdrew his name from the ballot. He started a security consulting company, the Albany police department being his flagship client. Joshua ensured there was plenty of work for him and gave him referrals to other agencies.

The View was blinded. Andrew's involvement in an officer's shooting was more negative publicity than advertisers cared to gamble with. Things fell apart after the bank contract fell through. Income filtered down to scrapings to pay the bills and finally offerings for persistent collectors. Selling the billboards and the building was his only strategy to pay the reaming balances from the funeral and break even without filing for bankruptcy. Andrew's empire was completely liquidated, just as he'd feared.

Work for ambitious MBA's with the bloodline of a murderer, albeit self-defense, after a natural disaster, was rare in Albany. Kyle was forced to look for a position up the road in Atlanta. He and Camilla journeyed up to the Southern Oasis for job-hunting. Within a week of interviewing, he was offered positions at Coca Cola, Lucent, and Motorola. All boasted salaries with several digits, but none more promising than the offer from the Good Times Plantation.

It was a start-up company owned by the same banker who co-owned the Pinefield Plantation. Apparently, the tax-write off had become somewhat of a tax liability due to increased profits at the hands of national and international clients. After buying out his partner, the banker decided to rename the facility with irrational irony. A golf and resort plantation named after his favorite television show, featuring a family that never climbed out of the ghetto.

He needed someone to run the complex with much more energy than he. Someone with a love of the city and the land which embodied it. Kyle was contacted after the banker learned of the View's outcome. There would be no signing bonus nor a touted MBA salary. He was offered meager compensation with perks promised if the business did well. Finally, the job offered an ultimate perk, a chance to return and live in precious Albany. Foregoing the courteous business etiquette and declining the other offers, Kyle planted a smile, grabbed his soon-to-be wife and drove.

બ૩૪ૈ

Months later, Kyle found himself driving with swift satisfaction. The longest stretch of the Georgia-Florida Parkway was a cool runway guarded from fear and danger by outstretched pecan tree branches. Gleaming with mature roughage and aged shelled fruits, the brown and green hands welcomed all coming, or returning, to take part in the experience of Albany.

Kyle and his fiancée, Camilla, would learn all too well this road home. And so would their children's children, who were all destined for prosperity.

Discussion Guide

Carter-Krall Publishers believes that books make people talk and when people talk with each other, the world learns about different cultures, thereby enhancing our existence. Included here is a discussion guide for your reading group, book club, classroom, or general gathering. We do hope you'll enjoy the topics listed here and even derive some interesting ones of your own.

1. Early in the story, Andrew begins to cover up his guilt. Is this intentional from the very beginning or is he too far into his own lie before he can reveal the truth?

2. Why was Kyle's love so important to Andrew? Did Andrew love his grandson more than his wife or his own children?

3. Andrew commits numerous acts of deceit and dishonesty although he believes they are justified. Does this make Andrew a bad person? Can people indulge in wrongful deeds yet still maintain their humanity. List some examples?

4. Virginia could have revealed the truth early in the story, yet she did not. Why did she have such an internal struggle with this dilemma? Does this speak to the loyalty of love or discerning right from wrong?

5. Andrew gives a vital piece of evidence to Kyle. What does this offering symbolize? How is Kyle's life affected by the evidence? Are generational burdens linked, in some way, to tangible objects or are most of them manifested through emotional traits?

6. What was symbolic about the flood? What did the flood mean to Kyle? Did the flood mean anything to Andrew? Did the flood mean anything to the city of Albany?

7. Virginia's ultimate demise occurs when the truth is almost revealed. Did Andrew's deceit cause her stroke? Had she confessed earlier, would the stroke have occurred? What does this illustrate about ridding ourselves of problems and burdens over which we have control?

8. The Mt. Zion Baptist Church held its worship service in the Jewish synagogue. How did the pastor's message parallel the events taking place in Kyle's life? How does the message parallel the tragedies in Albany?

9. Once Kyle returns to Albany, he is confronted by evidence of his grandfather's wrongdoing—the sins of his forefather. How does this affect his perception of Andrew? When individuals are placed on pedestals and their admirers watch them fall, what lesson does that teach about the reality of being human?

10. In the opening paragraph, the term 'dichotomous fusion' is used. What is a dichotomous fusion? Can you list some examples? Can you create some examples?

11. How do you feel about the author's use of dialect throughout the story? Did it make the characters more realistic? Did it add to the Southern setting? Did it illustrate how informal language is often widely accepted and understood?

12. What do think about the author's use of alliteration? Was it pleasing to read? Did it make words and phrases stand out?

13. Did the author paint vivid pictures with words? Were the places and people visible in your mind such as the pecan trees, the golf course, the quail plantation, Andrews' decrepit house? Was the path and behavior of the flood recognizable? What other writers have a similar writing style?

14. Discuss the dangers of generational burdens and list some examples. One day, in your own solitude, think about some generational burdens which may have been placed on you and the affects they may have on your life.

About the Author

Brian Egeston lives in Georgia where he spends his time writing, thinking about writing, and longing to write. An aspiring mediocre golfer, he lives with his incredible and lovely wife, Latise.

Carter-Krall Publishers
Literature that lasts forever

Books By Brian Egeston
Order the collection

☐ ## Granddaddy's Dirt
$24.00 Hardback ISBN 0967550599
$13.00 Trade paperback ISBN 0967550580
Circle one or both
Please send ＿＿＿copies.

☐ ## Whippins, Switches & Peach Cobbler
ISBN-096755021
$12.00 Trade paperback
Please send ＿＿＿copies.

☐ ## Crossing Bridges*
ISBN-09675505-5-6
$13.00 Trade paperback
Please send ＿＿＿copies.
*Anniversary edition available January, 2002

Available at your local bookstore or use this page to reorder.
Make check or money order payable to: **Carter-Krall Publishers**
GA residents add 6% sales tax.

MAIL TO:
Carter-Krall Publishers Order Fulfillment Dept.
P.O. Box 1388
Pine Lake, GA 30072

Please send me the items I have checked above. I am enclosing $ ＿＿＿＿＿
(please add $2.15 per book for postage and handling).
Name ＿＿＿＿＿＿＿＿＿＿ e-mail ＿＿＿＿＿＿＿＿
Address ＿＿＿＿＿＿＿＿＿＿
City/State ＿＿＿＿＿＿＿＿＿ Zip ＿＿＿＿＿＿＿
Please charge my Visa/MC/American Express # ＿＿＿＿＿＿
Exp. Date ＿＿＿＿＿ Signature ＿＿＿＿＿＿＿

Books By Brian Egeston
Order the collection

☐ ## Granddaddy's Dirt

$24.00 Hardback ISBN 0-967550599
$13.00 Trade paperback ISBN-0967550580
Circle one or both
Please send _____copies.

☐ ## Whippins, Switches & Peach Cobbler

ISBN-096755021
$12.00 Trade paperback
Please send _____copies.

☐ ## Crossing Bridges*

ISBN-09675505-5-6
$13.00 Trade paperback
Please send _____copies.
*Anniversary edition available January, 2002

Available at your local bookstore or use this page to reorder.
Make check or money order payable to: **Carter-Krall Publishers**
GA residents add 6% sales tax.

MAIL TO:
Carter-Krall Publishers Order Fulfillment Dept.
P.O. Box 1388
Pine Lake, GA 30072

Please send me the items I have checked above. I am enclosing $ _____
(please add $2.15 per book for postage and handling).
Name _____ e-mail_____
Address _____
City/State _____ Zip _____
Please charge my Visa/MC/American Express # _____
Exp. Date _____ Signature _____

Carter-Krall Publishers
Literature that lasts forever

Books By Brian Egeston
Order the collection

☐ ### Granddaddy's Dirt
$24.00 Hardback ISBN 0-967550599
$13.00 Trade paperback ISBN-0967550580
Circle one or both
Please send _____copies.

☐ ### Whippins, Switches & Peach Cobbler
ISBN-096755021
$12.00 Trade paperback
Please send _____copies.

☐ ### Crossing Bridges*
ISBN-09675505-5-6
$13.00 Trade paperback
Please send _____copies.
*Anniversary edition available January, 2002

Available at your local bookstore or use this page to reorder.
Make check or money order payable to: **Carter-Krall Publishers**
GA residents add 6% sales tax.

MAIL TO:
Carter-Krall Publishers Order Fulfillment Dept.
P.O. Box 1388
Pine Lake, GA 30072

Please send me the items I have checked above. I am enclosing $ _____
(please add $2.15 per book for postage and handling).
Name _____ e-mail _____
Address _____
City/State _____ Zip _____
Please charge my Visa/MC/American Express # _____
Exp. Date _____ Signature _____